Rosiebelle Lee Wildcat Tennessee

Rosiebelle Lee Wildcat Tennessee

A · NOVEL · BY

Raymond Andrews

WITH · ILLUSTRATIONS · BY

Benny Andrews

THE · DIAL · PRESS
NEW · YORK

Published by
The Dial Press
1 Dag Hammarskjold Plaza
New York, New York 10017

Copyright © 1980 by Raymond Andrews

Manufactured in the United States of America
First printing

Design by Francesca Belanger

Library of Congress Cataloging in Publication Data

Andrews, Raymond.
Rosiebelle Lee Wildcat Tennessee.

I. Title
PZ4.A5546Ro [PS3551.N452]   813'.54   79–28705
ISBN 0–8037–8336–1

TO

A Family's Album

PART · ONE

The Album

$\mathcal{N}$obody knew just how long she had been standing there. But when the oldsters sitting on Blackshear's Undertakers' front porch looked up, there she stood, silently watching them. Standing out there as if having risen from the dust of the undertakers' front yard itself. Yet what gripped the eyeballs of the porch sitters on that locally historic day even more than the sight of the woman herself or even her long, butt-whupping, coalblack hair, was that face—spellbindingly beautiful, an ageless, Circean face, with soul-piercing black eyes perched on their aerie atop high, flat cheekbones. The porch sitters were completely mesmerized. Though her skin was a smooth acorn-brown, she was definitely not anything like any colored woman the old eyes squinting out from the shade of Blackshear's porch had ever hit on before that hot Georgia summer afternoon back in 1906.

"What's the name of this heah town?" Nor did she even sound too much colored.

"Appalachee." Finally, a lone voice from the shadow of the porch. The rest of them were too stunned by the revelation that someone, even a woman, colored-looking or not, did not know the name of their town.

With the question of her whereabouts settled, the woman proceeded to drop right down in her tracks there in the middle of the front yard, crossed her legs beneath her ankle-length dress, and took a big hunk of cornbread from what appeared to be a dried cow bladder hanging from a piece of twine that encircled her wasp waist. And with that scorching mid-afternoon sun scowling down upon her bare head, she sat right out there in the near suffocating dust smacking that big piece of dry cornbread right on down her gullet and not even once taking those dark penetrating eyes of hers off the dumb-struck, gawking porch sitters.

All the cornbread eaten, she wiped her mouth with the back of her hand, let out a loud belch, broke wind silently, and rose to her feet. After brushing the dust from her dress, she again addressed her audience.

"Can any of y'all heah point me to the house of the richest white man living in this heah town?"

"You mus' mean Mist' George MacAndrew, ma'am." That same voice from out of the shade of the porch.

"Isaac! She said the riches' white man livin' in this *heah* town. Mist' George MacAndrew don' live in this *heah* town." Another voice cutting in, expressing a difference of opinion among the seated.

"Man, don' I know that! But what she said was to point her to the house of the riches' white man, 'n Mist' George MacAndrew is *the* riches' white man living *heah* in whole Muskhogean County!"

"He still don' live *heah* in town!"

"Whar 'bout he lives then?" The woman interrupting the two disputants.

"You mean Mist' George MacAndrew, ma'am?" The one called Isaac.

"If he's the richest white man of them all living round heah."

"Folks who oughta know says so. But he lives way down at Plain View."

"Plain View? Whichaway is that?"

"Take that there road right on through town 'n jes keep

on walkin' straight down it on ovah the bridge and pas' the river till you start comin' to the bigges' fields of the talles' cotton you evah did see—then you know you is there. But, ma'am, I heah tell Mist' George ain' takin' on no mo' field hands fuh the summer."

"Rosiebelle Lee Wildcat Tennessee ain't *nobody's* field nigger!"

Then she was gone. Walking barefoot down that long, hot dusty road to the biggest fields of the tallest cotton she ever would see—to Plain View.

Antedating Blackshear's Undertakers' historic front yard occurrence by a decade had been the sending "up North" from Appalachee to Virginia of seventeen-year-old Ira MacAndrew by his parents, George and Beatrice, for the purpose of attending that state's university at Charlottesville to study what the law was all about. But so impressed had young Ira been by his first train ride that he got no farther north than Norfolk, where, to his utter delight, he landed a job as cook's helper for the workers laying and repairing rails for the Norfolk & Southern Railroad. But his career was fated to last just as long as it took for his first letter to reach home and bring his daddy George roaring into Norfolk on the first train out of Appalachee, coming to fetch his son home from among the lowly railroad-working niggers, chinks, shanty Irish, foreigners, and other po' white trash and social dregs. Though in figuring Ira wanted work rather than college and in further figuring that he was willing to come back to Georgia to learn the family business, the business of cotton, his father figured wrong. For not even King Cotton itself proved capable of holding the interest of young Ira for long. Shortly following his return to the family's Muskhogean County plantation, he began to develop an interest in the new vehicle then very popular in the area—the bicycle. This interest proved so strong that, in partnership with a friend, he decided to open up the town of Appalachee's first bicycle shop. Yet despite the immediate commercial success of the shop (thanks largely to his partner, since Ira loved riding the bicycle more than trying to sell it), the desire to hit the open road on his own was to burn hotter and hotter in young MacAndrew's adventurous soul with the passing of each day. Before the century's end he'd sold his share of the shop to his partner and was off again—this time two-wheeling it for the wide open spaces of America's wild and woolly West.

Ira's dislike for the agrarian life proved a deep disappointment to his parents, especially to his aging father, George, who was naturally depending upon his only son to someday succeed him as head of Muskhogean County's largest plantation, officially known as Plain View and whose size rather than by acreage was referred to locally in miles. George's original plan as a young man had called for a house full of children, especially boy children, but the War had altered this early dream of his considerably. Going off at age twenty-two to fight for the Cause, George remained until the cold, bloody, and bitter end, when all the thunder's echoes had died. He returned home to a baffled and disillusioned family on a weed-infested plantation which they feared was about to be broken up by the land's newest, blue-clad conquerors. George MacAndrew took after his grandfather more than his father, Martin, the Southern Gentleman's Southern Gentleman. Grandfather Benjamin, of *the* Virginia MacAndrews, first came to Georgia back in 1806 to grab a piece of the vast territory that was then being parceled out by government lottery to land-hungry white settlers. After the War, since his father was no longer competent to the task, George himself assumed full responsibility as head of the family, and vowed to hold on to the largest and once most prestigious plantation in the area, no matter what the cost. And even later —when the President of the United States, Andrew Johnson, made the decision to pardon the Confederacy by letting the planters keep their individual holdings rather than sharing them with the nation's newest pioneers, the Freedmen—the cost of keeping such an enormous tract of land intact came high. Still, for more than thirty years, through all the South's postwar disasters (including the depressions of the Seventies, Eighties, and Nineties) George MacAndrew refused to sell one single acre of the place. Nor would he even put up so much as one acre of this land for credit or rental, despite local money being as scarce as hair on a 'tater during these long lean years. This was simply because the price of cotton kept dropping, from a full dollar a pound at the close of the War to twelve cents for that same pound in the Seventies, nine cents in the Eighties, seven cents in the Nineties. George's answer to all of this price nonsense had been to plant more cotton each year . . . and pray.

Yet a lifetime devoted to territoriality had left George with little or no time for life's many other pursuits, especially the pursuit of the fair sex, which perhaps best explains why he was nearing his fortieth birthday before he finally got around to marrying the much-courted Miss Beatrice Orr. But after suffering the animalistic humiliation of Ira's birth in the first year of her marriage, 1879, the very petite and even prettier Missis Beatrice developed a lasting distaste for the art of procreation and in place of it began concerning herself with the more important matter in her life, that of being a genteel Southern lady. Meanwhile, George, having gained a son and lost a roommate, went back to the land . . . feeling himself the winner in the swap. This left Ira free to become the *enfant terrible.*

But when Ira headed off for the Wild West, George didn't go chasing after to fetch his boy safely home, out of the clutches of the savages and outlaws. Instead he decided to teach the incorrigible a lesson by leaving Plain View to someone more deserving. So he, now approaching sixty, coaxed Missis Bea, teetering on the brink of the change of life, back to the drawing board for a last draw. But this time, as far as the sire was concerned, they drew a blank: a girl. Amanda.

Back to the land went George, this time the loser, and with damaged dignity Missis Bea returned from the unfamiliarity of the drawing board to the friendlier drawing room.

It was to be seven years before Ira returned home, looking more like some tramp than his father's son. After his return, by train—this time freightcar style—Appalachee's young Marco Polo had very little to say about, and, save for being seven years older, nothing to show for his adventure. Though word somehow got out about how, or rather where, he had parted company with the beautiful specially built bicycle he had gone wheeling westward on. It was just outside of a city called Saltino, down in Mexico, that he'd been relieved of his beloved bike (along with his money, tobacco, boots, and belt) by an armed group of banditry whose vociferous, droopy-mustached young leader kept referring to himself as something that sounded to the broken-Spanish-speaking Ira very much like *revolucionario*.

Several changes greeted an older, worldlier Ira upon his return to Plain View—the most significant ones being that King Cotton had regained his local throne; the once indestructible George, now approaching seventy, was a half step slower; there were two new arrivals at Plain View—a sister . . . and Rosiebelle Lee Wildcat Tennessee.

The instant he first laid eyes upon that high-cheekboned, glazed brown face, Ira fell violently in love with the long-haired, "Indian-looking" colored gal. Nobody's field nigger she, Rosiebelle Lee Wildcat Tennessee had made her way to Plain View straight from the front yard of Blackshear's on that very first day of hers in Appalachee. True to her words she had gotten herself hired immediately to a "house" job by none other than the lady of *the* house herself, Missis Bea, well known for her fetish for pretty and exotic things. Missis Bea felt her plantation house would be greatly ornamented by the addition to her domestic staff of this unusually pretty—but a mite mystic looking—barefoot negress with the long straight black-as-coal shiny hair hanging down her back. Yet Rosiebelle Lee's new co-workers weren't about to admit that this strange, non-nigger-looking new servant was any kind of ornament to their ranks, since they decided early that she was "too meddlesome and bossy." But it wasn't until after the prodigal Ira's return from out West later that year that the MacAndrew household servants were to feel the true potency of Rosiebelle Lee's meddlesomeness and bossiness.

Rosiebelle Lee realized early on and lost no time whatsoever in taking the fullest advantage of the unusual spell she cast over both Missis Bea and, especially, her son Ira. After less time than six months on the job she had taken unofficial charge of the MacAndrew house servants. Before her first year was up she had been the direct cause of the gradual disappearance of all of the old family faithfuls; in the meantime she had gone out herself and brought back her own hand-picked recruits, all of whom were hired on the spot by the lady of the house herself. Though by now Missis Bea was forming the tip of a suspicion that this very pretty negress was a mite pushy, or just plain "too much for a white lady." Ira just thought she was too much. And George's answer to the servant problem in the South in the year of 1907 was to come in from the fields one day for just long enough to die. Thus, death cheated him out of seeing his first grandchild. A girl. Luvenia. Born the very day of his funeral, to his son, Ira MacAndrew, and head household servant, Rosiebelle Lee Wildcat Tennessee.

Luvenia was Rosiebelle Lee's *coup de grâce*. This was the Old South, at a time when it was socially and, more to the point, economically acceptable among many black women to have bastard, or "love," children by well-to-do and responsible white men. ("Responsible" meaning that those prosperous white men were disposed to keep their black mistresses and their off-white offspring fed, clothed, and housed. Love affairs between black women and poor white men weren't at all

common in the Old South—that is, except for prostitution
. . . and, of course, rape.) On the streets of Appalachee one
could easily pick out the black women who had white lovers
by their clothing, since they were unquestionably the best
and most colorfully turned-out babes, black or white, strut-
ting the streets, dressed fit to kill. Yet these black ladies'
greatest source of self-esteem, and of the respect of their
friends, relatives, and admirers—and enemies—was a house
or a piece of land, if they were fortunate enough to obtain so
substantial a token of their white lovers' gratitude. Most of
the inherited land held by blacks in the South was originally
owned by a woman—in most cases a one-time concubine who
had acquired the property, or most of it, from her white lover,
or lovers.

Contrary to Southern lore these women weren't in the
majority, nor did they all enter into these black-white love
affairs willingly, nor did they necessarily benefit from them,
economically or socially. But in most instances it was an
accepted fact that the black mistresses of the wealthiest white
men would have the strongest voices, male or female, within
the colored community itself, and thus would serve as inter-
mediaries between local black and white folks. And yet most
of these women were married to black men whom they had
children by, along with those of their white lovers. Their
husbands were helpless to change their mates' outside mating
habits, unless they wanted to get their own asses run off the
land, or buried under it. Thus, they found themselves held
beneath the castration yoke by the same Southern white man
who had conveniently spayed his white lady, keeping her
imprisoned under glass in a stuffy drawing room, breathing
in the scent of magnolias, ennui, and self-importance. Most
important, though, she was safely out of the way, and her man
was free to wallow happily out back in the mire of life with
his black gal. This was truly the age of the American Cauca-
sian cat and his colored chick. The black *boy* and the white
lady stood—apart—in the wings, watching . . . and waiting.

· ——— ·

    Beginning just south of the soil-rich banks of the Oconee River—which poured out of Greene County in the east and flowed clear across the north-central section of Muskhogean before emptying over into Morgan County on the west—was the plantation of Plain View, consisting of just about twenty square miles of cottonfield and uncleared forest land. Near the core of this rich acreage rose the inevitable two-storied, white-columned Georgian style manor house, better known through the years to all black plantation workers as "the Big House." And it was down the hill in back of Plain View's Big House in a little one-room clapboard shack squatting humbly out in the middle of a field white with fluffy bolls of cotton that in the late summer of 1907 Missis Bea's first grandchild was born. Yet the newborn Luvenia and her mother weren't exactly doomed to a cramped cotton-patch existence, since the day after the baby's birth Rosiebelle Lee had taken Luvenia in her arms and headed straight up the path to the backyard of the Big House, where she met face to face with her white man lover Ira, whom she called "Mister Mac," and pleaded for (or demanded—none of the other house or yard niggers got within earshot) a *new* house where she could raise her Luvenia up in a decent manner. Whether out of charity, duty, decency, guilt, embarrassment, or love . . . or awe . . . of this beautiful, masterful, and mystic black gal, Mister Mac—now sole owner of Plain View—was eager to oblige. In a matter of weeks after that Big House backyard confrontation he presented Rosiebelle Lee with a brand-new six-room wood-shingle house built to *her* specifications and sitting on the periphery of a large tract of MacAndrew woodland.

    Rosiebelle Lee as mistress of the master of Plain View and mother of his child was no longer required to work there in the Big House, or any other house for that matter, to earn her daily bread. Her days were now mostly spent roaming the woods with a fishing pole and a mess of wet squirming worms in her apron pocket, in search of a brook, pond, stream, creek, river, branch, or trickle, in which to fish. Such was her love for fishing that it was often said that if no other body of water was available she would happily fish in a mudhole, or a water-bucket.

The most plentiful fish in those waters was the catfish and with her lightning-fast reflexes she oftentimes caught them with her bare hand. Being a southpaw, her left hand soon was decorated with scars carved there by the fish's famed razor-sharp whiskers. And since cooking was another love of hers, the very idea of a breakfast without fried fish to go along with her fried eggs, fried corn (in season), fried slices of Irish or sweet potatoes, fried pork sausage, grits, hot buttered biscuits, and cool buttermilk was unthinkable. Quite often she invited a neighbor or two over to enjoy with her this favorite of the day's meals. But *never* on Sunday morning would neighbors be invited over. This was simply because when Sunday came—the day she would have on her table a special treat of storebought fish (salmon, her favorite), purchased the Saturday before in Appalachee—Mister Mac himself always breakfasted with her, or at least he had breakfast at her house. Southern etiquette dictated that they could not sit down together at the same table. When he rode up to her house early on Sunday morning on his white stallion, Joe Boy, she would always have his breakfast steaming and ready, and while he sat chomping it on down at the table alone she waited out on the back porch with Luvenia until he had finished and left the kitchen, whereupon she'd come back inside and eat whatever was left. By then Mister Mac would be sitting out on the back porch himself, letting his food digest properly while he smoked, belched, picked his teeth, ears, and nose, and pared his fingernails, all the while wordlessly watching the doings of the alien little creature called Luvenia crawling around on the floor beneath his feet and chair. If he was convinced he wasn't being watched from the kitchen, on occasion he would extend his hand to pat the child softly on the head, though he was always hesitant in this, as if he were somehow afraid that

his fingers would be snapped off by the creature's little, tooth-
less mouth. Once she was finished in the kitchen, Rosiebelle
Lee would then meet him in a more democratic part of the
house. Although it would not allow them to sit together in the
kitchen, Southern decorum compromised by permitting
them to lie together in the bedroom. Left out on the porch
alone, little Luvenia just kept crawling right on.

Flowers were still another love of Rosiebelle Lee's. She
loved everything involved in their care and cultivation and all
year round her house and the spacious encircling yard were
alive with all kinds of beautifully colored flowers. But besides
flowers, fishing, cooking—and sewing—nothing else around
her place much interested Rosiebelle Lee, except the house
itself, which apart from being a status symbol gave her a sense
of independence, or, to be more exact, power.

At the outset her house had been completely equipped
with tasteful furniture, all still in excellent condition, as well
as kitchen fixtures, and other houseware and furnishings provided by the one person considered by her peers to be *the* lady
of exquisite taste in such matters, Missis Bea herself, who no
longer needed any of these objects for the Big House. But
other than those things used for her cooking, sewing, or her
flowers, or for her butt or back, then whatever it was it just
lay, sat, stood, or hung neglected in its own dust unless someone came around admiring it, whereupon Rosiebelle Lee
would gladly give it to them. Other than the house itself, and
the few useful objects she cherished, material things meant
little to Rosiebelle Lee and this coupled with her love of
giving—*and* receiving, since she continually accepted the
goods, and not so goods, given her regularly by Missis Bea and
many of her well-to-do cronies—meant that her house was
never more than half furnished. But half furnished or not,
everybody was welcome through the never-locked door of
Rosiebelle Lee's house (except for Sunday morning, of course,
or whatever other time Mister Mac happened on the premises) any time of the day or night for whatever reason and to

stay for as long or as little as one wanted to. (And everybody was welcome to bring something along with them, especially in the way of food, like a mess of greens, a chicken, or a ham, or peaches, plums, goobers, pecans, a watermelon, or anything else stomachable, because with all her love for growing flowers, Rosiebelle Lee had no space, much less time, left for the raising of non-flowering foodstuffs.) And she expected exactly the same kind of welcome when she went visiting, *anybody, anywhere, any time* of the day or night for *any* reasons feeling fit to, and stayed until she herself felt it was time to leave, which was just about always late. Rosiebelle Lee loved people. Rosiebelle Lee also loved hearing about people. Gossip. And as a result of her running an open house and at the same time running into every other house left open—Rosiebelle Lee, with her renowned golden tongue and gifted ear for the overheard word, soon had something on practically everybody in the colored community. In politics this is known as "getting the whip hand." And throughout the colored community on and around Plain View it was said that even more than her fishing, cooking, flowers, and sewing, Rosiebelle Lee Wildcat Tennessee loved whip cracking. In fact, some said she loved popping her whip over folks' heads something mighty close to sinful.

In 1906, when Rosiebelle Lee arrived in Appalachee, the local colored community numbered somewhere in the vicinity of seven hundred, mostly small farmers who owned their own land there on the fringes of Plain View, plus the several families who lived and worked on the plantation itself. And as with every other Southern colored rural community of that day, the focal point was the church. And it was here in the church that Rosiebelle Lee arranged her first real show of power, the consequences of which were to be felt throughout the community for generations to come.

When she happened on to the scene, the local church was a dilapidated building owned and operated by a full-time farmer and part-time preacher, the Reverend Willie Lee Williams. Reverend Willie Lee had always suffered occasional "spells," so that whenever he didn't feel up to preaching on a Sunday, he wouldn't bother showing up at the church at all that day. And since he had the only key to the building, this often created panic among the locked-out Sunday-go-to-church-dressed congregation, especially if it just happened to rain that day. When this occurred on an average of once or twice a year, just about everybody thought it funny. But the older Reverend Willie Lee got, the moodier he got, and with the passing years these Sunday lockouts became more and more frequent, which became less and less of a laughing matter to those serious churchgoers. And *nowhere* on God's earth was there a more serious churchgoer than Rosiebelle Lee Wildcat Tennessee, who loved her Sunday churchgoing better than Satan loved his sin. It was at these local pageantries, where everybody, dressed for all to see in their happy rags and their best Sunday manners and morals, met to talk, laugh, show off a little, sing, and pray together, that Rosiebelle Lee's star shone its brightest. And since she was not about to let any moody little jackleg preacher steal her Sunday shine, she went out and built her own church, less than a mile from her house on a ten-acre plot of land donated by Mister Mac, who also provided the workers and materials for the construction and furnishing of this new "Upper Church" (since it sat about a mile or more *up* from what was now Reverend Willie Lee's "Lower Church"). The new church was christened Plain View Baptist, and the job of finding a minister for it was left solely in the hands of Rosiebelle Lee.

It was just around this time that Mister Mac, still a lover of cycling, offered to buy Rosiebelle Lee a bicycle of her own. Rosiebelle Lee was no particular lover of vehicles, or machines of any sort, and a great lover of animals of all sorts, so she opted instead for a horse—a white horse like Mister Mac's Joe Boy. But here Mister Mac drew the line: No white horse for a black gal. Instead he bought her a pure black English mare, whom she named Nigger Gal. Owning a horse of her own added to the ever-growing stature of Rosiebelle Lee there in the community. She did not want a saddle nor, surprisingly, did she require any riding lessons, and every day the laborers in the fields would stop in the midst of their work to watch her, pulling a long cloud of dust in her wake, long coalblack hair trailing in the breeze, galloping endlessly up and down the roads and bypaths astride the shiny black Nigger Gal. Quite often Mister Mack rode beside her on Joe Boy —though never during the daylight hours—the two racing through the night with the only sounds heard above the horses' rumbling hooves the black gal's and white man's spirited laughter.

And it was on Nigger Gal early one Sabbath morning, dressed in her Sunday best, that Rosiebelle Lee Wildcat Tennessee rode into the town of Appalachee, with only one thought on her mind. She was looking for the one man of God who was considered by those who knew to be the best black preacher in the county and she was set on bringing him back with her to Plain View Baptist Church on that very day.

She found him in the pulpit of Bethel Baptist, not just the largest colored church in Appalachee but in all of Muskhogean County. Through his entire sermon she sat out in the congregation sopping up his every word and gyration. Immediately after the end of his soul-saving sermon, while the congregation broke out in booming soul-shaking song, Rosiebelle Lee strode up to the pulpit and stood for a few moments in back of the lectern talking to a seated, exhausted, and sweat-rolling-down preacherman. After listening stupefied to her speech, blunt, brief, and to the point, above the roar of the congregation, he suddenly looked up to see who she was. Hypnotized both by her boldness and physicality, he lost nary a second in getting his hat and was last seen by his flock that fateful Sabbath hanging for dear life to the slender waist of Rosiebelle Lee atop a galloping right down through the heart of Appalachee for all she was worth Nigger Gal.

Arriving at their destination, the captive reverend was led by the hand into the new, still empty Upper Church, where Rosiebelle Lee Wildcat Tennessee, automatically assuming the top half of the holy missionary position, ordained God's number one black man in all of Muskhogean County by fucking him into a state of blissful shock right there on the freshly sawed, piny-smelling planks of his brand-new pulpit.

At Bethel Baptist that Sunday there was no collection taken up for the preacher.

Amen.

Now that she had her church and her preacher, next came the most important step of all. The way in which she had taken it upon herself to establish a new house of God, and especially her method of acquiring a preacher for it, hadn't sat too well on the stomachs of the area's elder citizens. They felt that for such a momentous spiritual undertaking that affected the very souls of the entire colored community, they themselves should have at least been consulted. And as a result of this slight most of the community's oldtimers wouldn't bestow their blessings on the outlaw Upper Church and every meeting Sunday they walked right on past it and on down the road to the Lower Church, despite Reverend Willie Lee's gradually increasing lockout spells.

Yet this old folks' boycott of the new Plain View Baptist Church didn't put much of a crimp in the style of the eternally optimistic Rosiebelle Lee, who knew from the beginning that in peopling her church she would have to do so with the community's young folks. And the community's young folks and Rosiebelle Lee Wildcat Tennessee got along like hot biscuits and melted butter.

Whenever she was out riding during the spring and summer and she saw a whole passel of children picking and eating wild berries, cherries, plums, muscadines, or any of the other fruit that grew in abundance along the roadside, Rosiebelle Lee would pull up and jump down off Nigger Gal to join them. After filling their guts and bluing their teeth and lips with the wild fruit, she and the children would side up and engage in a fruit-throwing battle. As the battle heightened and ammunition became scarce, large pebbles would be substituted, soon followed by heavier artillery—rocks. And nowhere in the area could there be found Rosiebelle Lee's equal at skimming a rock 'cross a creek. She could put a mean spin on a rock. Later came the infighting, boxing and wrestling. Rosiebelle Lee was the first to admit that she was not exactly the best around with her dukes, but nevertheless there was hardly a youngster, girl *or* boy, in the community that she couldn't find a way of flipping on his or her ass. Afterwards, following the wiping of a bloody nose here, a tear and a scratch or two there, everybody got a ride apiece on Nigger Gal.

(That night, after too much wild fruit, the shadowy figure of Rosiebelle Lee could be seen streaking back and forth between her house and the necessary house out back of the barn, where until nigh sunup she transported a heavy case of the dysentery.)

Just as it was for the community's grownups, the door to Rosiebelle Lee's house was always open to these children. They were forever bringing her buckets and sacks full of the fruit and nuts that grew freely by the roadside, or were picked freely from some farmer's trees, and she was forever making them pies and other delicacies, as well as blackberry wine, everybody's favorite drink, including Rosiebelle Lee's. In return they performed such necessary chores around her house as chopping firewood, bringing drinking water up from the spring that was down the hill in back of her house, digging her fishing worms, and keeping the yard swept clean. These children, regardless of age or sex, weren't just faces or objects to be used by Rosiebelle Lee. She *knew* every single one of them, not only by name, face, and family but by personality and even down to such personal matters as which member of the opposite sex each one of them liked, or loved. And as a result of all this attention accorded them not only by a grownup person but by the community's most renowned grownup, the overwhelming majority of these youngsters, boys as well as girls, confided practically everything to her, much more readily than they would have to their own parents or relatives. This was the main reason why she was known by children throughout the community as "Momma Rosie-bellelee."

While Sunday school classes were conducted each and every Sunday, the practice of the rural colored churches was to hold meetings with a minister presiding only once a month, with each church selecting its own particular Sunday. Plain View Baptist's was the second Sunday of each month. This date, like the new preacher, was the personal choice of Rosiebelle Lee, and so were the new church officials, deacons, secretary, treasurer, Sunday school teacher, and sexton; all, as it happened, were in some way kin to one or more of Momma Rosiebellelee's young playmates. Led into the Momma's den of divinity by their children, it was these, mostly young adults, who at first made up the congregation of the Upper Church come the second Sunday of each month. (While down the road a piece the older heads gathered in the Lower Church, whose monthly meetings were, coincidentally, also held on the second Sunday of every month.) And "Second Sunday" was what lit Rosiebelle Lee Wildcat Tennessee's lamp.

Second Sunday at Plain View Baptist Church was more than just a day of worship, or even a social gathering. It was that and much . . . much . . . more. Second Sunday at Plain View Baptist Church was a real carrying-on.

Women began preparing for this big day each month days before by washing, sewing, mending, patching, starching, and ironing the outfits that would be worn by everyone in the family to church on Second Sunday. Then came the cooking. Since Second Sunday was practically a sun-to-sun carrying-on, wives and mothers would take baskets of food with them to feed their families out on the church grounds after the day's dependably long sermon. The contents of all these baskets would be spread out on the grass around the church and each basket bearer would spend all of the Saturday before and much of the night cooking and preparing food for the Second Sunday spread.

Second Sunday! The day began when the sexton rang the church bell. First on the scene were the very young and the very old who came to attend Sunday school, which on this day of days was shortened to no more than an hour or two. Plenty enough time for a massive buildup of folks, who had been arriving all morning from every corner of the community and beyond, by wagon and buggy, on horseback, muleback, and on foot. They formed up outside the church doors, flashing their number-one "rags," and stood, sat, or squatted, all lipping and laughing a bit louder, or lower, than was their wont in anxious anticipation of the trigger that signaled the official start of the long-awaited meeting. Then from far down the road would come that signal—in the form of a halo of red Georgia dust pulling up to the churchyard behind a galloping sleek, coalblack Nigger Gal hauling Rosiebelle Lee and Luvenia, both in their bright flower-patterned outfits, and a wicker basket filled with freshly cut flowers for the church and hot fried fish for the spread. Second Sunday was on!

Climbing down off Nigger Gal, Rosiebelle Lee would toss a greeting to everyone within earshot and, still without breaking stride, make her way jauntily along the path that was being quickly cleared for her and Luvenia by an always awed and respectful audience right up to the door of the church. Once inside, she would start humming her favorite hymn as she walked around filling every vase in the room with flowers before taking her specially reserved seat. This was the high sign for Sunday school class to end and for the folks waiting on the outside to begin pouring through the doors, led by the preacher himself, and find themselves seats. And at Plain View Baptist *everybody* had a seat.

Looking out over the room from the pulpit, the pews lining the church's right wall were the exclusive domain of the menfolk and the older boys who were soon to become menfolk. The middle row of pews held mostly younger children—the Sunday school set—along with mothers holding their inevitably screaming babies, and that handful of men, usually recently married, with gall enough to be seen sitting in public with their even more recently pregnant wives . . . and, of course, all those males labeled as "sissies," mostly Sunday school teachers. Over against the left wall sat the older women in the pews just in front of those occupied by the young girls of courting age and those still single females whose courting days were quickly passing them by. Nobody *ever* dared tamper with this seating arrangement.

In the uppermost corners of the room and at the head of the two rows lining the walls were a few selected pews turned to face the pulpit. This was the famed amen corner, so called from the custom of those sitting in these reverend seats of emphasizing in unison each potent point made by the sermonizing preacher with a loud and timely *amen!* Reserved for the senior and most Christian members of the congregation, the men's corner held the deacons and other selected brothers, while over in the women's corner sat the sisters and mothers of the church. Yet despite her obvious youthfulness alongside her pew sisters, *the* Mother of Plain View Baptist Church was undisputedly Rosiebelle Lee Wildcat Tennessee. From her front-row seat of honor over in the amen corner she punctuated the preacher's soul-shocking sermon with her well-timed bursts of loud soulful singing, handclapping, and foot-stomping. Snuff-dipping was the accepted ladies' vice in Appalachee, even among the mothers and sisters of the amen corner, but Rosiebelle Lee always had a plug of chewing tobacco bulging out her golden brown cheek, and she only would pause in her singing, praying, humming, moaning, and stomping to spit a thin stream of tobacco juice, with deadeye accuracy, right over the head of little Luvenia riding her momma's rhythmically bouncing knee and smack into the shiny brass spittoon that always sat several feet in front of her, right at the edge of the pulpit.

Rosiebelle Lee's position of eminence in the amen corner gave her a commanding view of the room and the entire congregation, which enabled her to immediately spot and quickly rush to the assistance of any sister who appeared to be feeling the spirit too strongly. These were the women that the preacher's "whupping it on the soul" sermon was just too much for, and the moment the spirit struck the right chord they would leap up and, with head thrown back, arms flailing the air, and feet stomping the hardwood, commence to shouting out loud enough to make good and sure of being heard and appreciated upstairs by the Man Himself, until tackled and subdued by the calmer sisters of the congregation. This sometimes took as many as three or four sisters, always led by Rosiebelle Lee, who saw it her duty to restrain these shouters with a rib-cracking bear hug, since once out in the aisle and on the loose they'd just flail, wail, stomp, and scream their way right on up to the pulpit in order to lay hands on or hug the hellfire and brimstone preaching preacher. Amen!

Not *all* of the Second Sunday "walking the floor" and carrying-on were being carried on inside the church. Many folks, mostly men and older boys, showed up each Second Sunday at Plain View Baptist Church with no intention whatsoever of putting the first toe inside its door, even if it rained. These were the sinners. To them Second Sunday wasn't inside the church at all, where the preacher was foaming at the mouth in his never-ending damnation of their kind, but outside, on the churchgrounds. Outside, where throughout the long day several crapgames and skingames would be underway, besides the selling of bootleg liquor . . . along with an occasional piece of *inbetween* leg. Then would follow the inevitable—the fights—which brought out fists, rocks, and eventually knives, culminating in the traditional Second Sunday cutting—"Who got cut at church?" would be a leading question in the fields the following Monday morning—with each generation guaranteed its one churchground killing. While inside the house of God the preacher preached, the brothers sang, and the sisters shouted on.

Immediately following the indoor services—climaxed by the joining of new members into the church and afterwards quickly cooled down by the collection taken up for the preacher—came the spread, and the members of every family, Christian and sinner alike, sat down on the grass outside and broke bread together, elbow to elbow. Besides bread, biscuits, and hoecakes, broken, chewed, or gummed down, all kinds of animals and fowl contributed to the spread, cooked in their own fashion—the rabbit, squirrel, possum, coon, cow, chicken, turkey, duck, and goose. The pig alone gave up its ears, jowls, tongue, brain, neck, back, shoulders, hams, loins, sausages, chitlings, chops, cracklings, heart, liver, kidneys, ribs, feet, knuckles, tail, rump, butt, and balls—everything, as the saying went, but the fart and the squeal. All of this meat went well with whole heaps of baked, boiled, fried, stewed, or raw butter beans, snap beans, blackeyed peas, English peas, Irish potatoes, sweet potatoes, sweet corn, cabbage, kale, collard greens, mustard greens, turnip greens, poke salad, turnips, beets, carrots, rutabagas, rice, okra, pumpkins, squash, onions, scallions, tomatoes, bell peppers, hot peppers, cucumbers, radishes, eggs, butter, dumplings, and stuffing. All sweetened by apple, blackberry, dewberry, mulberry, cherry, peach, pear, plum, pumpkin, and sweet potato pies, chocolate cakes and cocoanut cakes, cupcakes and teacakes and shortening bread, cantaloupe, and watermelon, and all washed down with gallons of buttermilk and lemonade.

Rosiebelle Lee brought the fried fish. And it was her basket which the preacher always dipped his hand into first each Second Sunday to officially launch that particular month's spread. Then he would faithfully work his way from one sister's basket to the next (the quality and quantity of one's basket goods being a matter of prestige, as most sisters worked hard at trying to outdo one another at each spread), tasting a little of each until he arrived, trillions of calories later, at the outermost reaches of the spread, whereupon with the assistance of timely burps and breaking of wind he'd gamely eat his way back across the vast churchgrounds, basket by basket. Since the "eating preacher" was a part of Southern black lore, by the time he returned to the starting point, with hands back inside Rosiebelle Lee's fried fish basket after a roundtrip excursion in the course of which he'd had a hand in *every* basket, going *and* coming, no one ever paid much attention when the reverend unbuckled his belt and unbuttoned his three top trouser buttons . . . yet there were those who could never get over the man's unlaced shoes.

When her basket was empty, Rosiebelle Lee would flip it and Luvenia atop Nigger Gal before jumping up herself and, after bidding the large crowd that always gathered to see her off a loud "Bye y'all," galloping off down the road, pulling behind her into the late afternoon that long string of red Georgia dust. Second Sunday was over.

Rosiebelle Lee was on the scene of every local birth, baptism, wedding, and funeral, and also administered her own special Second Sunday church collection for the sick and needy, mostly foodstuffs and clothing which she delivered personally—all of which brought her into nearly every colored home in the vicinity as often as kinfolks and kept her more closely attuned to the community's pulse than any other individual before or during her time. Yet since everyone in Plain View (as the area surrounding the plantation was quickly becoming known, thanks largely to the presence of the Upper Church) had enough to eat, clothes to wear, and a decent place to live, nobody there considered himself poor. Thus, rather than food or clothing, many sick people needed help working their farms or taking care of their homes while they were laid up. And when this was the case then Rosiebelle Lee lost no time whatsoever in summoning much needed help for the afflicted by voluntarily volunteering the services of

every able bodied man, woman, child, and mule available for
work in the community. And *nobody* refused a favor asked, or
given, by Rosiebelle Lee. Besides yet continuing the unofficial
hiring and firing of the Big House servants, she was also
serving by this time as semi-official mediator for the colored
community in all its dealings with Mister Mac and Missis
Bea, or any other white who had business in the Momma's
province. With gerrymandering of this sort, it was not long
before Rosiebelle Lee had caused the doors of Reverend Willie Lee's Lower Church to be closed permanently.

By the rest of Muskhogean County's white ruling class
Mister Mac was looked upon as somewhat of an enigma. They
were willing to accept that the growing pains of youth had
lured him away from college to work on the lowly railroad—
though this was certainly not an action befitting a person of
breeding—and that this was the reason behind his bicycle trip
to the Wild West, where it was rumored around the county
that he'd lived among the wild and *naked* savages. However,
the local elite were not about to look the other way when he
took up his peculiar relationship with the negress with the
long straight hair and even longer name. This was a relationship that was peculiar indeed, since it *was* an accepted Southern custom for a white gentleman of means to keep a black
concubine (in fact if he didn't he would soon find his *manhood*
being questioned by both his peers and his inferiors), but it
was also expected that he have a white wife and a brood of
legitimate children. This was especially expected of an only
son like Mister Mac, and Missis Bea in her ladylike, refined
way never ceased dropping hints around that it was high time
for him to settle down and marry, if for no other reason than
to keep the MacAndrew name alive. But about the only thing
Mister Mac seemed interested in keeping alive was his ardent
affair with Rosiebelle Lee, and it seemed there was nothing
under Georgia's sun he wouldn't do for her, or especially give
to her. He had spent his early adult years away from Musk-

hogean and this had put division enough between him and his
contemporaries, most of whom had already started families of
their own. Then, after his return home, by all rights he should
have plunged right back into the social mainstream and
started to make up for those seven lost years by courting and
marrying one of the county's many young and available
belles. There was no denying that they were attracted to the
wiry, sunburnt maverick, with his long yellow hair and spar-
kle-toothed smile, who was actually rumored to have lived
(and loved?) among the savages of the Wild West. Instead,
Mister Mac immediately took up with that long-haired negress. Thus, his obstinate refusal to marry, and the obvious
impossibility of his black mistress being introduced into soci-
ety, gradually widened the rift between Ira MacAndrew and
the white world outside Plain View.

Mister Mac was not much of a businessman, or even too
interested in business affairs, nor did he involve himself in
local politics, which also did not help endear him to the local
elite. His father, George, had taken a very definite interest in
all levels of business and politics, from the courthouse and
cotton warehouse on up, and he spent most of his day riding
back and forth across the plantation, personally seeing to it
that his workers treated the land the way he felt it ought to
be treated. Mister Mac did none of this. He was content to
leave everything to do with the soil and its tillers to the
family's long-time and trusted overseer, just so long as the
largest cotton-producing plantation in the county continued
to show a profit. Mister Mac's great love, besides Rosiebelle
Lee, was hunting. Not fishing, since just sitting and waiting
by the hours bored him. He was a man of the trail, tracking
down rabbits and treeing squirrels, and most of all, bird hunting. And when he wasn't hunting, and to the perplexity of
everyone who knew him, he spent hours reading books, a
suspect act that only alienated him further from the rest of the
white community.

Then there were those mysterious disappearances of his.

About twice a year, without a word to anyone about where he was going or why, Mister Mac would vanish for anywhere from a week to a month—completely disappear. And after his reappearance he *never* bothered explaining anything to anybody, not even Missis Bea, young Amanda, or even Rosiebelle Lee, all of whom, like everybody else, quickly learned not to ask any questions, since all they ever got from him was that silent firm stare of his that told them to mind their own business.

When he was not hunting, reading, or vanishing into thin air, Mister Mac could usually be found in and around Rosiebelle Lee's house, where he began spending more of his non-hunting hours the older that little Luvenia got. As soon as he discovered that the alien little creature crawling beneath his feet there on the back porch while he sat contentedly digesting one of Rosiebelle Lee's Sunday morning breakfasts didn't bite when he hesitantly patted its tiny head, Mister Mac began to take a liking to the little thing. It wasn't too long after this astounding discovery of his that he got up enough nerve to take the child on his knee and begin to talk to her in a low, nervous voice until he heard Rosiebelle Lee's love call cooing from the bedroom. From that day onward the white man and his colored daughter were pretty nigh inseparable.

In the meantime he tried hard to keep his affection for the little girl hidden from Rosiebelle Lee, always pretending to ignore the child whenever she was watching them. But as Luvenia got older and started to show how fond she was of him, Mister Mac no longer cared if Rosiebelle Lee saw him playing with her daughter. Yet in spite of this peculiarity of his about Luvenia, he was still a white man and he made sure that he was *never* seen by anyone besides Rosiebelle Lee while enjoying the company of the little colored girl, even if his MacAndrew blood did run through her veins. So whenever he dared to venture outside the house with her for walks, he always made certain they went out the back way, down the hillside, across the spring, and back into the dense woodland, where they'd stroll unseen. Luvenia was long of body and limb, like Mister Mac, and he taught her how to climb trees, how to recognize them by name, and especially how to tell those whose branches bore edible fruit and nuts. It was back among these same trees that she learned how to swim, set rabbit traps, collect wild honey and, most important of all to him, to identify the many kinds of birds that inhabited the woodland. (As for teaching the child how to fish, Mister Mac wisely decided to leave this matter to her mother.) But when it came time to learn to ride a horse, Luvenia had to leave the woods for Rosiebelle Lee's spacious backyard, where Mister Mac taught her, unseen from the main road some two hundred or so yards from the front porch. He even went so far as to teach her how to read, along with giving her lessons in grammar, script, history, and geography. But when he felt it was time that she be taught those subjects he himself had no knack nor interest for—arithmetic being the leader of this group—he decided the time had come for Plain View's first little black schoolhouse.

Plain View's colored population had never had their own schoolhouse, and their children had always had to go outside the community for their schooling. The main reason for this was that, besides a distinct lack of encouragement from the local whites, prevalent colored thinking held that there was no sense whatsoever in *wasting* their children's time by sending them to school, since no matter how much they learned out of books, to the white world they were still niggers. Doomed. So, taking its cue from Rosiebelle Lee herself, the prevailing mood in Plain View was that once a child had gone to school long enough to learn to read and write its own name and count up to at least one hundred, then it ought to be taken out of the classroom and set to some more *useful* task in life. Like work, or marriage. But all because of little Luvenia, this was to change.

Unlike the new church though, the Plain View school, a neat little one-room log cabin, and its ten-acre plot were

donated to *all* the colored folks of Plain View. Mister Mac
even went so far as to interview applicants for the teaching
job himself and, after looking over everybody the county
board of education could scrape up from the area's colored
communities and not finding a single one he felt Luvenia
would get the proper learning from, he disappeared one day
and reappeared a week later with a teacher he'd fetched back
all the way down from Spelman College for Colored Women
in Atlanta.

All of this uncustomary attention given young Luvenia
by her white daddy throughout her childhood was certain to
tell on her character. Being the constant companion of Mister
Mac left the youngster little time for that other busybody,
Rosiebelle Lee, much less the time to develop any real close
ties with other children, even her schoolmates. And since it
seemed to them that Luvenia was totally uninterested both in
them and in their world, Plain View's young people, along
with many older people, quickly branded Luvenia a
"stuckup," who thought herself white, just like her daddy.
Yet despite her aloofness, Luvenia had light, sweet-milk skin,
long, straight, yellow hair, and a vast wardrobe (even Sunday
dresses for the middle of the week!), and, later on, even her
very own horse to take her to school every day, and all of these
attracted the rest of Plain View's children to her side like
green to grass.

There were, of course, other mulatto children in Plain
View at that time, but, unlike Luvenia's, their daddies almost
seemed not to know they existed. The best examples of this
were Luvenia's two younger brothers and her sister, all just
as fair of skin and straight of hair as Luvenia, but Mister Mac
never expressed the least bit of paternal affection for any of
them.

The arrival of Rosiebelle Lee's first son by Mister Mac,
in 1909, so delighted her that she immediately named the baby
her "Sugar Boy"; another boy was born nearly two years later,
and his little red body was so speckled with freckles even at

birth that she laughingly called him "Speck"—and the name stuck. Then came Doris Virginia. And *nobody* in Plain View who was old enough to remember at the time could ever forget the events surrounding Doris Virginia's birth. This occurred in the fall of 1918, at a time when there were several other newborn babies in Plain View who were still feeding on their mommas' milk. Plain View was hit hard by the flu epidemic, which afflicted all of those breastfeeding mothers. That is, all but Rosiebelle Lee. While the rest of the mothers lay helpless with flu, she would jump on Nigger Gal and gallop from house to house, nursing each one of these babies (the exact number increased with each telling of the story) from her two substantial and well-stocked tits until their mommas recovered enough to resume their maternal duties. This was the crowning achievement that ennobled Rosiebelle Lee Wildcat Tennessee as the true Mother of all Plain View. Amen.

Never one for farm work, nor much of any sort of work, for herself, Rosiebelle Lee still wanted her two boys to grow up to be *real* men, which by the standards of that place and time meant farmers. This also meant that their mother was obliged to go see Mister Mac and this time come away with a hundred acres of the woodland that adjoined her house. Half Mister Mac had cleared so that young Sugar Boy and Speck could begin their apprenticeships as farmers; the other half, with its small ponds, streams, and branches, Rosiebelle Lee reserved solely for her fishing.

While Sugar Boy and Speck were still youngsters, Mister Mac did at least offer to foot the entire bill if Rosiebelle Lee promised to keep them in school. But seeing how she was slowly but surely losing her older daughter to this man who was molding the child's young mind with his many big books, Rosiebelle Lee began to get increasingly suspicious of the new schoolhouse. But what perhaps frustrated her most of all about the entire learning mess was that the new schoolhouse came under the jurisdiction of the county, and so this was the *one* black thing in Plain View that she exercised no power over at all. And to pour salt on the sore, she had *no* authority at all to fire the schoolteacher and hire a new one—the way she could with the maids at the Big House—nor would Mister Mac grant her such authority. As a result she was always to remain cool both toward the teacher and the school itself. This left only one way for her to combat the schoolhouse mystique—when Mister Mac offered to educate Sugar Boy and Speck at his expense, she yanked both of them right out of school, and out from under the mystic spell of the new, *young,* pretty schoolteacher with the white folks' talk and manners and her mysterious schoolbooks. The boys headed back to the farm just as soon as she felt they had gone to school long enough to have learned to recognize their names after scribbling them down and to count their money. Rosiebelle Lee, like most of the area's colored, believed that the schoolhouse was a place for girls to learn how to teach school—teach other girls.

But when it came time for Luvenia to go to the county's colored high school up in Appalachee, Mister Mac himself reneged. He told Rosiebelle Lee, who had long since left practically all the decisions that affected Luvenia up to him, that he didn't want the girl, who was just entering her teens, going up there to Appalachee and mixing in with all of those worthless "town niggers." He had other plans for Luvenia. He sent her off to a girl's private boarding school, on out of the county, state . . . and South. To Ohio. Cincinnati. Luvenia was not to return home for many years, and nobody but Mister Mac knew her address. When she wrote home, she wrote *only* to him, and any time her mother wanted to find out about how she was getting along up North, she had to ask Mister Mac . . . because Rosiebelle Lee Wildcat Tennessee never did learn how to read, even her own name.

With land and equipment provided by Mister Mac, Rosiebelle Lee became a farmer herself in order to prepare her boys, even though most of the sweat she worked up came when she was sitting on Nigger Gal out in the hot sun, over-seeing the fieldworkers who were also provided by Mister Mac. Still, during those first eight years of farming, her land produced some of the finest cotton in the area, but it was in that last successful cotton year of hers, 1922, that the first sign of the end of the Old Order, and of Plain View's prosperity, first appeared on Rosiebelle Lee's front porch.

For every single cotton crop since the end of the Big War in 1918 there'd been talk around the country that It was on the way—from as far away out West as Texas. And each year It was said to be getting closer. And closer. Then, in 1922, the opening of the cotton-picking season found the whole of Muskhogean and neighboring counties overrunning with folks up from South Georgia who hoped to find work in the local cotton fields, and had brought their cotton sacks along . . . and terrifying tales of It. Bringing even more devastation than W. Tecumseh Sherman nearly sixty years earlier, It had struck South Georgia, wiping out *all* the cotton crops. Yes, It was coming! Plain View got a big share of these South Georgia migrants, even including a few white folks, whose farms and lives It had completely wrecked overnight. It had sent these folks scampering with their cotton sacks to the north end of the state to beg work in the cottonfields. When-ever they were lucky enough to find work, they stayed on to pitch camp, sleeping in barns, cribs, yards, underneath sheds, on and under porches, along roadsides, and even in the cot-tonfields themselves. Since they had seen It and what It could do to a boll of cotton with their own eyes, the faces of these South Georgia refugees expressed nothing but shock and dis-belief, like having just witnessed doomsday long before its time. And *all* they could talk about was It, in voices verging on whispers. Yes, they had *seen*. Then once the local fields were picked clean, they took up their sacks and moved on as quickly as they had come. They never returned. Instead, It followed them to Plain View before the next year's picking season began. Thus the Old South which fetched forth Rosiebelle Lee Wildcat Tennessee and her Mister Mac was finally dead. Killed not by anybody's Civil War, nor even by some Emancipation Proclamation. But by It. A little bitty ol' bug. The boll weevil.

> *Boll weevil's here, baby,*
> *Boll weevil's everywhere.*
> *Well, I would go to Arkansas City,*
> *Lord, boll weevil's over there.*
> *Boll weevil, boll weevil, cut down all my cotton*
> *and corn.*
> *I'm gonna pack my suitcase,*
> *And down the road I'm going.*
> *Boll weevil, boll weevil.*

Plain View was almost entirely a community of small farmers—and one big farmer; cotton was everybody's bread and butter, and the boll weevil *wasted* Plain View. Crawling onto the scene right at the height of the region's greatest period of prosperity for colored folks, when all those acres upon acres of fluffy white cotton were providing most with money enough to care for their needs as they never were able to before. Besides having plenty enough to eat and wear, most everybody owned their own homes and farms, and many of these farmers were able for the first time to afford modern equipment and machinery—not to mention such formerly unheard-of luxuries as rubber-tired buggies and even a few automobiles. Then came the bug—completely wiping out the *entire* cotton crop and breaking up farms, homes, and families in the process. Folks who were forced off the land either sold it if they could, left it to their creditors, or just left it, heading off into the nearby towns and faraway cities, where they had to find some other way of earning their daily bread.

But the boll weevil wasn't destined to ruin *everybody* in the county. Some it hatched. Perhaps the foremost of these were the white Nicholson brothers, Ike and Mike. Twins, from over in Walton County around the town of Monroe, west of Muskhogean, Ike and Mike arrived in Appalachee in 1911 and opened up a small grain and seed store. But by the end of the Big War, and thanks largely to the business boom it had created in the region, the brothers had branched out into farm implements and the little store had expanded into the biggest of its kind in the area, stocked with the newest in farm machinery and other equipment, plus the choicest quality grains and seeds. Ike and Mike sold most of their products on time, with payment usually due at harvest. But after the boll weevil's arrival on the Muskhogean scene in 1923, when there was no cotton harvest to speak of, only a handful of farmers were able to meet their payments. The next year's harvest left even fewer who were able to pay. Even in these lean years, the gifted brothers Nicholson still found ways to extract their pound of flesh. The innards of those farmers froze when they saw the tall silhouette of the Nicholsons' false-bodied two-horse wagon, drawn by two mules, looming up on the horizon—just like a giant vulture coming to pick their bones clean —and creaking slowly over the boll weevil-ravaged landscape. They drove from farm to farm, repossessing all the unpaid-for implements and machinery that were all still in good shape. On those farms where the equipment was not considered to be worth recovering, the Nicholsons' wagon would be seen leaving the premises with a cow, calf, mule, horse, or pig tied to the tailgate. Grain, vegetables, fruit, and fowl were also collected in lieu of payment. But the brothers Nicholsons' biggest coup during this Hour of the Boll Weevil was seizing the land itself. And at *every* land sale or auction that high false-bodied two-horse wagon stood above all the rest, waiting for the brothers Nicholson, while they busily bought up every available acre of this new rock-bottom-priced real estate. And while the boll weevil destroyed the cotton crop, the great droughts that hit the region in the mid-Twenties, right on the ass of the bug, made sure that all the other crops were practically wiped out in turn, thus

uprooting even more folks and sending them scampering off the sod and into the city. While across the county creaked that big old false-bodied two-horse wagon, with those two pulling mules all harnessed up in brand-new gear that smelled of hot leather and oiled wood—right behind the droughts and the bug, and almost half the folks in Plain View running off ahead of it.

What the two brothers really had their eyes fixed and hearts set on was the Big House. The Plain View Plantation itself. As with practically every one of the other plantations, Plain View had only one real cash crop, cotton. But even though this source of earnings was now all but cut off, all the workers were permitted to remain on the land. Mister Mac, not much of an entomologist, figured the boll weevil scare would blow away in a year or two, whereupon Plain View would return to normalcy. Besides, and despite his reputation for having little interest in business, Mister Mac (no big spender except when it came to Rosiebelle Lee and Luvenia) had banked most of the plantation's yearly profits. This, and whatever mortgage could be scraped up on the house and land, kept all the calamities then besetting the area from affecting his accustomed manner of life.

But, to the disenchantment of Mister Mac, the boll weevil just kept right on coming those next couple of years, and the droughts that killed the crops seemed to be about the only thing that would stop it. Although the plantation started showing a deficit that grew larger by the year, Mister Mac still refused to lay off or send away any of the dozen or so families who were still doing what little work was to be done while they remained on his land. Also, Mister Mac made a decision that recalled an earlier one made by his late daddy George (though here all similarities between the sire and the son began and ended) and absolutely refused to sell even one single acre of the plantation to anyone, anyone being the brothers Nicholson for whom Mister Mac had at one time publicly expressed his contempt. Also it was along about this time that everyone who knew him started to notice that his little disappearing acts were occurring more and more frequently and lasting longer every time. In the meantime the Nicholson brothers' wagon pulled by two "town" mules kept right on creaking from farm to farm on the land bordering the plantation . . . and the twins never kept their eyes off the Big House.

Meanwhile, thanks to Mister Mac, the life of Rosiebelle Lee and her three children hadn't changed one whit during those lean years. She still had her hundred acres, unmortgaged, with her two teenage sons old enough now to manage the farm without her help. With the community's population suddenly cut almost in two, Rosiebelle Lee's hold over Plain View tightened even more. Since she and her children were still living comfortably while everyone around them was visibly suffering, the Mother of Plain View was enjoying a measure of local power that even she had never even dreamt of. Since she was now in a position to literally starve out anyone who opposed her philosophy, the doors of Rosiebelle Lee's house were now open to her flock even wider than ever, and more of her time was now spent giving away everything she'd been given by, or had taken from others. And since she had been the official midwife of Appalachee, with a certificate on file in the courthouse, since the birth of Doris Virginia, this only helped to increase the size of her flock.

Ironically, the Mother of Plain View was looked upon by most parents of the community as a poor, or at least an unorthodox parent herself. While spending plenty of time with other folks' children, cajoling, scolding, *and* molding them, Rosiebelle Lee found little time for her own and more or less let them go their own way, as if she figured that merely being hers made them automatically capable of handling their own problems without anyone else's help. Yet one thing she did expect from her offspring, if not discipline, was *allegiance*. Allegiance to the Momma. This she made sure of early by making and keeping them dependent entirely on her for their material, if not spiritual needs. And thanks to the willingness of Mister Mac to grant whatever she asked whenever she asked for it, her children in their early years wanted for little materially, and with their white folks-like complexion and hair and pretty momma with the pretty black horse they were the envy of every colored child, and most grownups, in the community.

Yet in spite of her socializing and organizing, and though her soul fed on the amenities of friendship, sisterhood, and all other kinds of togetherness, Rosiebelle Lee was a loner. She didn't have, nor did she ever seem to need, a single close friend. Though she never tired of listening to the woes of others and helping out however she could, she herself was never once heard to complain even one little whit about *any* problem of her own. Rosiebelle Lee wasn't a complainer. Whenever she was down, or felt herself sliding, her true loner soul would emerge, sending her out with a pole and an apron pocket full of squirming, rebellious worms in search of a fishing hole. Hypnotized by woods that seemed especially hushed in honor of their respected guest, with only the soft trickling sound of water moving lazily below the bank, she would sit by the hour fishing. This was the only time Rosiebelle Lee ever *insisted* on being alone; even her children were not allowed to disturb her, and when they were babies she would put them to sleep before leaving them alone in the house.

Another oddity of Rosiebelle Lee's was that unlike the vast majority of colored women with white lovers, she had no black husband nor boyfriend on the side. Not because she was unable to get one, though she did weigh *only* about a hundred and twenty-five pounds (despite the huge amounts of food she was capable of absorbing) in an age and culture where the highest compliment a woman could be paid was to be told that she was fat, a visible sign of affluence and contentment. Yet the sight and thought of her slender, fine-boned figure topped off by that long butt-beating night-black hair burned in a way that was just on the verge of uncontrollable in the minds, hearts, souls, and britches of nearly every colored male in the area who was old enough to spew sap. Over the years few of them ever dared put their lifelong fantasies of Mister Mac's black gal on the line, and as for that less than a handful who did, after only one try each, they quickly found themselves faced with the choice of leaving the land . . . or hanging around to fertilize it. They *all* got their hats.

Also, at that time, when all of the area's colored babies were born at home, few of these births were officially recorded and many people went through life without ever knowing their correct age. Some knew the year they were born, but not the month (December 31 being a popular birthday for many every year); many others knew the month but not the year. And then there was Rosiebelle Lee. With her ageless looks, she professed ignorance of it all, the year, the month, and the day of her birth. In fact, Rosiebelle Lee, who figured that anything said, done, felt, or thought yesterday was of no importance whatsoever today, professed total ignorance of her entire past before her appearance in the front yard of Blackshear's Undertakers in the summer of '06. (This from a woman who could remember the name of *every* baby born in Plain View since that year of her arrival.) The *only* thing the local citizenry could wrest from her concerning her life before Plain View was that her daddy had been from "up at Chattanooga, Tennessee," and that he loved to chop wood. But whenever they asked what the colored folks up at Chattanooga, Tennessee, did, her reply was always, " 'Bout the same thing the niggers down here do"—a door-slammer on any further poking into her past. Though this had no effect at all on local speculation, which as the years slipped past became local lore, regarding the past history of the Mother of Plain View. Everybody's favorite Rosiebelle Lee story told how she had *had* to leave from up at Chattanooga, Tennessee, because of man trouble. White man, or more to the gut of the story, white *men* trouble. Rosiebelle Lee, according to the talk, had left behind up at Chattanooga, Tennessee, a whole mess of lovers, children, and messed-up homes, souls, and heads. So the stories went.

Unlike Rosiebelle Lee herself, Mister Mac was an extremely jealous lover. This, along with his renowned quick temper, made it risky business for any man, especially a colored one, to make an attempt at wooing the ever provocative Rosiebelle Lee. Yet there still were that rare few destined to have their moments.

The kidnaping and rape of Bethel Baptist's preacher by the Mother of the church was never followed up. However, the blame for this inaction couldn't be attributed to the man of God, and every Second Sunday, while he was ranting and raving the Good Word back and forth across the pulpit before his rapt congregation, his mind and eyes were never far away from the spot just beneath his traveling feet where he'd first felt the "good feel." The memory of that feeling and the eternal hope that one day the Mother of the church would lower it all down onto him just one more time kept him dancing and ritualizing over that sacred spot on the pulpit for more than thirty years ... or until he went to meet his Maker, holding that same, now holy hard. Amen.

Those were the days when in small towns time revolved around (at most) one or two local phenomena—like that unforgettable day back during the Big War when Plain Viewers looked heavenward and beheld with their own God-given eyes their first flying machine. For days afterwards the dogs barked at the empty sky way into the morning hours, and the cows refused to give milk. But most important, from that day onward everyone who remembered the event, and their numbers increased with the years, always referred to events in the past as having happened either before or after "the airplane." Though not the first one to see it, yet *never* one to be outdone, Rosiebelle Lee claimed that the flying machine had had a long chain attached to its tail that had dragged right over the roof of her barn. No one else at first recalled having seen any such thing, but the passing of time and the persistence of Rosiebelle Lee convinced them all that they too had seen that long chain hanging down from the flying machine.

Another happening were the Gypsies. Every few years or so these here Gypsies would pass through the area, and everyone working out in the fields and woods would drop whatever they were doing and go running for home like some dog gone mad, because if you didn't get there ahead of this caravan of grasshopper-like folks then there just might not be any house left to go running home *to*. The Gypsies took *everything* that moved, and if it didn't, then they turned right around and sold it straight back to the original owner. Now, that is, they did with everybody but Rosiebelle Lee. Never having been much of an accumulator or hoarder of material things, Rosiebelle Lee had little or nothing around her house for these long-haired, grinning, funny-talking *and* smelling, brown-skinned (but still white) folks to take. Instead she would inspect the wagons of these collectors of everything and *take* from them anything that she wanted—beads, rings, earrings, bracelets, necklaces, sandals, anklets, scarves, and any other richly colored pieces of cloths. (This caused many a Plain Viewer to suspect that perhaps some of these strange folks' blood just might even be flowing through the veins of their community Mother.) The same band of Gypsy folks *never* returned to Rosiebelle Lee's house, as many were known to do to many other houses in the area.

Another type of Gypsy also roamed the region during this time. This was the tramp singer or entertainer. Nigger. Looked upon both with contempt and awe by decent, hard-working, God-fearing colored folks, these nigger men who rather than work—

> *I ain' gonna pick no mo' cotton,*
> *I declare, I ain' gonna pull no mo' corn,*

—roamed the countryside with banjo, guitar, harmonica, or just voice or feet, singing, picking, blowing, or dancing wherever they could for a day's meal or a night's pallet.

> *I ain' gonna dig no mo' 'taters.*
> *Oh boy, I ain' gonna pick no mo' peas,*
> *'Cause everything I do on the farm you gotta*
>   *git down on yo' bended knees.*
> *I've been walking, I've been walking. . . .*

Since the rural colored, before the coming of the boll weevil, were more numerous and generally more prosperous than their town brothers and sisters, these nigger Gypsies appeared in abundance throughout the countryside, around harvest time especially. That was when money and food were most plentiful and every night after work in the fields the farmers sat digesting their suppers on their porches and stoops while being sung, picked, played, joked, and danced to by these non-working, worthless—but Lordy, Lord, talented —tramp niggers by lantern, star, or moonlight. The next morning these homeless folks would be gone on to the next farm or county, sometimes taking along with them a farmer's stray chicken . . . or daughter.

> *I've been walking, I've been walking. . . .*

And it was one of these Gypsy-type nigger tramp singers, a blues-singing one, who came back every year to serenade Rosiebelle Lee personally. No one in or around Plain View knew anything about this particular singer of the real mean and low-down dirty dog blues, who performed *only* before the Mother of Plain View. But what everybody *did* know about him for sure was that the man's timing was pretty nigh unbelievably perfect, since he showed up with his expensive-looking guitar (said by those who did all the saying that it had been bought by Rosiebelle Lee) on the Mother of

Plain View's front porch *only* on those nights when Mister Mac was away on one of his mysterious little trips.

Unfortunately though, all of God's children weren't blessed with such a perfect sense of timing. One such unfortunate was Mike Nicholson, the sporting twin (as opposed to Ike, the brain of the partnership). While riding alone from farmhouse to farmhouse on his repossessing route after the meager harvest of 1928, Mike got it into his head to try possessing something bigger—and more dangerous—than mere farm tools. Big game. Rosiebelle Lee Wildcat Tennessee. Amen.

The more than twenty years since she first made the Plain View stop had been good to Rosiebelle Lee. Her black hair had managed to remain segregated, keeping out that token strand of gray, and not a hint of a wrinkle had touched the firm skin of her still striking face. And since she was just as well off as ever—owing her soul to nobody's company store, notably the Nicholsons'—there was no cause whatsoever that anyone in Plain View knew of for Mike to drive across Rosiebelle Lee's hundred acres, right on up to the front door of her house where someone was said to have seen those two gray town mules, that nobody ever saw eating grass or hay like other folks' mules, still hitched up to that false-bodied wagon, which was standing, empty, in Rosiebelle Lee's front yard for over half the afternoon. It was never known who it was that saw the Nicholsons' wagon, since whoever it was knew that such a sight meant trouble. White folks trouble. The worst possible kind of trouble a colored person could possibly get messed up in, especially in a situation like this one. Mister Mac, whose jealous eye for Rosiebelle Lee was even well known by now to all the local white folks, had been seen and heard by his colored workers on occasion exhibiting that renowned quick temper of his and ordering the Nicholsons and their "scavenge wagon" off his land, and threatening them with sudden death if they didn't comply. So, it came as no surprise whatsoever to most of Plain View's colored when, early that very next morning, a Saturday, Mister Mac rode

Benny Andrews
Feb. 19, 1979

into Appalachee, right up to the front door of the brothers Nicholson Farm Implement, Grain, and Seed Store, right on the town's main drag where without bothering to climb down off his horse, he called the twins outside, in what was an unusually loud voice for him, and asked which one of them had been minding the store for the whole afternoon of the day before, and, when Ike said he had, Mister Mac drew from beneath his sporty black jacket a pearl-handled Colt .45 and shot the overall-clad tobacco-chewing Mike's brains out right there in front of several onlookers, then rode slowly back to Plain View, where he calmly packed a small suitcase, and left on one of his mysterious little trips.

The law didn't come looking for Mister Mac. Local mores didn't invest law officers with that kind of authority. This was an open and shut case; a member of one of the county's most reputable families had rid the scene of a nonentity, a piece of poor white trash from redneck country over around Monroe, who had flourished during a time of trouble for nearly everyone else in a career that was only equaled by that of the boll weevil itself. Mike's funeral had been eagerly awaited in Appalachee, but was not particularly well attended. In fact, the only person there besides Mike himself, the preacher, and the undertaker, was Ike, who at the graveside was said to have promised his dead brother not to worry about a thing wherever he was right then, because *all* of the expenses for the funeral was gonna be paid for by a MacAndrew. Well, Mister Mac wasn't around for the first installment, but Rosiebelle Lee was. That night after Mike's funeral, and before he had even had time to get his new grave cold, Rosiebelle Lee was awakened by nightmarish animal sounds coming from the direction of the barn. Running buck naked out to the back of the house, she threw open the stable door, and in the lantern light she saw a terror-stricken Nigger Gal running crazily around in circles, filling the night with vein-splitting squeals. Somebody had gone and thrown potash in Nigger Gal's face!

Nigger Gal—like her mistress, aging though still beautiful—survived the potash. But never again was she seen galloping proudly along Plain View's dirt roads and paths, giving
all the fieldworkers an excuse to put aside their chores for a
few moments just to stand up and wave, letting their envious
eyes follow the sleek animal and rider until the two merged
into a black speck pulling behind it that long string of legendary Georgia red into the far distance and on over the horizon.
Nigger Gal was blind.

Unlike his return from the Wild West nearly a quarter
of a century earlier, when he found the plantation in much
better shape than he had left it in, Mister Mac, when he
returned home for the first time since shooting Mike Nicholson more than a year earlier, saw that what the Civil War and
the Carpetbaggers and Freedmen, and even the boll weevil,
hadn't been able to do to his family's estate, the stock market
crash of 1929 had. Bringing the old plantation crashing down
at the feet of the MacAndrew family and workers where it all
was swept up and taken away by the bank. Mister Mac and
his family were left as broke as haints.

The first of the many pressing matters that awaited Mister Mac—who hated any kind of pressure and, worse, anything that had a business sound to it—was to find a new home
not only for himself but for Missis Bea and Amanda and her
two young daughters as well.

To her father, Amanda had been a *big* disappointment,
for Amanda was the result of old George's attempt to spite the
runaway Ira, and he had been expecting that an all-knowing
God would oblige a God-fearing man with a more reliable son
and heir. But when the boy was born a girl George instantly
lost *all* interest in babies and how to make them, and God, and
decided that the only way to make sure the plantation was run
right would be to just go on living forever.

Arriving when her mother was well into her forties, little
Amanda had been something of an embarrassment to Missis

Bea; her friends' childbearing days were already an unmentionable memory of the distant past, and as a result Amanda was reared entirely by her black mammy. She saw little and knew even less of her mother while she was growing up, since Missis Bea expressed more of an interest in her friends and local social events than in raising a child.

And another thing which didn't endear Amanda to her mother's heart was the girl's downright plainness, both in looks and personality. This was an unpardonable sin in the eyes of Missis Bea, that well-known lover of all things exquisite, romantic, and exotic. (Perhaps this best explains why she had never been heard publicly or privately condemning her son's relationship with that negress, who his mother secretly felt must have been the most beautiful creature that God ever let walk the earth.)

After having gone for twenty-one years without a sister, plus another six not even suspecting he had one, Ira never really got used to the idea of Amanda.

Adrift on this sea of family indifference, Amanda was to grow up totally alone, absolutely in awe of her brother Ira, though unlike him she was not a loner—quite the contrary. It seemed that need for the attention, love, and companionship she never got from her family was the reason why she got married at the young age of seventeen. It was a "tainted" marriage in the eyes of Missis Bea, who considered the bridegroom's family a notch too far down the social scale to think of marrying into hers. But since she suspected that Amanda had gotten herself in the family way somehow, Missis Bea felt she had no alternative but to give the match her blessings. Missis Bea's suspicion, a girl, was born six months later, and the following year another daughter was born to Amanda, who was by this time already a widow, since her husband had gotten himself killed off in the Great War—not in battle though, not even across the pond, but in training camp. This was a disappointment for the young soldier, and an embarrassment for both families, especially her husband's people.

They had never been fully accepted by the area's old families, who still hadn't forgotten that not a single one of them had marched off to defend the Cause in '61. And now this. But with two daughters of her own Amanda had no more cause to be lonely.

In deference to the MacAndrew name and its place in the county's history, the Appalachee National Bank gave Mister Mac permission to remain at Plain View until he could find suitable quarters elsewhere for himself and family. Amanda took her two daughters to live with their father's family in Appalachee. Missis Bea, in spite of the catastrophe, refused to raise any eyebrows by lowering herself a rung down the social ladder and declined a similar invitation from her son-in-law's family and decided instead to put her future in the hands of her son, Ira.

One hundred and twenty-five years earlier Mister Mac's great-granddaddy Benjamin, then a young man of twenty-seven, had come to the region and unlike the other pioneers who were then settling Muskhogean County, with their frontier-style crude box houses, he built himself a mansion, Georgian style. It was constructed of specially cut and fitted wood hauled overland, in an oxcart he drove himself, from as far away as Augusta, and the furniture and fixtures, including a Napoleon bed, were all made of French mahogany instead of the plentiful local raw oak and pine. Now in the Year of Our Lord 1931 it came to pass that—aboard a one-horse wagon driven by his bastard son and drawn by a slow, old, and blind Nigger Gal and with his mother sitting beside him, dressed in her Sunday finest and protecting her pale, delicate skin from the hot Georgia sun with a tiny, once white parasol— the great-grandson of Benjamin MacAndrew took leave of the Plain View mansion for the last time. Originally Mister Mac had wanted his mother to move into Rosiebelle Lee's house with him, and he planned to build another, much smaller house for his black gal and their children on that same land. (The bank couldn't foreclose on that hundred acres at the estate's northwestern corner, which was still owned outright, unmortgaged, by Rosiebelle Lee.) But here Missis Bea let her son know that the former mistress of Plain View would *never* live in a house that had been built for a negress, no matter how pretty. Missis Bea was too proud to live with Amanda's in-laws in Appalachee, even too proud to go back to her own people, the Orrs—so her son's black mistress's two boys built the two white folks a cabin, which, as a last humiliation for Missis Bea, was hardly big enough for Bonaparte's bed. Thus, a two-room log cabin, all the way downhill, across the spring and back into the woods *below* Rosiebelle Lee Wildcat Tennessee's house, became the MacAndrew—white—clan journey's end. Amen.

PART TWO

The Family

CHAPTER · ONE

*T*he Momma was dying. This was the brain-busting bulletin that was flashing across Speck's mind as he walked from the sawmill back to the Hundred Acres that sunnyhot, dusty Saturday in August of 1942. Saturday meant a half day's work in the woods, from sunup to noon, with the rest of the day religiously set aside for going into town to buy the next week's groceries, socialize, fraternize and, for some, to get their heads all bad on bootleg liquor. It was a three-mile walk from the mill to Speck's house and the sound of the unmuffled motor of the truck that was hauling the workers home from the woods had faded out somewhere up the long dirt road, leaving behind a reddish film of dust settling softly on the cap, neck, shoulders, and fast-moving shoes of the younger son of Rosiebelle Lee Wildcat Tennessee. Wiry, freckle-faced Speck was a familiar figure on that particular route, walking straight ahead with long, purposeful strides, but with his head hanging and his eyes firmly fixed on the road. Ever since the Accident four years earlier, Speck had not just out and out refused to ride the sawmill truck back and forth from the woods everyday, he wouldn't ride, or even handle, *anything* running on a motor. Speck's faith didn't lie in the future of the machine—thanks to Sugar Boy, for it was when he was riding in his older brother's car that the Accident happened.

Sugar Boy was known throughout the county for his fast driving, and on that late rainy Saturday night Sugar Boy had brother Speck and his brother-in-law Ezell Moore clutching onto a sack full of groceries, a head full of moonshine, and the footfeeder on his old Model-B Ford flat down on the floor as he came barreling down the four miles of rutted dirt road that led from Appalachee out to Rosiebelle Lee's Hundred Acres. Just about a mile up from the Hundred Acres the road sloped down in a steep incline for a half mile before the wooden Sugar Creek Bridge, then just as suddenly took off on a sharp upgrade for about another half a mile before finally leveling off. This stretch of the road was walled in by red-clay-coated hills topped off by rows of tall Georgia pines, and according to local lore the white man who owned this land back in slavery time used to tie his disobedient slaves to the branches of these pines and bullwhip some discipline into their disrespectful souls before leaving them for a day and night so that the rest of his niggers who passed along the road below could look up and see them hanging there marinating in the sun and rain. And to those few down through the years who dared to walk this stretch of road after dark those tall Georgia pines outlined against the sky presented a ghostly image, and the wind whispering eerily through their branches was said to carry the moans and screams of those slaves, long-since dead . . . unearthly sounds that gave this mile-long stretch of road its local name, Haint Hills.

While they were bearing down on Sugar Creek Bridge on that late Saturday night, it felt to Speck like Sugar Boy's ol' Model-B had suddenly forgotten its way home and unintentionally run a rut wrongly, for the next thing he knew the car was flying through the air just like an airplane, and with them all in it too, right up and off the bridge, over into the creek more than fifty feet below, taking the railing down with it. The only thing Speck remembered about the landing was the

sight of Ezell lying inexplicably in front of the car, water up
to his neck, his family's next week's eats floating away down
the creek—except for a string of smoked link sausages that
encircled his face like a wreath while he stared blank-eyed
right back into the car's still-burning headlights. Ezell was
deader than a doornail. That was when Speck started screaming, and he didn't stop completely until early that Monday
morning, when it came time for him to go back to work for
the WPA.

Physically, Speck suffered little damage from the wreck,
and since he had a wife and six children to feed at the time,
it wasn't nearly serious enough to keep him home from work.
But *mentally* was something else. He hadn't been able to forget the picture of death on Ezell's face, poking up out of the
water, staring with unseeing eyes right into the headlight of
the flipped-over Model-B, and decorated with that string of
storebought sausages. Since that night Speck couldn't stomach the sight of a link sausage on his plate, much less eat one.
(Though he still ate the hell out of the pattie-style sausages.)
But worse of all he himself had felt responsible for Ezell's
death. Ezell Moore, the brother of Sugar Boy's wife, Pecora,
had been a good, God-fearing Christian man, and like the
majority of those who knew Sugar Boy's fast driving habit,
Ezell really hadn't wanted to get in the car with Sugar Boy
and Speck at all that Saturday night. Ezell wasn't a drinking
man, and he had already been heading home with his sack of
groceries that night when he bumped into Speck on Appalachee's busy back street—the town's main drag for the colored
and known as "the Alley." Speck himself was always scared
to ride home with Sugar Boy, and on this particular night he
had been frantically looking around for someone else, anyone
else, to ride with who would share his scare all the way home.

Not much of a churchgoer, Speck hadn't sat in on Ezell's
funeral. Instead, he'd just stood around on the churchgrounds
watching the going-ons out there . . . but his mind's eye could
only see Ezell's body lying there in the church with everyone

singing, praying, mourning, eulogizing, and crying over him.
Then the night of the funeral came the storm. Speck had been
sitting with the rest of the family in Momma Rosiebellelee's
living room listening to the lightning cracking across the sky
like it was being shot out of the barrel of a .22 rifle. But the
wind was what made that storm a storm, and it kept howling
and moaning around the corners of the house just like it had
been sent down by a God who was out to get Speck personally. Sugar Boy's wife, Pecora, who was sitting there in the
dark listening to the storm still dressed in her funeral black,
claimed she could hear pigs squealing through the thunder,
wind, and rain. According to superstition, pigs were the *only*
ones of God's creatures who could see the wind, and, as pro-
claimed by Pecora, the high priestess of the superstitious, on
this particular night the pigs of Plain View were watching
from their pens while a supernatural wind carried the spirit
of her dead brother Ezell from his grave to join those of the
slaves on Haint Hills, where he would remain until Judgment
Day, haunting *every* car that dared to drive that mile between
sundown and sunup.

But one thing Momma Rosiebellelee wasn't was superstitious, which is probably why her children grew up disbelieving in signs. But after the very night of Ezell's funeral, Speck
had started to be deathly afraid of storms, especially high
winds and lightning, and every such storm found him huddled off in a corner with his head bowed, elbows dug into
knees, palms tightly clapped over his ears to keep out the
squealing sounds of pigs that were still echoing in the wind,
and eyes squeezed tight to shut out the lightning flashes. Also,
though he was constantly telling himself that he didn't believe in haints, when he had to walk that one-mile stretch
through Haint Hills every Saturday afternoon to buy the next
week's groceries in Appalachee, Speck would set his famous
fast feet down a bit faster than usual, never once taking his
eyes off the toes of his shoes to look up at the whispering
red-clay-coated hills. The overturned Model-B still sat in the

creekbed, half-submerged, with fish, tadpoles, frogs, and snakes swimming in and out of its rusted frame. The car was something of a local tourist attraction, and the guardrail was still down, but Speck kept carefully away from that side of the bridge, and never once stopped to look over the side. On his way back from town, if the sun had gone down and there was no one else in sight, Speck would pick up his feet and run that one-mile stretch through Haint Hills.

Speck was both unable and unwilling to confide his true feelings to anyone else, so no one besides himself knew the real impact Ezell's death had had on him, and certainly no one could figure why at his age he'd suddenly grown so knee-knocking scared of thunder, lightning, and high winds. All that everybody knew for sure was that ever since the Accident he'd refused *all* rides offered him by everybody, regardless of the time of day or night or the temper of the elements, in or on anything running on a motor. He walked back and forth into Appalachee every Saturday, and every workday morning found him rising hours before daybreak to eat breakfast and walk the three miles from the Hundred Acres to the sawmill, though his long, fast stride always got him to the woods ahead of the truck that brought in the other workers. As the memory of the Accident faded in the minds of the folks of Plain View these little kinks of Speck's became a source of amusement for the community at large. Yet when they climbed down from the truck and walked into the woods, these co-workers of Speck's made sure to leave their smiles, grins, smirks, and jokes about him back on the truck. For once they were in the woods there was one truth that no amount of their devilment could give the lie to. Speck was a *worker.* A sawmill man.

During the Depression—which Plain Viewers just thought of as Hard Times—the only available work around besides farming—which paid no money to talk about even if you owned your own land—was with the WPA. But, fortunately, the Japs came along and bombed a place the newspaper and radio folks called Pearl Harbor, and for those men who were left out of the draft all sort of jobs, paying good money, began opening up in the area, led by the sawmill and later on the pulpwood mill. With an unheard-of offer of fifteen dollars a week staring his stomach in the face, Speck picked up the empty lard bucket that he carried his lunch in, split the WPA scene early one Monday morning, and struck out for the woods. Walking. When he got to the sawmill, he was immediately thrown into the bullpen. So the mill's foreman could see whether their backs were made of something more than a bone with a piece of rubber stretched over it, all new hands went to work alongside the sawmill bums, malcontents, doggers, and young boys in the bullpen. Here, underneath a red pepper hot sun, they picked up the long slabs of bark that were sawed off the logs just before they were sized up into lumber, toted them up a steep embankment that was just past the always growing pyramid of sawdust, and threw them over into the "pit," a deep gully where local people collected the scrap wood after the mill closed for the day and hauled it home to burn in their stoves and fireplaces. The men in the bullpen were supposed to keep the area around the huge motor-driven saw clear of these slabs, and Speck, moving up and down the steep incline twice as fast as anyone else, accomplished this almost singlehandedly. The foreman knew a *real* worker when he saw one, and he wasted no time in pulling Speck out of the bullpen and putting him on one end of a two-man crosscut saw, felling trees in the deepest part of the woods.

Before he had been in the woods six months, Speck's equal on the crosscut saw couldn't be found on any of the mill's several teams. In fact, the foreman had trouble finding someone *man* enough to handle the other end of Speck's fast and smooth gliding crosscut, for ten hard-sawing hours with only one break, who wouldn't have to resort to "riding the saw" or letting the "monkey" get them.

In felling trees with a two-man crosscut you pull your

end of the saw toward yourself with a steady, swift, and firm
motion, then quickly loosen your grip on the handle so that
your partner can snap the saw back toward himself on the
other side of the tree. This would build up a rhythm which
usually took several days, sometimes even weeks, for even a
good crosscut team to perfect. In reaching this rhythm, these
back and forth motions had to be *all* pull, and then let go
. . . pull and let go . . . pull and let go. If one partner didn't
loosen his grip on the handle so the saw would snap back free
when his partner pulled, he was said to be "riding the saw."
This usually started to happen during the hottest part of the
day, when the overseeing sun stood directly overhead and
sealed the woods off from infiltration by fresh breezes and
anything else suspected of feeling cool. Then the trees held
in the sun's heat—the "monkey"—and the monkey descended
to sit heavily on the shoulders of the sawyer; this added hot
weight forced him to lean on the saw, and his partner would
have to put out more energy to pull all three—the saw, the
rider, and his monkey. The most common saw-riders were the
sawmill bums, grumblers, and doggers, none of which a good
saw man wanted to have on the other end of a crosscut which
was the main reason why this unwanted group had a monop-
oly on the bullpen.

The backcracking task of toting slabs didn't bother Speck
so much as the stigma of working in the bullpen—anything
or anybody tainted with controversy or nonconformity made
him uneasy. Still, Speck himself hadn't really wanted on the
saw either. What he still secretly wanted to do in the woods
was to snake logs. Once a tree had been felled and the
branches trimmed off, the trunk was chained to a mule and
dragged, or "snaked," through the woods all the way up to the
clearing where the big motor saw would slice it into lumber,
which was then stacked aboard a truck and hauled to the big
lumberyard in Appalachee. But all the snaking jobs were held
by those experienced millhands who were getting a little too
old to put in ten hours on the crosscut but were still invalu-

able for their knowledge of the woods, sawmilling, and mules. And deep down, Speck dug mules.

From as far back as he could remember until the time he was twenty years old, Momma Rosiebellelee had had a farm. A farm which he'd loved *everything* about, especially the mules. He'd learned to handle mules and plow by the time he was eight years old, and those had been Speck's happiest years —so happy that even the boll weevil and the long drought hadn't been enough to spoil his love for farming, as they had for Sugar Boy and many another Plain View farmer. But then came Hard Times. 1931. And Mister Mac.

Whether it was Hard Times, or just plain ol' log-cabin living, or perhaps even the cabin's location—downhill, across the spring, and back into the woods *below* Rosiebelle Lee Wildcat Tennessee's house—something had happened that finally made Mister Mac show his true colors. White. First, after failing to persuade Rosiebelle Lee into signing the Hundred Acres back over to him, he did what he felt would be the next best thing for himself and his mother. Mister Mac still harbored a strong feeling that he had been personally betrayed by ol' King Cotton, and he forbade his mistress—now his landlady as well—to plant any more of the traitorous plant on the Hundred Acres, ever. Instead, he conscripted Sugar Boy and Speck and set them to planting pine seedlings on the cleared land—hitherto mostly devoted to cotton—so that all of the Hundred Acres would eventually revert back to woodland. The Hundred Acres were set aside as his private hunting preserve—and private it was. He permitted no one else to hunt anywhere on this land, though he himself continued to roam all over everyone's woods and fields in quest of wild birds. This prohibition did not apply to Momma Rosiebellelee, who continued to fish wherever she could find a trickle of water, but it did apply to Sugar Boy and Speck. If they felt the hunting urge, or a hunger pang, then they had to go find someone else's land. And Speck also loved to hunt—but just rabbits and squirrels, the wild game favored by local colored

palates, not birds. Mister Mac even had a special dog, a short-
eared white creature with black spots that he called a
"pointer," that hunted *nothing* but birds—and Speck
wouldn't bother wasting a shotgun shell on a bird. Looking
around for other woods to hunt in hadn't bothered Speck so
much, but when Mister Mac decided to let those trees grow
back over the rich farmland of the Hundred Acres—that had
hurt, and it kept on hurting. As for Momma Rosiebellelee
though, she had never particularly cared for raising much of
anything—except for a little hell, lots of flowers, and other
folks' children. And there was still plenty of room for that
right around the house, and all over Plain View. Also, since
her firstborn and favorite son, Sugar Boy, after the coming of
the boll weevil had become more interested in the manmade
motor than in the Maker-made mule, she hadn't objected too
loudly at all when her land was replanted with pine trees—
just so long as it didn't in any way mess with her fishing, and
it didn't. That left only Speck, and *nobody* had ever been
accused of listening to *anything* Speck ever had to say.

But in the woods they *all* listened to his saw, and whatever else they might've thought of him, they all knew that
there wasn't to be found, in any woods anywhere, a better
crosscut sawing man than Speck. And *this*, like mules, farming, and hunting, Speck deep-down dug—even though he
knew that once they were out of the woods, these very same
admirers of his would say to one another, "Yeah, man, o'
Speck's all right, but he jes ain' the man his bro' Sugar Boy
is." And that is what deep down dug at Speck.

He was halfway home now. At this point in his journey
he never failed to lift his eyes from the toes of his brogans,
now slowing up slightly, to gaze almost reverently off to his
right, some three hundred yards back from the main road to
the top of the rise, where a grove of weeping willows seemed
to be like a hedge between the present-day world and Plain
View Plantation. Now he stopped, stared up the long tree-
lined drive leading to the front steps beneath the still immacu-

late white façade. Speck knew that for as long as he lived he would never forget that day back in 1931 when Mister Mac and his momma had moved from the Big House to the log cabin. Speck had driven the wagon. That was not too long after Momma Rosiebellelee had told him and Sugar Boy that there would be no more farming on the Hundred Acres and, on instructions from Mister Mac, they had gone about selling all of the farm equipment that Momma Rosiebellelee hadn't already given away. During Hard Times they were offered precious little . . . and paid even less. (When it came time to sell the mules, ol' Red and Clyde, Speck had taken off down into the woods in back of their house, where he stayed well into the night, crying like a lost baby.) Whenever anything was sold, the money had to be turned over to Mister Mac immediately, so he could plow it right back into the tree-planting business. So when moving day came around, nearly everything from Momma Rosiebellelee's farm was gone, and a wagon had to be borrowed from a neighbor to move Mister Mac and his momma, Missis Bea. Ol' Nigger Gal had pulled the wagon, a one-horse job, on that day . . . Speck loved her because she'd been in the family since even before he was born, but as a rule he didn't care much for horses—too high-strung to make good workers, totally unlike the dependable, much cooler mule. As it turned out, that move of Mister Mac's and Missis Bea's from the Big House on the hill to the little two-room log cabin downhill, across the spring, and back into the woods *below* Momma Rosiebellelee's house was ol' Nigger Gal's last journey.

Momma Rosiebellelee had been dead set against their using her Nigger Gal, *nobody's* workhorse, but since that just happened to be the very first day of spring plowing, not a horse or a mule was available for loan anywhere in Plain View. Still, blind and all, ol' Nigger Gal completed the entire trip with no audible complaints. Later, Momma Rosiebelle-lee had known that something wasn't right; she got up in the middle of the night and went out to the barn. Nigger Gal kept wheezing loudly, twitching, and kicking for a while, then grew absolutely still. Rosiebellelee sat with the horse's head in her lap until sunup, then went into the house, woke Sugar Boy and Speck, and sent them with shovels down into the woods. In a clearing no more than a good stone's throw from her favorite fishing hole they spent nearly the whole day digging a long, deep trench. Nigger Gal was later dragged by a borrowed mule-team down to the clearing and thrown over into the grave, then the grave was filled in. Momma Rosiebellelee was determined that the way to horse heaven wasn't going to take her Nigger Gal through any buzzard's gut.

Speck had never seen his Momma Rosiebellelee cry before, and for the first time ever the community of Plain View saw its Mother get deeply shook about something—she had lost the only living thing that she had really been close to in her quarter-century in Plain View. After Nigger Gal's burial, Momma Rosiebellelee was never the same again . . . for at least a week.

Now a half mile on down the road past the Big House, Speck suddenly heard it. He jumped quickly into the ditch and stood holding tightly onto the bib of his cap as he looked back down the road at the pile of dust surging toward him on the tail of the brand-new, black-topped white '42 Buick. Behind the wheel was Rockee Ryder, the pretty young speed-loving wife of Mr. Ike Nicholson, or Mister Nick, as he was known to his workers, who now lived in the Big House on the hill.

The MacAndrew smell hadn't had time to pack up and leave the Big House and settle into the little two-room log cabin downhill, across the spring, and back into the woods *below* Rosiebelle Lee Wildcat Tennessee's house before Mister Nick had done some business with the bank and moved into the old plantation house. He also bought up most of the original MacAndrew land—though Rosiebelle Lee's Hundred Acres were not for sale—which he immediately began littering with clapboard shacks, while chopping the acreage up into sharecropping plots; before long he had more tenant farmers working his land, and owned more farmers' souls outright, than anyone in the area. Next, he went out and got himself a suit, a tie . . . and a wife . . . Rockee Ryder, a pretty town girl who could run everybody and everything in Plain View off the road. And now, with her colored maid sitting up in the back seat holding on to the white lady's four-month-old daughter, Rockee Ryder shot past Speck standing there in the ditch, holding on to his cap with one hand and shielding his eyes with the other from the blast of dust and flying gravel that followed the speeding Buick up the road leading into Appalachee. Dust down, Speck climbed out of the ditch and quickly got his feet back into the rhythm of the road for that last mile home.

He stopped out of habit to open the white-painted mailbox with the name MACANDREW in black letters he had painted himself on both sides, even though he knew it would be empty. Every weekday morning Mister James Bacon, the mailman, just had to reach out the window of his car without bothering to open up the box, because, come rain, sleet, slime, or shine, someone was always standing there at the side of the road, waiting with hand outstretched to pick up and whisk over to Mister Mac his *Atlanta Constitution.*

From where he stood Speck could look across the road right into the rarely closed front door of the Prickards' house, a three-room shotgun shack (one of those Georgia tenant farmhouses whose front and back doors were lined up so straight that you could fire a shotgun clear through the house without hitting a thing inside). In this case, though, you'd be likely to hit one of the nearly twenty Prickards that lived inside, the only white family besides the Nicholsons and MacAndrews in Plain View. Apart from their color though, the Prickards struck the colored community as an odd bunch of folks.

They were said to be from up in the mountains somewhere in North Georgia. Joel Prickard—called "Cotton Eyed

Joe" because of the constant twitching and blinking of his left headlight—appeared in Plain View, along with his wife, parents, children, grandchildren, in-laws, brothers, sisters, and cousins, during the worst of Hard Times to squat on Nicholson's land, just across the road from Momma Rosiebellelee's Hundred Acres. Some said that where they came from up in the mountains there were no colored folks and that the family had never seen a black face until they got to Plain View. Anyway, they had little to do with the rest of the community, since they kept too busy among themselves—mostly drinking, fighting . . . and having more of one another. The only one in Plain View who had much to do with them was Momma Rosiebellelee. She almost singlehandedly fed the Prickards (along with many another Plain View family) during Hard Times. This was not to say that Momma Rosiebellelee put herself to the trouble of cultivating a garden of her own just to feed the hungry during those many eatless days when practically every belly in Plain View was French kissing its backbone. She drew from the gardens of those who had to feed those who had not, and despite their God-given whiteness the Prickards had not. Still, when they showed their appreciation of what she had done for them, the Prickards, being white, didn't go so far as to address her as "Momma Rosiebellelee," or even "Missis" or "Miss," nor did they refer to her as simply "Rosiebelle Lee," as many a white was prone to do who was much younger than she was. To them she was Aunt or "Aint" Rosiebellelee. Respect.

Even though they lived in the midst of a colony of sharecroppers, the Prickards weren't farmers of any sort, by any stretch of anybody's imagination. Local gossip claimed they had just moved into the first empty house they spotted on their trek out of the mountains heading nowhere. Besides what was provided by Momma Rosiebellelee, the family's subsistence depended on its working members finding whatever jobs were available in the area, mostly those menial jobs better known as "nigger's work." Thus the Prickard family became Plain View's first specimens of genuine "po' white trash."

From where he stood at the mailbox Speck could see the Prickards' youngest children running in, out of, and around the house—buck naked, as was their custom. Even though they had a big yellow schoolbus stopping in front of their house every day—something Plain View's colored children didn't—they hardly ever boarded it to go to school. Nary a chair or swing did the front porch hold, nor could a stick of furniture be spotted through the open front door, not even a shade or curtain inside the two windows in front, whose many broken panes made the Georgia red dust-covered shack look like a snaggle-toothed old woman cackling away at passersby. But what piqued Speck's curiosity most about the Prickards was that they didn't have a mailbox . . . and no lamplight was ever seen shining through those mad cackling windows, which to him meant that they *never* read *The Atlanta Constitution,* or at least not at night. But even if they didn't, one thing they did do and that was sing. God! How they sang. They surely had rhythm. They had only one old guitar, but everyone in the family must have known how to play it, since it sounded like it *never* got any rest, day or night. Since Plain View's colored didn't much care for white folks' singing of any kind, they responded to these hillbilly sounds with annoyance, or laughter . . . but always out of earshot of the forever singing, picking, drinking, fighting, and fucking Prickard family, of course.

There was one colored in Plain View who didn't conform to local standards of music appreciation, and every Saturday night, weather permitting, Speck crawled on hands and knees across the road to the ditch alongside where, right by the MacAndrew mailbox, he lay hidden while secretly enjoying the strange mountain sounds twanging from the Prickards' house, front porch, stoop, or yard just a few feet away. He especially loved the singing of ol' Cotton Eyed Joe's teenage daughter, Betty Jean, who he felt sure was the best singer—and looker—of the lot. . . .

A sudden uneasy feeling brought Speck back from his reverie. That old Southern colored man's malady—guilt and, especially, fear of loose thinking about a white woman—had his soul in a vise. Meekly closing the door of the mailbox and hanging his head, he turned away from the white folks' house with its front yard and porch filled with running and screaming little buck-naked bodies and began walking on down the narrow turnoff that led right past his house and down into the front yard of Momma Rosiebellelee's.

CHAPTER · TWO

*W*hereas the Prickards' shingle-roofed, dust-col-
ored shotgun shack with its backdrop of acre upon acre of
open cotton fields sat right near the main road, Speck's two-
room, tin-roofed house on the opposite side of the road was
set much farther back, right on the edge of a forest. For the
first few years of their marriage he and his wife, Theophilia,
had lived with Momma Rosiebellelee, along with Sugar Boy
and his wife, Pecora, and the young Doris Virginia. But
Theophilia, who didn't quite see eye to eye with her mother-
in-law on enough subjects to suit Speck, informed him that
whether he planned to stay or go, *she* was moving out of
Momma Rosiebellelee's house, and taking the children with
her. Speck was always scared by the idea of anyone putting
asunder what Momma Rosiebellelee had joined together, so
he immediately requested and was granted an audience with
his mother. He started to explain that with all due respect to
Momma Rosiebellelee, Theophilia was just too headstrong by
nature to live under the same roof with her in-laws. At first
Rosiebelle Lee was not much disposed to favor a petition that
seemed to imply that the Momma was no more than a common mother-in-law, but she relented finally and gave permission for Speck and Sugar Boy to cut down enough of her trees

to build a cabin on her land, just a long spit up the path from her front porch—and let no more be said about it.

Bordered on the east by tall pines and cedars, the long yard leading up to the front porch of Speck's house was spotted with several corroding rubber tires filled with dirt and planted with brightly colored flowers, and tended and watered by Theophilia, whenever she found the time. These neat, circular beds of flowers served as oases in a yard grown grassless from the daily pounding of children's bare feet. Now two pairs of them—followed closely by the bloodhound, Belle, ears flopping, tail wagging, tongue lolling, thin ribs heaving in and out—were running out of the house to meet Speck.

"Daddy! Daddy! Daddy!" Accompanied by loud barking.

Speck could never get enough of his children's affection, even though anyone else's emotions always made him feel a little self-conscious—so, without a word or a break in his long stride, he leaned over, scooped a child up in each arm, and headed for the door, with Belle still right behind.

Their first four children were born under the roof and the direction of Momma Rosiebellelee, certified midwife. In fact, it was right after the birth of their first child that the coolness between wife and mother-in-law first breezed in. Theophilia wanted to name the baby, a boy, after her daddy, though Speck thought that Momma Rosiebellelee ought to have first crack at naming her first grandchild born under her roof. Well, Theophilia went ahead and named the baby after her daddy—Hamilton. But never one to be outdone by *anybody,* at *any time, anywhere,* or for *any* reason, Momma Rosiebellelee got in her usual last lick. As the attending midwife, it was her responsibility to record the child's birth at the county courthouse in Appalachee, and there were those in Plain View who were convinced she must have put down the name "Ham" on the birth certificate. Why else, they asked themselves, would she go around calling the child "Ham," against his mother's wishes . . . and encourage everyone else to do the same? This led many to believe the boy's grandmother just called him Ham out of spite, since she hardly bothered to hide how disappointed she was that her first grandchild had not been sired by her favorite son, Sugar Boy, but instead by Speck, whom no one, especially his family, ever took too seriously. Also, unlike the light-skinned, almost red-skinned Speck, little Hamilton's skin was the color of his mother's—tar black.

But no matter how much encouragement they got from the Mother of all Plain View, *nobody*, not even other children, dared call Hamilton "Ham" within earshot of Theophilia. Theophilia had this here real funny thing about names—hers, for instance. She wouldn't tolerate anybody, including Speck and her own kinfolks, shortcutting her name to "Theo" or "Thee," something everyone who heard her name naturally seemed to want to. Instead, every time somebody felt the spirit and took one of these shortcuts, she would quickly, though always nicely, make them backtrack to where they started from and spit out the whole Theophilia. And in a culture where practically everybody had a nickname of some kind, she never had one and never allowed one to be bestowed upon any of her children. Theophilia was funny that way.

Their next child, born two years later, was also a boy and the father wanted to name this one Speck Junior. But not wanting any little Speck running around under her feet, Theophilia once again took charge of the christening herself —Benjamin.

But with the third child, a girl, Theophilia offered the privilege of naming it to Momma Rosiebellelee, who flatly refused this well-meant offer. By now, the Momma was growing more and more impatient with Pecora, who still had not presented her Sugar Boy with a baby. So, by default, the new baby was also named by her mother—Olivia.

And with Speck, surprisingly, still the only one of Momma Rosiebellelee's sons who was siring any grandchildren, by the time of the arrival of the fourth child, another boy, Mister Mac suddenly got into the baby-naming business. Word came from the two-room log cabin back in the woods, over across the spring, downhill *below* Momma Rosiebelle-lee's house, that this fourth child of Speck's and Theophilia's was to be christened Richmond. Nobody knew why Mister Mac, who had never even seen him, would want to give such a name to a little-bitty baby, but Richmond was the name the white man sent from over across the spring that early June morning and Richmond the little-bitty colored boy baby stayed.

Their last two children, the two now in his arms and the only two born in the new house, Speck himself had named— Marian Anderson and Joe Louis. Unlike their older brothers and sister, who always seemed to Speck to be too busy doing something else whenever he came home, little Marian Anderson, age six, and Joe Louis, four, always ran up to meet him, screaming for their daddy. And of the six these two were by far his favorites.

Built in 1936, Speck's house with its yellowish, dirt-free, raw-lumber face beneath a shiny cap of tin still had about it a look of newness. He was proud of this house, for even though his older brother had gotten most of the credit for the building of it, Speck had done all of the carpentry work, while Sugar Boy's and Ezell's contributions had been mainly muscular. Speck loved building things. He'd made the long wooden bench that sat up against the wall in the middle of the porch, right in between the two front doors—and he'd also made the frames for the screendoors, along with the two smaller pew-style benches, painted green, at each end of the porch, which was enclosed on each side by climbing rose-bushes. In fact, there were times when he himself wasn't quite sure which he loved the most—farming, hunting, or carpentering. But there were those, including Theophilia, who said he could never make a living as a carpenter, because he was forever making and fixing things for folks for nothing.

Still, he could never bring himself to charge somebody for doing something he enjoyed so much.

Coming to the front porch, built so low to the ground that even a child needed no stoop to reach it, Speck lowered both children to the porch, and their little bare feet touched down running on ahead of him into the house as they shrieked, "Momma! Momma! Daddy's home!"

When Speck appeared in the door, Marian Anderson was jumping up and down and shrieking while Joe Louis hopped excitedly from one foot to the other, grinning widely, both looking from the front door to their mother, who was standing with her back turned over the hot cookstove, both impatiently awaiting her reaction to what they'd just brought back alive into her lair.

"I've told both of y'all to stay outa this here kitchen—"

By the time the screendoor banged shut behind their little butts, they were already off the porch and halfway around the house, running. . . .

"—and *don't* slam the screendoor!"

Left stranded just inside the doorway by his favorite welcoming committee, Speck just stood for a moment, mustering up the right amount of gruffiness, as befitted the man of the house, before addressing his wife's back.

"Hi long fo dinner's ready?"

She turned her head around, without shifting her body from in front of the stove—since she was already well into her eighth month, and the baby was expected any day. She stood just a head shorter than Speck, tiny stationary beads of sweat glistening on her polish-black face. Speck could never meet her gaze for long, and she spoke in a voice that was just as steady and unyielding as those dark, deep-set eyes:

"Just as soon as you wash your hands and face."

Without another word he lowered his eyes and walked across the kitchen, over to the washstand in the corner between the stove and the back door. The kitchen itself wasn't all that large—crowded, but not junky, with the black wood-burning cookstove sitting on a rectangular strip of tin, burnt dark brown by heat, nailed to the floor alongside a wooden box half-filled with short sticks of stovewood. Straight across the kitchen, next to the room's only window, was a bare table with two backless benches, all, including the table and stovewood box, built by Speck. Standing almost arrogantly in the corner between the table and the front door was an ornamental, glass-fronted kitchen safe, its storebought green beginning to fade; it had once been part of the more elegant decor of Theophilia's mother's kitchen, and now seemed miscast beside Speck's homemades. On the wall above the safe were several nailed-in shelves with Mason jars full of recently canned peaches, snap beans, blackberries, corn, and watermelon rind, while a bed occupied the farthest corner from the front door—a bed that was not quite large enough to sleep three boys comfortably (ages fourteen, twelve, and eight) but still slept Hamilton, Benjamin, and Richmond, nevertheless. High up on the wall between the foot of the bed and the back door were several well-spaced nails, on which was hung the family's wardrobe, mostly for winter.

In the corner next to the washstand (straight across the room from the foot of the bed), on a wooden shelf fixed to the wall by two metal brackets, stood four tin water buckets. Speck took the gourd that hung alongside, dipped out some water, and poured it into a small tin washpan. Dropping the bar of strong-smelling homemade lye soap into the cool spring water and without bothering to roll up the sleeves of his sweat-dyed guanosack sewn workshirt or to remove his cap, he proceeded to wash his hands and face in a most splashing manner. Dripping water heavily, he quickly dried himself on the rough towel, also sewn from a guano sack, that hung on a nail alongside the stand, before taking the soap out of the pan, kicking open the screendoor with his left foot, and heaving the water out into the backyard, scattering sunbathing hens and their chickabiddies. Walking over to the table, he pulled out his chair—straw-bottomed and backed by

Theophilia—and sat down. Sitting at the head of the table, cap perched firmly on his head, the man of the house was ready to eat.

From this seat of authority he sat for a few moments looking at Theophilia; her swollen belly hanging out over the stove made him think the baby must be straining to bust out right that very second and drop right over into the pot its mother stood stirring. His appetite having left the kitchen temporarily at this sight, Speck quickly turned his head away from his wife's *predicament* to screw his eyes into the wall directly above the boys' bed before he spoke.

"You sent Ham'ton to town wit the grocery bill?"

"He went. You still ain't going in today?"

"That's why I tol'ja to send Ham'ton in to git my pay from the sawmill boss 'n then go on ovah to Mist' Frank Few's store wit the grocery bill so hit kin be sent out on the 'livery truck. No, fuh the las' time I ain' gwine in 'n don' wan' any of the chillun gwine in 'cept Ham'ton wit the bill. You heah?"

"The boys all want to go to the picture show."

"*No* picture show t'day! You tol' Ham'ton to git straight back here wit the res' of my pay soon as he give Mist' Frank Few the bill, didn'ja?"

"He know."

"The Momma said jes las' night she wan' *all* the chillun 'n gran'-chillun close by her bedside *all* day t'day *an'* t'morrow. Any word from down at the house?" A solemn, reverent tone suddenly swallowed up the heretofore gruff voice of the man of the house sitting at the head of the kitchen table with cap on waiting for his food.

"Nobody told me nothing." Then, "But somebody down there oughta be told something . . . to go get a doctor before your momma won't be needing one at all."

"There you go agin!" Gruff voice returning at the head of the kitchen table. "You know good 'n doggone well the Momma don' have nud'n to do wit Doc Allen."

"There's two white doctors up there in town."

"The Momma says she don' need to pay no doctor jes so he kin tell her that her time is done come." His voice dropping at these last words.

"Only God can tell her that." Resting her swollen belly halfway between the stove and the table while looking directly down at Speck.

"Do you think fuh one minid the Momma would be send'n all the way up Nawth to Cincinnati, Ohio, fuh her oldest daughter Luvenia, who she ain' seed in mo' than twenty years, to come back home if she didn' know her time was heah?" His eyes, getting red at the corners now, were still screwed into the wall directly above the boys' bed.

"When she do that?"

"Las' week."

"She hear anything yet?"

"Got a letter jes yest'dy."

"Is Luvenia coming home?"

"Be heah sometime this even'n. 'Ginia's Geechie gonna pick her up in the taxicab at the train station in town 'n bring her back down to the house."

"Is she coming with her family?"

"Wha' family? Her family's heah."

"I mean her husband and children. She's married, ain't she?"

"Sho' she's married. But I don' know if she's bring'n them wit her. The Momma didn' say if Mist' Mac said she was or not."

"Mister Mac?" She was back over at the stove now.

"Yeah. He the one who got the letter."

"I pray to God no child of mine ever do that to me."

"Do wha' to you?"

"Don't think enough of me to even write me a letter on my deathbed. That's what!"

"You know good 'n doggone well the Momma can' read!"

"Doris Virginia can read. Sugar Boy can read. *You* can read!"

"Now don' you go git'n started on that agin. That's hi
come I nevah tol'ja nud'n 'bout the letter in the first place,
'cause I jes knowed you be talk'n lak that. All the Momma said
Mist' Mac said Luvenia said was she would be com'n home
t'day. An'. . . ."

"And what?"

"An' . . . er, somethin' else the Momma said Mist' Mac
said 'bout Luvenia. Luvenia ain' her name no mo'."

"*Ain't* Luvenia? What *is* it then?"

"Shirley Temple."

"What?"

"Shirley Temple. That's wha' the Momma said Mist'
Mac said Luvenia said."

"When did it get to be this Shirley Temple stuff?"

"A long time now, the Momma said Mist' Mac said."

"How come she waited till her momma was dying before
she told her that she wasn't going by the name her momma
gave her when she was a baby no more?"

"I guess she jes wanted to let evahbody know what name
to call her by when she gits heah."

"If she went through all that time and trouble just to
change her name from Luvenia to a name like Shirley Temple, then she sure ain't gonna bring no husband and children
down here to Georgia to see her family."

"Hi come you say that?"

"You just wait and see. Didn't you ever think it mighty
peculiar she never sent home no pictures of her husband and
children?"

"Hi do you know she didn'? She jes might've sent them
to Mist' Mac."

"Why'nt he show them to her momma, her brothers and
sister then?"

"I said Luvenia . . . er . . . er . . ."

"Shirley Temple."

"She *might've* sent some to him. I don' know."

"If she sent some to him, then he sure ain't gonna show

them to nobody else because that's how come he sent her up North in the first place."

"*Hi* come he sent her up Nawth?"

"So when she got grown and ready to marry, she wouldn't have to marry no colored man. *That's* how come!"

"That's a lie! The Momma tol' us when we were lil' chillun that Mist' Mac sent Luvenia up Nawth 'cause the schools up there was bettah fuh cullud chilluns than the schools down heah in the South."

"If she come down here this evening by herself and don't let her dying momma see her oldest grandchild for the first time, it means only *one* thing."

"Wha' hit means?"

"It means that her husband is as white as clabber."

"Hi come you always think you know so much 'bout folks you ain' nevah evah seed befo'?" A crimson shade of annoyance beginning to cover his freckles.

"Oooh, but I've seen *her.*" Theophilia was standing with her back to the stove now, the firm, fixed expression in her eyes suddenly relaxed, staring out the kitchen window, as if she were looking straight back into another time. Then, in a wistful tone, she began to speak. "We other children use'ta wait down yonder at the crossroad every school morning for her to come by on her pretty white-and-black spotted horse. And for two miles we would run behind her and her, oh, so beautiful horse all the way up to the schoolhouse door. The first time I saw this happen was on what was suppose' to be my first day of school when I was five years old. Luvenia, who must've been every bit ten or eleven, came down to the crossroad that morning and *all* those other children took off like rabbits running behind that horse of hers. My two older sisters left me standing there in the middle of the crossroad, crying my eyes out. I was so scared I ran back home, more than a mile, hollering my head off all the way. That night Poppa told the girls that if they ever ran off and left me standing all alone there in the road like that again, he'd run behind them all the way up to the schoolhouse door with a hickory switch burning their behinds. The next day when Luvenia got to the crossroad one of my sisters—I can't for the world remember now which one of them it was—grabbed me by the hand and pulled and dragged me with her running behind the horse. I guess I must've fell a hundred times during that two-mile run. But with knees, nose, elbows, chin, and hands all skint, I made it to school for the first time. And from then on until I was eight years old and Luvenia went away up North, I was part of the crowd. Even now about all I can remember of my first three years of school is *every* morning and evening having a mouth, nose, and eyes full of dust, or mud, and running like a jackrabbit gone mad behind that pretty white-and-black spotted horse.

"Oh, but Luvenia was soooo pretty! She had real long yellow hair that shined like it had gold in it. And wore the prettiest clothes . . . something different *every* day, even around the house, I heard. And she always wore long white gloves. She *never* got herself and her clothes all messy and dirty like the rest of us children did. She was too old to play with me, but from what I heard she didn't even take up time with the children her own age. Always with her daddy, Mister Mac, they said. But I can still remember the children talking about the mannish little boys who use'ta crawl up the hill behind y'all's house real early every Second Sunday morning and peek at her and your momma out on the back porch taking their before-church bath in the same tub . . ."

"Stop talk'n nasty!" A quick snap of the neck unscrewed Speck's eyes from the wall above the boys' bed. He glowered at Theophilia, and his freckles were now completely hidden by a crimson flush of anger and embarrassment.

"You won' nevah theah! You jes gwine by wha' you heard other folks say!" Ever since their marriage nearly all of their conversations had ended this way—with hot words, usually his, since she always seemed to say something that got under his extra-sensitive skin. "Don' evah let the chillun heah you talk'n 'bout that. Put somethin' to eat on the table heah, 'oman!"

Without speaking, Theophilia went to the back door to call the children. One moment they were scattered over the yard and the woods, the next already piling in through front and back screendoors to line up at the washstand, then quickly wet, then even more quickly dry their hands and faces, before finding their respective places on the benches on each side of the table. These were five of Speck's and Theophilia's six children, ranging in ages from Benjamin's almost twelve down to Joe Louis's just past four and in complexions from Marian Anderson's Bermuda brown to Olivia's Tennessee tallow.

Despite the presence of five youngsters at one sitting, all the noise and cutting-up came to an abrupt end once they sat down at the kitchen table. The only child talk the man of the house sometimes tolerated at the table was that which was addressed directly to him.

"Daddy, is Grandma dead?" Like this by Joe Louis.

"She *ain't* dead! She's jes on her deadbed! And it ain't Grandma, its *Grandmomma!*" Marian Anderson enlightening her younger brother, then taking over the interrogation herself: "Daddy, how come we don't call Grandmomma Momma Rosiebellelee like all the other folks and children do?"

"Because she ain't your momma. She's your *grand-momma.*" Theophilia answering before Speck could get his out.

"They kin call her Momma Rosiebellelee jes fuh t'day . . . 'n t'morrow. . . ."

"I'm the *only* momma they got and ever gonna have. Today, tomorrow, and the day I lay down on my deathbed I'm still gonna be the *only* momma for them. These here are one bunch of children in Plain View Missis Rosiebelle Lee ain't gonna make *her* children. They her *grandchildren!*"

Doggonit! He *hated* Theophilia for that. Not letting the children call the Momma "Momma Rosiebellelee" like the rest of Plain View did, and was glad to do. Everybody called her that out of respect, young and old, except, of course, for Theophilia, who Speck was convinced thought herself better than everybody else in, or outside, Plain View. He was so mad at her right at that particular moment that he didn't even notice her bulging belly when he swung his eyes down off the wall over the boys' bed to glare at her while she busily shuttled the hot food from the stove to the table. But between his thoughts, throat, and lips the rush of words got so jumbled up that nothing could break this logjam to make it out of his mouth except a few unintelligible sputters coated with spit.

"Daddy, we kin call . . . ?"

"Hush yo' mouth, Marian Anderson, so you kin eat!" The logjam was broken. But food was on the table now, and Speck's sawmill-hungry stomach was frantically sending up distress signals to the brain to stop trying to spit it out and start trying to stuff it in. This time hunger whupped anger.

Despite the availability and richness of the soil, food raising on the Hundred Acres had an unbelievably young history. From the beginning Momma Rosiebellelee, a natural-born flower-grower, and her children had lived mostly off of what came out of other folks' gardens and orchards. Even after she herself became a farmer, she only raised cotton and enough corn for her animals—Nigger Gal and the two mules. Cows and pigs and chickens and ducks and such had never much interested Momma Rosiebellelee, except as pets. Alive, they presented too much of a hazard to her yard full of flowers and they and their produce were readily available for the Mother of Plain View for not even so much as the asking in most cases. The local stomachs hadn't been starved directly by the boll weevil; Plain View's food crop was just as bountiful as ever for those who stayed on the farm after the coming of the bug. But these stay-at-home bellies were severely pinched by the droughts, which, unlike that little connoisseur

of unborn cotton, messed with *all* the crops, edible and inedible. Then came Hard Times.

As late as 1928, the year Speck and Theophilia got married, the only food growing on the Hundred Acres was still the wild kind, mostly fruit and nuts. Momma Rosiebellelee and her family were then eating mainly out of Mister Mac's many gardens on Plain View Plantation . . . and also out of his pocketbook. But Hard Times ended all this, suddenly making Mister Mac and his momma dependent on Momma Rosiebellelee for their daily bread. (This—as many felt but few dared express—was a situation that Momma Rosiebellelee just wallowed in—the great-grandson of the first lord of Plain View abandoning the Big House to go live in exile downhill, across the spring, and back into the woods *below* her house. And this automatically exalted her to the title of queen of *all* Plain View. Even she felt that Mr. Ike Nicholson's takeover of the Big House had not changed her status, since he would always be an outsider, and no matter how white his new shirt collar his neck would always be red.) And when Mister Mac had to move off the plantation, with its abundance of garden patches, orchards, and livestock, Momma Rosiebellelee, almost ten years after Its arrival, finally felt the bite of the boll weevil. Plain View was hungry. Even the farmers who grew their own food were finding it hard to feed themselves and their animals . . . not counting their landless relatives who lived nearby, and faraway—distance never being a problem when harvest time came . . . and Momma Rosiebellelee, who still commandeered the farmers' food to feed not only her family but *all* Plain View's needy.

The hardest times now came during that in-between time when most everyone had already eaten all the food stored up for the winter—hogmeat, canned fruit and vegetables, dried peas, beans and nuts, hilled Irish and sweet potatoes—and was only just planting their spring gardens. This was when the woods and fields were always full of folks, mostly women and children, hunting for patches of poke salad or any other wild greens, just about the only available food for many folks during the long, hungry weeks of late winter and early spring.

When Speck and Theophilia got married in early 1928, and she moved in under Momma Rosiebellelee's roof, the teenage bride, who came from a very self-reliant family of hard-working farmers, couldn't get used to the idea of living out of other folks' gardens. That was why during that very first year of their marriage she went to Momma Rosiebellelee, whom she called "Missis Rosiebelle Lee," and got permission to use about two acres of the Hundred, then went straight back home and returned with her daddy's mule and plow. She broke up the ground herself before sowing the seeds of what was soon to be known throughout Plain View during those Hard Times as "Theophilia's Garden." And whatever went into Theophilia's Garden, and whatever came out, did so only because Theophilia herself wanted it to. This applied to folks as well, including Momma Rosiebellelee. Even though she owned the land these vegetables grew in, this garden of her daughter-in-law's was the *only* one in Plain View that the Momma had absolutely *no* say so over at all—even the tenant farmers who worked Mr. Nicholson's land kept on paying tribute to Momma Rosiebellelee. As long as she lived under the Momma's powerful wing, Theophilia shared her home-grown food with her in-laws, even though she did *all* of the work herself. (Momma Rosiebellelee was too busy tending her flowers, Doris Virginia entertaining her many friends there in the shade of the porch while swaying and dancing to the sound of the Victrola coming from the sitting room, and Pecora doing all of the housework momma and daughter were too busy to do themselves.) But Theophilia refused to let *anyone* tell her how to take care of her garden, one reason—along with a handful of others—why Momma Rosiebellelee's house was soon divided against itself. Then, when Theophilia's daddy died right at the beginning of Hard Times, she inherited his cow, pig, chickens, and mule. The mule she sold,

since she had no more use for it, but these other alien creatures she brought back to the Hundred Acres. The inevitable
disagreement arose between Theophilia, a devotee of the kind
of charity that begins at home, and Momma Rosiebellelee,
who favored rural free delivery of milk, butter, eggs, poultry,
and pork all over Plain View. And that, along with other
disagreements about childrearing, was why Theophilia and
Speck were living where they were. The move to the new
house proved both embarrassing and unsettling to the spot-
light-shy, non-boatrocking man of the house, Speck, but
Theophilia was glad to have a place of her own, where her
vegetables, cow, pig, chickens, and children's growth weren't
about to be stunted by a lack of sunlight there in the long
shadows beneath the wide, wide wing of Momma Rosiebellelee.

Everything that grew in Theophilia's Garden that her
family didn't eat she either canned, dried—blackeyed peas,
hot peppers, and goobers—or hilled—sweet potatoes—for the
long winter months ahead. It was the height of the canning
season now, August, but Theophilia never found the time to
can on Saturday, since she had to have Speck's midday dinner
ready for him when he got home from the woods so he could
eat before going into town in the afternoon to buy those few
staples her garden didn't provide. But Momma Rosiebellelee
wanted all of her children and grandchildren within hollering distance of her bedside on the day she was expecting to
cross over and Speck, who was scared of death but even more
scared of the wrath of Momma Rosiebellelee, wasn't going
into Appalachee, for the first time in a long Saturday afternoon. This was why he had Theophilia send Hamilton into
Appalachee with the week's grocery list to pick up Speck's
pay from the sawmill boss over in front of the bank at noon
and then head over to Mister Frank Few's General Store. But
Speck had specifically told Hamilton the night before not to
wait for a ride back home on the delivery truck, nor to go to

the picture show, but to get back with the leftover money just as fast as his two feet would bring him home. Momma Rosie-bellelee was sure to count heads at her bedside when she got ready to cross over.

Theophilia always fixed all the plates at the table, Speck's first. She set in front of him this early Saturday afternoon a plate of garden-fresh, steaming-hot green butter beans flecked with tidbits of fatback and balanced on one corner by nearly half of a thick hoecake. She put long strands of fresh, green, boiled okra on the children's plates and then on her own—but not on Speck's, okra being a vegetable he considered too slimy and nasty-looking even to watch someone else eat, much less sit still and let it slide down his own throat to his queasy belly. Nor did he drink milk, so Theophilia filled each child's tin cup with buttermilk and set a glass of fresh spring water beside his plate. While he liked butter beans, and most other vegetables, Speck's favorite food by far was rabbit and rutabagas. Speck could eat rabbit and rutabagas by the potful, daily. But rabbit was not in season and Theophilia didn't grow rutabagas in her garden, so they had to be bought in town every Saturday, which meant, to the sorrow of Theophilia and the children, a dinner of rutabagas *every* Sunday as long as they were in season.

"Did'ja put rutabagas on the list?"

"They on there all right." Theophilia's answer coming out sounding more like a sigh.

"Daddy, we hafta eat rudubugus . . . ?"

"They *ain't* rudubugus! They's *rutabagas!* Ain't that right, Daddy."

"Marian Anderson, you leave Joe Louis 'lone. Joe Louis, you hush up."

Except for those winter months when hogmeat was available—from the one pig a year they could afford to fatten and kill—meat on Speck's family's plates was, like the rutabaga, reserved primarily for Sunday dinner. From time to time, though, a little money could be spared for fish, fried by Theophilia for either Saturday night supper or Sunday breakfast, or sometimes both. These were the meals the children looked forward to so much.

It was Olivia's turn to say the blessing:

"Lord, make us thankful for this food
We are about to receive,
To nourish and strengthen our bodies,
For Christ's sake,
Amen."

"Now, Olivia, next time don't say it so fast, you hear?"

"Yes'm, Momma." Speck never said the blessing himself but honored it by not starting in until it had been said by Theophilia or one of the children. Now, he began chopping up over his butter beans scallions, tomatoes, green and red-hot peppers, before dousing everything with vinegar. Ready. As usual, he ignored the fork Theophilia always put besides his plate. Speck hovered over his food, hemming the plate in with his elbows before breaking off enough cornbread to fit snugly just inside the tips of his fingers, to sop up his food from his plate, and bring it up to his mouth, dipping so low down to meet his fast-sopping, dripping fingers that the bib of his weather-worn, grime-smeared, greasy leather cap, which he *never* took off to eat, nearly landed in his plate at each dip of his head. And for the rest of the meal the loud smacking noises sent forth by Speck's fast-working lips ricocheted off the stove, safe, and walls, and back over the table, drowning out the sound of the children's spoons scraping their tin plates and teeth, along with the buzzing of the lone fly happily flaunting the fact that it had solved the screendoor defense system.

$\mathcal{T}$he other room of Speck's house was where he and Theophilia slept, in a large wooden-post, cotton-ticked bed in the far corner, directly across from where Olivia, Marian Anderson, and Joe Louis slept. The narrow aisle separating the two oversized beds ended at a curtained window looking out onto the road that ran past the house and ended up on down in the front yard of Momma Rosiebellelee's. The backyard window, also decorated with a thin, white, stiffly starched curtain, was between the foot of Speck's bed and the dresser that stood back in the corner. Rising up almost to the ceiling between the foot of the girls' bed and the front door was a huge chifforobe, the same dark brown as the beds and the dresser—all of which, like the kitchen safe, had had much more show-off room when they still belonged to Theophilia's mother. At the end of the aisle between the beds, and just to the right of the door to the kitchen, was the fireplace, complete with firedogs, poker, and mantelpiece, with each end held down by two large kerosene lamps. Directly above the mantel, looking out into the room from behind a large glass frame through a pair of deep, dark, soul-puncturing eyes in an adamant African face under a thick crop of woolly hair, was the portrait of Theophilia's now-dead daddy, Hamilton Crawford. Speck hadn't wanted his dead daddy-in-law hanging up there; instead he'd wanted to paste on this wall space his large and still-growing collection of pictures of the World Heavyweight Boxing Champion, Joe Louis, cut out of newspapers and magazines over the years. This fight about who belonged above the mantelpiece, Hamilton Crawford or Joe Louis, was eventually won by Theophilia through sheer persistence, which was not one of Speck's qualities. He finally did get Joe pasted up, beyond the fireplace over in the corner above the dresser, the darkest spot in the darkest corner of the room. Unlike the kitchen, this room was completely wallpapered, sky blue, but at this particular moment Speck could hardly see anything, because the front door and the door to the kitchen were both latched, and the green window shades were drawn as well. All for Speck's Saturday-afternoon bath, prepared for him each week by Theophilia in the big tin tub she used for her weekly Monday washing and with the water boiled on the back of the stove in the two big black kettles given her by her momma when the latter broke up housekeeping to go up North to live with her oldest daughter's family following old Mr. Hamilton Crawford's death.

During the week the only things of himself Speck washed were his hands, face . . . and his feet. Theophilia wouldn't let him near their bed until his feet had been washed. After sliding and squishing around inside a pair of sockless brogans all day, Speck's feet would slip out of their sunup-to-sundown calaboose all capped with toejam, sending out a smell that was somewhere in between something else and too much. This emancipation ceremony always took place out on the front porch, where Theophilia would send him to sit on one of the benches and soak his feet in a washpan full of hot soapy water until the air indoors was clear of that nose-wrinkling smell. Meanwhile, his brogans were left under the front porch overnight, and neither dog, chicken, *nor* child dared go near.

Now that the big tin tub had been placed between the hearth and the foot of his and Theophilia's bed, his rocker and three other straw-bottomed chairs pushed back into the narrow aisle between the two beds, Speck sat with his knees up in the big tub, soaking in the relaxing warmth of the soapy water, the heaviest thing on his mind being his cap.

Speck *never* took off his cap, even in bed, except when he wanted to wash and cut his hair, which he did himself with the aid of a pair of scissors, standing in front of a looking glass and behind a latched door. Alone. For Speck was ashamed of his hair. He'd always been ashamed of his hair, his color, his talents . . . himself.

Speck had *never* wanted to look, act, think, or be different from everyone else. Even as a child he longed to be just a regular fellow. But being a regular fellow in Plain View didn't mean having light skin and long, straight, ashblond hair, belonging to the first colored family, with a rich white daddy who owned the community and a pretty brown-skinned momma who ran it. Instead it meant having dark skin and short, nappy black hair. Shy and sensitive, Speck carried a heavy burden of guilt about his skin, hair, and social station —everything that made him stand out like a haint at midnight, and not wanting to be different, he had spent most of his thirty-one years trying desperately to meld with the mold. Long before the color ever dared dream of someday being beautiful, Speck had actually *wanted* to be black. So badly did he want to be just like everyone else that he'd spent all of his life working hard at doing, saying, acting, and thinking *nothing* different—which in itself made him different. He'd tried to keep himself innocent, in word or deed, of *any* kind of originality. As a child in school he had had at first no problem whatsoever with his studies, but he still felt uncomfortable; his classmates looked on him as being uncanny, or a sissy, since all that book stuff came so easy to him while for the majority of them learning books was a struggle. But, and to the utter consternation of his teacher, this was quickly remedied when Speck started pretending to be just as indifferent or unhandy at learning as most of his colleagues were. And by trying so badly to belong, he ended up always trying to please everybody, which left his overly sensitive soul vulnerable to attack by the most vicious assailants of them all—children.

Speck had a face that bordered on pretty to go along with his light skin and long, straight, ashblond hair, and all of the young Plain View girls were crazy about him, while most of the boys were either jealous or contemptuous of him, because of these same qualities. True, there was a smattering of other children around whose daddies or granddaddies were white, but their mothers weren't named Rosiebelle Lee Wildcat Tennessee. In fact, Speck went out of his way to avoid the company of these other "lights," solely because of their haint-at-midnight appearance—the very reason they, *and* he, drew others to them like flies to buttermilk and molasses.

What others thought of him meant *everything* to Speck, which was why he shied away from anybody and anything considered to be different by the other boys around his age, and shunned the company of all lights, and especially girls, ever fearful that too much popularity with them would damage his chances of winning the approval of Plain View's young males. This never quite worked out that way though; most of these youngsters still felt Speck, with his light skin, straight hair, and uncanniness with the printed word, to be somehow unlike them. Still, they all liked him in a way, even if it was only as the target of their devilment. Nobody could really hate Speck.

The one these youngsters did like, envy, and, in a few cases, worship, was Speck's older brother, Sugar Boy. Now Sugar Boy was something different and *then* some more. The girls, *and* womenfolk, just didn't like Sugar Boy—they *loved* him. And he spent his entire adolescent and adult years trying his doggonedest to love as many as he could right back. Sugar Boy was the local lover, Plain View's own *sport,* and somebody the rest of the boys—and men later on—looked up to and tried their damnedest to emulate. Sugar Boy didn't feel the least bit guilty about his color, his hair, or his social station. He took all of these things for granted and went around using them to their fullest advantage among a race brainwashed to believe that black was bad and white was right. Younger sister Doris Virginia, like Sugar Boy, just went along with and loved the whole idea of being the child of Rosiebelle Lee Wildcat Tennessee and all that entailed so much that many felt the Mother of Plain View's youngest child was mighty close to being a *stuckup*.

Even though he was unable to be and do like his brother and sister, Speck still envied them their boldness—especially Sugar Boy, whom he simply idolized, or better, loved. Yet there was little about Speck that anyone could've pointed out that Sugar Boy and Doris Virginia—who were tight as ticks themselves—actually liked (not including his ashblond hair, which enflamed the redheaded Doris Virginia with a jealousy that verged on hatred). In fact, around the house Speck was always the object of most of their devilment . . . even on the part of Momma Rosiebellelee, though his strong need for her approval, respect, *and* love always seemed much greater than Sugar Boy's or Doris Virginia's. These two she somehow seemed to take more seriously than Speck, and she—hardly ever without that chuckle in her eye or throat—still always referred to him as her "Speckled Baby."

Since Speck was always the hind end of all the devilment around his own house, Plain View's other children, especially the boys, felt free to make him the butt of many of their jokes, all the more so since he himself never seemed to object, and Sugar Boy and Doris Virginia never came to his rescue—like they always did for each other—when these other children were forever getting the better of him, whether with words or fists.

Despite wanting to belong at any cost, Speck was secretly glad when Momma Rosiebellelee pulled him out of school to work full-time alongside Sugar Boy on the farm. Like Speck, Sugar Boy had found that there was nothing at all to learning, so that by the time Momma Rosiebellelee took him out of school in the fourth grade he figured he'd about learned all from books that was worth learning anyway. Sugar Boy had enjoyed farming well enough, just as long as it proved profitable come the end of cotton-picking each year. But after the coming of the boll weevil, and unlike Speck, he had absolutely no objection to giving up the unequal struggle to till the soil at any and all cost. For his twelfth birthday Momma Rosiebellelee had bought him a brand-new Model-T Ford, a "Tin Lizzie," so by the time the boll weevil struck, two years later, his chief interests in life had become the car, chicks, and clothes, in that order, and he went speeding through the Twenties, Thirties, and on into the Forties, letting the good times roll on his way to becoming Plain View's all-time legendary *sport.*

Meanwhile, that other fourth-grade dropout, Speck, no social bug like his brother, mother, or younger sister, was finally finding the one place he did belong—on the farm. Speck loved everything about farming, from the seedtime to the harvest. *Everything.* But most of all he loved the mules.

Back before the Big War, when Mister Mac presented her with the Hundred Acres, Momma Rosiebellelee decided to put forty into cotton, ten into corn, and fifty into fishing. And up through 1922 this rich land produced just over a bale of cotton per acre, averaging more than fifty bales a year. During those first few years all the work was done by outside help, provided by Mister Mac and everyone who owed Momma Rosiebellelee a favor here and there. Then, when Sugar Boy and Speck came of age, they took over all the plowing, but after the boll weevil came to stay and Sugar Boy became more interested in cars and girls than in mules—and had to start seeking outside, cash-paying work to keep his cars and girls running—all of the plowing was left to Speck, who loved every single furrow of it.

The outside help did all of the chopping, hoeing, and picking of Momma Rosiebellelee's cotton, but Speck, who had learned to plow at age eight, was handling practically all of the mule-work on the farm by the time he was ten. This began in late winter—first, ridding the land of all the dead cotton stalks left from the year before with a rolling stalk cutter and then clearing them away with a harrow so they could be piled up alongside the field and burned. This required both mules, Red and Clyde, the only ones Momma Rosiebellelee ever had on the farm. Then came the first spring plowing, or "breaking up," of the land, followed by the most difficult part of plowing, plowing that separated the butter from the milk, the grit from the grime, the man from the boy—middle busting. The field had to be lined, or "rowed," off for cotton planting. With all the ground markers left from the previous year's crop now plowed under, what you needed for this next, crucial step was an instinct for the straight and narrow and a mastery of the art of guiding two strong and stubborn mules down that line in the mind over forty acres of field spotted with hills and low spots for ten long, hard, sweat-popping hours a day. But when it came to plowing and mules Speck was both instinctive and masterful.

Plowing was lonely—man and mule turning the soil one long lonesome furrow at a time. But the shy Speck, who always walked barefoot behind the plow in the cold, newly turned earth, loved the solitude of plowing. He took extra good care of his mules seven days a week, only taking time out from the farm to go into town on an average of once a month to pick up whatever supplies the Hundred Acres required. He always rode in by mule and wagon, rather than with Sugar Boy and his Tin Lizzie the way Momma Rosiebellelee, and especially Doris Virginia, did. Even as a youngster and long before the Accident, Speck hadn't liked or trusted the machine. He was purely a mule man. He even hated tractors, which were then being used extensively on the many farms bought up by Mister Ike Nicholson in the wake of the boll weevil, and he was convinced that the tractor's performance was far inferior to that of the mule-drawn plow. He rode in to church on Sunday behind a mule—though without letting on to God, he went not in order to go inside the church, but to hang around outside, comparing the many mules standing out there with their wagons and buggies or just by themselves, waiting patiently like only a mule could for the day's festivities to end so they could take their owners back home. Out here, except for those involved with crapshooting, drinking, wrestling, and fistfighting in the woods behind the church, the talk was crop talk. Ever since he'd learned to plow, Speck had looked forward to church on Second Sunday just so he could hang around outside listening to the grown-ups discussing crops and, especially, mules. And as he entered his teens he became respected throughout Plain View for his knowledge of mules and his ability at handling them, from plowing down to knotting the tightest hame-string in the community. Mules were a man's thing.

Yet despite all the manliness behind this mulishness, Speck's masculinity, like all the rest of the men's and perhaps even more so, was continually being gauged against that of his good-time-loving older brother, Sugar Boy. And in the eyes of everybody—men, women, children, and family—the shy, withdrawn Speck, whose only social life consisted of hanging around on the churchgrounds each Second Sunday listening to mule talk, didn't even flick the needle on that gauge.

But to the surprise of everyone, including himself, in the winter of 1928, when mule work stood at its yearly low, the teenage Speck left the mules just long enough to go courting. He married Theophilia Crawford (who for years had come to sit on the bank alongside the field and watch him plow), after a short official courtship, even by Plain View standards, of three Second Sundays. The marriage didn't turn out to be too popular with their folks and not just because of their ages— he was seventeen, or almost, and she was nearly sixteen. It was more that the girl's proud father, ol' Hamilton Crawford, and the Mother of Plain View, Momma Rosiebellelee, both had a way of looking at the same thing in the same place at the same time and seeing something different every time. On purpose. And they both saw this marriage their same different ways.

Even though they were living under Momma Rosiebellelee's roof, those first three years of their marriage went fairly well, mainly because the farm work kept them both as busy as ants in a sugar mill, and farm work was something they both loved. Then came 1931, and Mister Mac. Out went farming, and the mules; in came the pine trees. And nobody could eat trees—even pines—not even the white Mister Mac, and not even during Hard Times. Suddenly, after twelve gratifying years of plowing and farming, Speck no longer had his mules and for the first time in his life he would have to go off the Hundred Acres to look for work. Hard Times for sure had come in off the porch and now stood inside Momma Rosiebellelee's front door, just a-watching and a-waiting, while Momma Rosiebellelee wallowed in it.

With his mules and farm being suddenly yanked from beneath his brogans, Speck sank into a deep blue funk that he never really ever came all the way out of. He even refused to go out looking for day work that first year to support his family, and it was then that Theophilia's Garden got to be so important. Though he was never talked about behind his back for being aggressive except where mules were concerned, during that first year off the farm with no mules to mind Speck suddenly became overly aggressive, and oftentimes plain mean, toward Theophilia and their two young boys, Hamilton and Benjamin. Speck didn't even start looking for work until he was finally ordered to by Momma Rosiebellelee herself. (It happened that Sugar Boy's liquor still was raided by the law; he was sent up the Oconee River to Yankee Town, the state prison farm, to work on the chain gang for a year, and Momma Rosiebellelee's main source of income suddenly dried up.) Still, Speck would only look for something to do that was going to involve mules. Having spent most of his years toiling alone, Speck was suddenly competing and working with others for the first time since his school days, and he

found it even more difficult dealing with outsiders as an adult than he had as a child. But most farmers trusted their mules to no one but themselves, and those few in the area who were still hiring during Hard Times only hired outsiders, mainly to chop, mop, hoe, and pick cotton—jobs that pitted people row to row, elbow to elbow, which would leave Speck no choice but to mingle with the masses. Farm work was available from spring to mid or late fall, but during the long winter months of Hard Times many a Plain Viewer sat listening to his deflated belly creeping hungrily up his backbone, trying to peer up his throat to see if his mouth had lockjaw. But those who lived under Momma Rosiebellelee's roof—*and* those downhill, across the spring, and back into the woods, too— during those barren months lived mostly off what Theophilia canned, dried, and hilled from her garden.

Meanwhile, Theophilia was not only busily trying to get Speck to move her and their (now three) children out from under Momma Rosiebellelee's wing, but out from under her shadow entirely—off the Hundred Acres and onto Mr. Ike Nicholson's land, where they would once again be able to farm for themselves. Theophilia's father had owned his own farm and she didn't think much of the idea of sharecropping, but by this time she was willing to take her chances as one of "Nick's Niggers," instead of staying on with her husband's family, who didn't show him the respect she felt he rightly deserved, even though Speck, and Theophilia, were supporting them. And to make matters even more frustrating for her, whenever she brought this matter up, which as time passed was nearly every day, he *always* sided with his family against her. And as for moving onto Mr. Ike Nicholson's land—word came from over across the spring on uphill to Rosiebelle Lee Wildcat Tennessee's house that as long as Mister Mac drew breath *nobody* living on the Hundred Acres would ever be allowed to hit one single lick of work for Ike Nicholson. Bye-bye Nick Niggerism.

Speck and Theophilia moved into their new house between the births of Richmond and Marian Anderson. And it was after they moved here that Speck went to work for the WPA, where he stayed until the Japs got around to bombing Pearl Harbor and opening up the sawmills. Now, for the first time, Speck wasn't working on a farm and was working with town niggers, not farmers, mostly a rough crowd. But Speck never got caught up in any rough stuff because of his unique ability to agree with *everybody* on *everything, every time.* The last thing in the world Speck wanted to be was someone's enemy. He was always being offered the job of straw boss by the white foreman, and he always refused. Apart from the acute embarrassment he would naturally suffer from being under the spotlight, he felt he had been considered first for the job solely because of his light skin. Even though the straw boss job paid more money—which he certainly could've used at home—Speck wasn't about to accept any favors from *anyone* on account of his color—a color he hated while everybody around him cried out in their dreams to have such light skin —and instead went around outshuffling, outscraping, out-kowtowing, and out-yassuhing the job's blackest black. The white man's nigger. All Speck wanted to be was a regular fellow. He couldn't hide his light-skinned, freckled face, though he tried to by always keeping his head hung down and never looking above anyone's shoetops even when he was talking to them. But he could hide those ashblond locks of his —under his cap—by not *ever* taking his cap off, except to cut and wash his hair. From early childhood the first thing after he got up, he would go over to the looking glass to see if during the night the good fairy had come and made him black *and* nappy-headed like other folks.

Though nobody's enemy, Speck was still nobody's friend either. No matter how badly he wanted to be, Speck never really became just one of the boys. One of many possible reasons for this was his habit, very odd for a grown man's habits, of reading the funny papers. Also, every Saturday in town he would buy himself a funny book, or a Wild West, detective, crime, or adventure book, and once a month he bought himself a *Film Fun.* This one was full of pictures of moviestar women practically buck naked, wearing nothing more than their underskirts, bloomers, silk stockings, and garterbelts. These he kept out of the children's, and Theophilia's, sight in a specially built, padlocked wooden box pushed far back under the bed. Also kept in here were many other books he ordered through the mail, a great number of them about Africa and other places around the world where the womenfolk went around with their titties flopping and bare asses showing. Whenever he pulled this box out from under the bed and unlocked it, he always made sure that both doors were latched from the inside, and he was in here alone looking through his growing collection of what Theophilia told the children were his "grownup folks' books." He also kept in this box a small black radio, a Philco, he'd bought not long after the Japs bombed Pearl Harbor, so he could listen to the war news. Speck was deathly afraid of getting drafted and having to go way off to the army, where he didn't know anybody, and eventually on across the pond where he was sure they would kill him for something he didn't know the first thing about, or cared. Speck was scared of the war. That's why the day the Japs dropped their bombs, he dropped one of his own . . . going to work that very night on making a baby in Theophilia, for he knew that the more children a man had, the less chance he had of getting called up. So precious was this radio, with its direct line to a war he somehow felt must have been declared solely to get Speck, that no one else was allowed to so much as touch it. Whenever he went out, he kept it under lock and key, hooking it up himself each night after work to listen to the news. When he wasn't listening to what was happening in the war, he tuned in each Tuesday night to the *Mystery Theater,* a real scary show, and on Wednesday nights to *Mister District Attorney,* his favorite crime show. Then on Saturday night he enjoyed the joke program, *Can You Top This?* But more than any of these he enjoyed the Saturday night barn dances. The WSB Barn Dance from Atlanta, the Chicago Barn Dance from way up North, and then the Grand Ole Opry from Nashville, Tennessee. (No one but Theophilia and the children knew he listened to these "hillbilly" programs.) And though he had never joined the church—was still classified as an official sinner—Speck, an early riser, woke the whole house every Sunday morning with the little black box blaring out the spiritual sounds of such gospel groups as the Golden Gate Quartet, the Deep River Boys, the Sprocos, the Golden Bell Quintet, and more. But of all the gospel singers he listened to, his number-one was the great Sister Rosetta Tharpe, who, Speck had heard, along with her fine singing, picked her guitar, an electric one, right there in the Holiness Church. But of all the radio programs his favorites were the Joe Louis heavyweight championship fights and *Amos 'n' Andy*. These two things coming over the radio could make him forget all about the war news. Almost.

When the radio was on, Theophilia and the children could sit in the room and listen if they kept quiet, but *all* the button-turning and tuning on the magic little black box was done by the man of the house. Speck.

While to others Speck may have seemed like a pussycat, at home with his wife and children he was *all* lion. A born perfectionist, he had no patience to spare little bumbling, imperfect children and a wife whom he felt thought her doo-doo didn't stink the way other folks' did. And this kept the little two-room house alive with arguments and quarrels whenever he was home. In contrast to her husband, timidity around outsiders wasn't Theophilia's style. Yet what got Speck's back all up around his neck was her bullheadedness in insisting on not doing what everybody else in Plain View was doing—like not talking like everybody else, going around trying to talk that proper talk like white folks and always correcting the children, and even him, who *purposely* went around talking regular nigger talk. Now that was something other folks in Plain View just didn't go around doing. With her eighth-grade town schooling—she had gone for one year to the colored high school in Appalachee—Theophilia seemed to think she was better than everybody else, and was busy every day, working the children's heads along the same row. She insisted on sending them to school every day it was open, rain, sleet, or shine, never thought of keeping them home when there was plenty around the house and garden for them to do, the way other folks did with their children. It was true that Speck wanted his children to learn how to read, write, and count, but what he *didn't* want was for other folks to think that *he* thought his children were better than theirs— even if it meant pulling every one of them out of school *before* they had learned to read, write, and count, and, doggonit, he knew he would, just to keep them from acting different from other folks' children.

Standing up in the tub and stretching to unlatch the door to the kitchen, Speck called out "Theo'phy!" before quickly sliding back under the water to wait. The door opened just wide enough to let her in, and she turned the latch, stepped across the hearth, and knelt down beside the tub. Taking the soapy washcloth that he handed over his shoulder, she began scrubbing his back. After more than a minute of hard rubbing she rinsed the soap off his back, then rose to her feet, took off his cap, and started soaping his hair. Without being able to see it in the darkened room, Theophilia stood there, slowly running her fingers back and forth . . . back and forth . . . back and forth through her husband's long, cornsilk hair. But this squelching noise didn't quite drown out the sounds of the couple's heavy breathing. Long minutes later, after rinsing off the soap and drying his hair as gingerly as possible with the rough, guanosack towel, Theophilia stepped around the tub and picked up from the bed, where she had laid out his clean clothes, his Big Apple brand Sunday cap, which she brought back over and pulled tightly down on his head. Then she walked out of the room, without a single word having been spoken between husband and wife.

Left sitting in the tub underneath his gray Big Apple, waiting for his underwater part to get soft, Speck's mind was still on Theophilia. Though he never dared let on to her, he would've given *anything* to be her color, and for the rest of his children to have been born as dark as Hamilton was. That was the main reason why he'd married Theophilia, figuring somebody as black as she was would produce *all* darkskin children. But look what he'd gotten instead. Doggonit!

When he stood up in the tub, the corner of the drawn window shade let in a streak of sunlight which fell right across the middle of his lean, pale, almost hairless body. Looking down at what this streak of light revealed, his eyes came to rest automatically on his hanging, now limber *thing*. And here was something else that greatly bothered him. While the rest of his body, from his neck to his toes, was almost pearl-white, his thing was red! As a child he'd soon stopped going swimming with the other boys because they had always poked fun at him and called him "Ol' Red Dick." And ever since then he'd tried not to ever let anyone see it . . . including himself, and around Theophilia he only took it out during those necessary times and *always* in the dark. When working in the woods, he *never* dropped off the saw to go take a leak. Most of the other sawmill workers would pull out their things right in front of everybody and empty their bladders just as easy as drinking water—but not Speck. He would take care of business before he went to work, and then right after lunch when most all the mill hands were gathered at the edge of the clearing near the big saw eating, talking, or dozing, he'd sneak off back into the woods where he could be alone, and finally after he got off work. Speck definitely was not a public pisser. And when it came time to do the *other* thing, that was a chapter unto itself.

One thing that *didn't* bother him about his thing, for all

its redness, was its size. True, it wasn't the biggest thing in all of Plain View—that honor belonged to one Cousin Tater —but still, it was, as even Speck modestly admitted to himself, of more than acceptable size—even bigger than Sugar Boy's! This *he* knew for sure, even if nobody else did—excepting, of course, Sugar Boy himself and Speck doubted he went around telling folks that his younger brother's dick was bigger (and much redder) than his own, believed to have been the busiest in the whole history of Plain View. Still another thing Speck had over his older brother, something everyone could see for themselves, was six children, plus another one in the heater. Not counting Doris Virginia's *girl,* these were Momma Rosiebellelee's *only* Plain View grandchildren. Speck's. And Sugar Boy, married over ten years, had none. There was one on the way though now . . . but not by Pecora. Despite having a bigger thing and more children than Sugar Boy, Speck still knew that it moved no rocks with the rest of the male community with their "Oh, Speck's all right but you 'n me both know he jes ain' the man his bro' Sugar Boy is" attitude. Doggonit!

Stepping out of the tub onto the brick hearth, Speck dried himself off, then walked around the tub to the bed, where he began to dress: first, his ironed and stiffly starched Second Sunday dress shirt with long sleeves—no short sleeves to show off Speck's ivory arms—followed by a brand-new pair of dark blue overalls, which he was wearing that Saturday for the first time. So new were these overalls that just above the left hip pocket was still sewn a large fiery-red paper tag that spelled out in blue letters the brandname, LEE, which Speck wouldn't allow to be taken off before the first washing. During the summer Speck wore no underwear or socks. Normally he wore brogans to go into town, but due to this Saturday's solemn occasion he put on the light brown Sunday shoes, or "slippers," that were sitting polished, shined, and ready for the day down beside the bed.

Capped, gallused, and shod, Speck topped off his Saturday dressing by tucking into his right hip pocket a freshly washed and ironed long red-and-white bandana, with the tail left stylishly hanging out of his back overall pocket. Having already shaved off his light growth of beard with a straight razor at the washstand while Theophilia was pouring his bath, Speck, preceded several seconds earlier by the combined aroma of lye soap and new overalls, walked out of the dark bedroom into the sunlit kitchen feeling fit and ready for the second—and more important—half of Saturday.

CHAPTER · FOUR

$\mathcal{I}$nstead of going out and taking the road that ran past his bedroom window, which would've brought him right up on Momma Rosiebellelee's front porch, Speck walked out of his back door on this sunnyhot early Saturday afternoon and took his usual route to his mother's house. He was worried about running into somebody sitting on Momma Rosiebellelee's front porch, which was rarely empty even when its owner was at the top of her health. Now that she was bedridden the porch was always full of folks who had come by to pay their respects, and the steady stream of foot traffic over the floorboards began in the morning with the early-rising old and ended long past sundown with the late-to-bed young. And Speck knew that today, Saturday, it would be especially packed with *all* sorts of folks looking out at him and his "haint-at-midnight light" skin during that long, long three-minute walk from his house up to the porch, with them sitting, squatting, leaning, and standing around staring out at his approaching lightness from the cool shade of the porch and the comfort of their God-given darkness. Speck took the back way to Momma Rosiebellelee's.

The sun in a field of pure blue sky overhead was now just about to hit its hottest for the day, sending out a film of heat waves that slithered in slow motion across the landscape. This was Speck's kind of weather. Each day he said good morning to sunup by scanning the sky for the dreaded thundercloud, but today there was not a cloud of any kind in the Hundred Acres sky and the possibility of a storm coming up was one thing less he felt he had to fear on this Saturday afternoon.

Hemmed in on the east, like the front yard, by a woodland of long-needled pines and short-fingered cedars, Speck's long, funnel-shaped backyard gradually tapered off into a footpath that took him past the henhouse, empty at this time of day except for those few hopeful mommas left behind on their nests, then the pigpen, whose sole occupant had been castrated, or "cut," just a few weeks earlier and moved into the fattening house in the middle of the sty to eat himself into shape for the winter, and on down through a grassy, unfenced pasture where Theophilia's cow, Peg, who'd been with the family ever since ol' Mister Hamilton Crawford's death, grazed with a long chain tied around her neck, the other end hooked around the trunk of a pine sapling. By now the path was curving and sloping down a hill rising gradually higher on the right, or west, side of the trail, taking Speck on around the other side. Down at the foot of the hill was the spring which provided the Hundred Acres with drinking and cooking water, and where Theophilia and Pecora did their families' weekly washing. Just a few yards below the deepest part of the spring, almost hidden from view by a cluster of overhanging shrubbery, and where the drinking and washing water was drawn from, was the spring's most noticeable and best-known feature. Extending clear across the water here was a long narrow plank, its far end resting on the densely wooded bank on the other side of the spring. This plank was Mister Mac's private footbridge and nobody . . . nobody . . . else dared cross it without having been summoned downhill, across the spring, and back into the woods *below* Rosiebelle Lee Wildcat Tennessee's house by none other than Mister Mac himself. Speck stopped by the nearer end of the plank and stood staring across the spring over at the motionless trees, though he couldn't make out the legendary two-room log cabin, and there was no sound coming from beyond the trees. He turned and began making his way slowly up the steep hill to the back of the Momma's house.

Both sides of the path up the hill were lined with pine saplings, and in fact, the whole hillside back here was green with young pines. Speck loved this land. He didn't like it to, but sometimes his mind would act on its own and start wondering what would become of the Hundred Acres when . . . or *if* . . . the Momma, God forbid, crossed over. He hadn't heard anybody, including the Momma herself, talking about such a thing, but he supposed that, since Sugar Boy was the oldest and all, the Momma would look to him, the way she always did, and leave Sugar Boy in charge of things. All Speck wanted for himself though was just a little piece of land, but Theophilia had already put something of a damper on his hopes here by declaring, without even being asked, that the Hundred Acres and everything, and everybody, on it was *all* going back over to Mister Mac. That was why, she said, if they ever wanted to farm again, then they'd better go somewhere else and rent themselves a farm or just take up and move on over across the road and throw in with Mister Nick's share-cropping niggers. At the time he had pretended not to pay any attention to this, and he told her she was just having one of her usual "know-every-damn-thing spells." But, doggonit, there was still Mister Mac and his doggone pine trees—something even his mind couldn't keep out. Why, Speck wondered, wasn't it Mister Mac dying, instead of the Momma? Lord God, the thought of the Momma dying and leaving him all alone in the world brought hot tears to fog his vision. The Momma and her well-being were the *only* excuses he had to offer Theophilia for keeping his family there on the Hundred Acres he loved so. It just wasn't in his farthest imagination to think of ever leaving this land. That was why it was so dog-gone . . . no . . . *damn* important that when—if—the Momma died, she left him a piece of land to work, so he'd be able to stay on this land, instead of leaving it to rent or sharecrop somewhere, like Theophilia kept on him all the time to do.

At the top of the hill the path led Speck on around Momma Rosiebellelee's big barn, which had once housed cotton, corn, hay, goobers, farm equipment, Red, Clyde, and Nigger Gal. But all of that was now just a memory, and the old barn seemed to realize how useless it was now by putting on a weary pose of slow dilapidation. Still, the doors and shutters swung on well-oiled hinges and the inside was swept free of rubbish and junk—thanks to Speck, who loved this building better than his own house and dreamed that someday it would once again serve the purpose for which it had been built. Farming.

But the day the barn had become more than just an ordinary barn came right after Momma Rosiebellelee sold her two mules back in '31. Walking out of her back door on the way to the stall to feed Nigger Gal, she looked up and saw it. Painted in blood red on the front of the barn was a giant-size airplane, its bottom wing down near the ground and the top one clear up by the loft. Momma Rosiebellelee had never in her life. . . . For the first, and only, time in anyone's memory Rosiebelle Lee Wildcat Tennessee was said to have been totally, absolutely, no-question-about-it speechless on the spot. Her first thought was that the airplane had been painted on there by one of the tramps who'd been seen roving the area lately. But, she thought, how could he have reached from the ground up to the loft to paint the whole airplane? And at night too! Haints, along with tramps, God, the devil, children, or drunks, got blamed for all inexplicable events, and Momma Rosiebellelee could very easily have attributed this mysterious painting to a regular ol' haint without fear of being officially declared tetched in the haid, because the airplane was definitely *there* for all to see. And a pretty one it was, too. Instead, the Mother of Plain View explained the airplane to all her children thusly: After all these years, the flier of the flying machine that had passed over Plain View way back during the Big War had found his way back to the scene of his greatest flying stunt—dragging a long chain across the roof of Momma Rosiebellelee's barn. And just in case anybody doubted that he'd really done it—and after all, the chain must've been pretty close to invisible—he painted a picture of his plane on the Momma's barn. And, true to Momma Rosiebellelee's words, the very next morning when she went out to feed Nigger Gal, a long chain had been painted on to the tail of the airplane. (While Momma Rosiebellelee, as in all similar, and dissimilar, cases, never once allowed herself to be cross-examined by her subjects . . . yet to herself she secretly prayed that no other barn in the area would wake up one morning with a big red airplane across its face.) The airplane itself, painstakingly painted, became a local attraction and many who passed along the main road stopped off to walk around in back of Momma Rosiebellelee's house just to see the giant mural of the red flying machine with the long chain hanging down.

The path ran alongside the barn and took Speck on around to the front to the airplane and also to the spot where early every Saturday afternoon Sugar Boy attended to his car. This Saturday afternoon was no exception. Since Nigger Gal's death, the barn's chief occupant had been one of a successive string of Sugar Boy's cars, the most recent being a kale-green 1936 Ford V-8 convertible, equipped with fender flaps, whitewalls, a long, whippy radio aerial (but no radio) topped off with a bushy foxtail, that was parked with the top down between the barn and Momma Rosiebellelee's back porch while being readied for the day by head-under-the-hood Sugar Boy and water-bucket and wet soapy rag toting Doris Virginia, who quickly spotted the visitor.

"Hey, Speck!"

"Hey, y'all!" Walking on around to stop in front of the car, with his back to the barn—and the airplane, something he *never* let anyone catch him staring at.

"Sugar Boy gonna take her today!" Anticipation riding Doris Virginia's voice.

"T'day?" Speck didn't believe his ears.

"Is the bear?"

"Miz' Rockee Ryder?"

"*She's* the bear."

"When?"

"When she comes from town."

"She jes passed me on the way in, drivin' up a storm."

"Already? You hear that, Sugar Boy?"

Except for the sound of pliers scraping against metal there was silence under the hood.

"Whar he gonna take her?"

"Haint Hills. Nobody knows that road down through there like Sugar Boy knows it. Ain't that right, Sugar Boy?"

Still no answer was forthcoming from under the hood. And the mention of Haint Hills had sent a shudder creeping up under the back galluses of Speck's brand-new overalls. Also, the thought of Sugar Boy racing his car against a white lady's while the Momma lay up in bed readying herself and her family for her crossing over left Speck aghast. But he knew he would be the next after the last one to voice his disapproval to Sugar Boy about *anything* he did. Sugar Boy never bothered explaining his reasons for doing, or not doing, anything to anybody, not even to the Momma, least of all to Speck.

"What'cha wanna bet he takes her?"

"I don' know." Speck wanting to please his brother and sister but unable to work up any real enthusiasm for the upcoming race. "How's everythin' inside?"

"Inside where?" Then watching Speck nod his head piously toward the house. "Oh, in there. All right. Don't *always* be worrying so. She'll let us know when she's ready to. I bet you a dime Sugar Boy takes her."

· ——— ·

Doris Virginia wasn't worrying one bit. Despite her shapely slimness (to go with her quicksilver moves and mind), the most striking thing about Rosiebelle Lee Wildcat Tennessee's youngest was her hair—hellfire red. And she *hated* every single strand of it. She wanted Speck's ashblond hair, and she hated him not only for his having it but even more for his not ever showing it off to folks. The way he kept *every* last bit of what she felt to be the prettiest hair in the county hidden under his ol' cap twenty-four hours a day really got her gizzard like nothing else did. And it was Doris Virginia who *always* did the gizzard-getting.

As a youngster she had just about had her way with everything and everybody. In school, like Luvenia before her, she was always the center of attention, even though, unlike her older sister (whom Doris Virginia had never seen), she hadn't had the help of a horse. But when she went on to "town school," the colored high school in Appalachee, she did go back and forth each day in a car, Sugar Boy's car. (When Sugar Boy was sent up the Oconee to the Yankee Town chain gang, she stayed out of school that whole year.) Doris Virginia was just as quick to learn her schoolbooks as Speck was, and not at all ashamed of it, but she got bored pretty quickly too. This, she claimed, was the reason she hadn't finished town school. But many others believed that she quit because she couldn't ride back and forth from school in Sugar Boy's car anymore, and more important, because away from Plain View she was a pond fish lost in a big river. Although she did have more than her share of town friends, they were all boys. This was all right with her, too, except that it turned most of the town girls against her, and she still craved their friendship just as strongly as the boys'. But the one thing folks always noticed about Doris Virginia's friends was that they were *all* dark-skinned. Untouched black. Some said she picked dark friends, both boys and girls, because alongside them she really stood out, looking even prettier than she already was. And

Doris Virginia was something else *and* some more pretty already: long red wavy—not curly—hair, darting green eyes beneath whip-tip lashes, a pink—not red—rosy skin stretched smoothly over a sharp-featured face whose only drawback, in her mind anyway, was a pair of lips that were too thin to hold enough lipstick to suit her. (Besides her red hair and thin lips, Doris Virginia's titties presented another problem. She thought them a bit too tiny for her needs—though most everyone who'd seen her even once felt that her long, well-formed, slightly bowed legs running smack up into a set of rippling hips holding up a prettily proportioned, elastic ass more than made up for that red hair, too-thin lips, and those tiny titties she hated so much.) Yet no matter how much she disliked her hair, the rest of Plain View, men and women, just loved Doris Virginia's long red something sinful. But, as many were to learn to their sorrow, *nobody* went around calling Doris Virginia "Red." Nobody—no matter how dark-of-the-moon their skin might be.

Doris Virginia's only real problem, though, was finding something to do. Anything, that is, but work. Even Momma Rosiebellelee—never a known, or suspected, workhorse—toiled among her flowers, over the cookstove, the sewing table, or at the end of a fishing pole. Not Doris Virginia. Apart from her mother, of course, she was the only colored in Plain View who'd never done *any* field work, had never even planted, chopped, mopped, hoed, or picked cotton in her life, and had no intention of ever doing so. During the hot summer months, when everybody but the too-young, too-old, and too-sick was out in the fields, Doris Virginia, surrounded by her harem of housecats, sat loudly popping chewing gum there in the swing on Momma Rosiebellelee's front porch while fanning herself slowly, sipping cool spring water or looking through her stereopticon, just swinging back and forth . . . and always listening to the sound of the Victrola moaning from the sitting room the low-down dirty dog blues.

Although not the insatiable Speck-type reader, Doris

Virginia still liked her reading (though she didn't particularly like men who read a lot). This was limited to true romances and moviestar magazines, thus preserving her sanity during the long weekdays when everybody else was out in the fields. (As a woman, Doris Virginia could get away with reading. With the exception of the Bible, the almanac, the war news, and cotton prices, reading in Plain View was looked down on as a womanish trait. A *real* man didn't have the time to waste on reading, which was why Speck never let anyone catch him in the act. Whenever someone came around, he would quickly put whatever he was reading—unless it was the newspaper—back into the box under his bed before sheepishly walking out to greet his visitor—but they *always* knew when Speck had been reading.)

As a child Speck had also loved the picture show, and he often took Doris Virginia along on Saturday afternoons when he wasn't plowing. But after he got married, he stopped going altogether, because he was a *man* now. And in Plain View going to the picture show was a "child's" thing. A *man* didn't have the time to waste on picture shows; he was too busy being a man. But Doris Virginia still loved the picture show. She *never* let a week go by without going into town at least once to The Appalachian, Appalachee's only picture show, with shows Monday through Saturday nights, plus a Saturday matinee, and no shows on Sunday at all. Doris Virginia never went on Saturday, because that was the day they only showed cowboy shows, or others involving folks killing folks —which she didn't care for—and Saturday was country day in town, the one day in the week when all of the country colored poured into Appalachee from all around the county to take over the back street and the balcony—"nigger heaven" —of the picture show. And if there was anything that girl from the piny woods of Plain View didn't want to be called, that was "country girl."

But, country or not, Doris Virginia's first love was the blues. The blues as sung by her main man—Tampa Red.

Doris Virginia loved Tampa Red's singing something sinful. In fact, "something sinful" was precisely what most Plain Viewers, especially the older heads, thought of Rosiebelle Lee Wildcat Tennessee's youngest.

Apart from her red hair and pink skin, Doris Virginia was different from the rest of Plain View's females—mostly because she spent all day sitting up there fanning herself in the shade of her front porch for all the working world to see, only moving off her pink ass to go around to the back porch when the sun pushed the shade on around there. Her town school education was another thing. Most of Plain View's women had dropped out of school to go to work or get married, and later had little time, and even less inclination, for reading, except for an occasional letter from distant relatives. And they had no time whatsoever for something like the picture show. Besides, the picture show was sinful! Which brings us to Doris Virginia's sins.

Even though their momma was *the* Mother of Plain View Baptist Church, once they were into their teens the children of Rosiebelle Lee Wildcat Tennessee weren't turning out to be what the community considered real churchgoers. Oh, Speck showed up faithfully each Second Sunday and at funerals and such, but only to stand around outside the building talking crop talk. And Sugar Boy, with the top rolled back on his car and his head all bad on bootleg liquor, would speed around and around the church in one continuous maddening circle, stirring up all the women and girls, who'd be gawking out the window at his long black wavy hair blowing crazily in the wind. Then Momma Rosiebellelee herself would rise from her amen corner throne and, still holding her fan, would come out to flag him down and send him speeding on his way back down the road toward town just ahead of a cloud of Georgia red. But once Doris Virginia got the notion to go to church *nothing* stopped her, though this notion only came on those special Sundays of baptisms, weddings, and homecoming—but *no* funerals for Doris Virginia, as she wanted nothing at all to do with anybody dead. And when she did show up, arriving after things had gotten well underway and sitting throughout the service loudly popping her chewing gum, she was *always* the center of everyone's attention. But after church was when Doris Virginia's lamp was lit.

Long before she reached sixteen, the accepted age for receiving company, the front porch of Momma Rosiebellelee's house every Sunday after church would be crammed with young boys, mostly there on the pretext of seeing Sugar Boy, and sometimes even Speck . . . but their eyes and ears were alert for every second of their stay to the sight and sounds of young Doris Virginia. By the time she reached sixteen, the back porch and yard were already overflowing with these young, and some older studs, many coming from as far away as Appalachee and even beyond. Yet despite the vast number of boys *and* men (plus a few of Doris Virginia's closest girlfriends who happened by to catch some of the overflow) around Momma Rosiebellelee's house every Sunday, the official courting day, only a privileged few ever made it to the sitting room, where the queen bee swooned to the sounds of her Tampa Red on the Victrola.

> *I know a gal by the name of Mary Lou,*
> *She shook it so much she had the German flu.*
> *No matter how she done it,*
> *She done it just the same.*

Though in order not to disappoint those left outside in the sun, cold, or rain, Doris Virginia would appear on schedule at the front door each Sunday shortly before sundown, walk out on the porch, on down the stoop, and on around the house to disappear from sight out back of the barn. This automatically brought an abrupt halt to *everything* (talking, laughing, shooting marbles, boxing, wrestling, playing ball, pitching horseshoe) while that rubbery, jerky ass went switchering and twitchering through their midst like two cats fighting in a croker sack, and *everyone* kept their eyes and minds right on it, without muttering a sound this side of heavy breathing, until she reappeared from around behind the barn and wordlessly vanished back through the front door to be engulfed by the blues sounds of Tampa Red . . .

> *She shakes all over when she walks,*
> *She made a blind man see,*
> *And a dumb man talk*

. . . after having completed her pilgrimage to the family necessary house to, as she so devoutly put it, "take her Sunday after-church pee."

Except for that privileged few left sitting there in Doris Virginia's sitting room with her, including a select few of her girlfriends, most everybody at Momma Rosiebellelee's that day, having seen what they came to see, would then begin heading home to do their evening chores—bringing up the cows, slopping the hogs, cutting firewood, and the like—since for them the week's courting day was over. Meanwhile, back at Momma Rosiebellelee's, Tampa Red wailed way on into the night.

> *The cop brought her in,*
> *She needed no bail.*
> *At the judge she shook her tail,*
> *And he had the cop thrown in jail.*
> *No matter how she done it,*
> *She done it just the same.*

Though she never lacked for boyfriends, Doris Virginia never kept any special one in her early courting days. Her only requirement, most folks said, was that they be dark-skinned. That is, she had nobody special until the winter of her seventeenth birthday when onto the Hundred Acres came Plootsy Perryman.

Plootsy Perryman was a road man—Florida in the spring and summer, and New Jersey, or "Jezzy," in the fall. Riding with the crops. Pulling 'maters in the South in the spring and summer and picking up 'taters in the North in the fall. And Plain View was his winter home. He came back just before Christmas every year driving a different car, never new but always clean, with four fender flaps and whitewalls. But what *was* always new, colorful, and in the very latest style, was his clothes, from his wide-brimmed hat all the way down his lean-as-a-snap-bean body to his smartly shined shoes. It was Plootsy who introduced Plain View to the zoot suit, knob shoes, and the long jiving chain—all of this plus jive talk. Every time he came home he brought back some new jive expressions that caused the locals, especially the younger set, to marvel over the man's extensive outside-world vocabulary. A social soul, Plootsy spent most of his time, and *all* of his money, with his many friends in Plain View, bringing them new, old, updated, and renovated tales of his travels back and forth across the Mason-Dixon line each year. Plootsy Perryman was, in his own outside-world words, a "hepcat."

But the thing about Plootsy that really aroused the envy and awe of the local males was the talk that he—the blackest of niggers—had done the unbelievable. Plootsy Perryman, son of a black sharecropper, had fucked a *white* woman. Now whenever he took time out from talking, or whatever else, to go take a piss, many of his admirers would suddenly realize that they, too, had to empty their bladders and would go stand proudly pissing right alongside, while glancing from the corner of their eyes at the black dick that had been inside a *white* pussy.

Plootsy was much older than Doris Virginia and her crowd, but this didn't stop him from driving over to the Hundred Acres every Sunday afternoon whenever he was back in Plain View. First he'd stop to talk to Sugar Boy out back at the barn about cars, then mosey on into the house through the kitchen to pay his respects to Momma Rosiebellelee, before sliding on up to the sitting room, where Doris Virginia was sure to be listening to her Tampa Reds. Momma Rosiebellelee herself always appreciated the gesture, but nevertheless, she still didn't trust the man, and she was constantly reminding her daughter of the reasons why. It was not on account of his being way older than Doris Virginia, or that the man shot dice . . . or was said to have toted a switchblade knife. It *was* because of the dark sunshades the man *always* wore, day or night, rain or shine, plus that gold tooth he forever flashed. Momma Rosiebellelee didn't trust anybody who sported in the middle of his mouth a tooth God didn't put there—and whose eyes she couldn't see. Yet she didn't refuse Plootsy permission to come courting her daughter which, as the Mother of Plain View, she could easily have put a stop to. She did tell Doris Virginia, though, that she didn't want to ever hear of her getting into Plootsy's car. And this in itself was highly unusual for Momma Rosiebellelee, because she rarely ever bothered with her children's courting life; it was after they got married that the Momma laid the *real* raw red meat out on the table before their very eyes.

Other than this warning about getting into Plootsy's car, Doris Virginia had no bit at all in her mouth controlling her courting life, and she kept seeing whomever whenever she wanted them to come see her. But she was most fascinated by the man Plootsy. His worldliness, coolness, dress, and, most of all, his dancing. Doris Virginia loved her blues, but she was no dancer worth talking about. Then along came Plootsy, and so Plain View and the Hundred Acres saw the return of the shimshamshimmy, truckin', and the jitterbug—*all* having been born in the South and just going North to get their white names.

Whenever there was a dance in the area and Plootsy was around, he'd be sure to be there with his many followers coming from miles around just to see him do some real mean and low-down cutting up. But Doris Virginia never went with him to any of these places since she couldn't get into his

car—instead she settled for those Sunday afternoons when, right there in her sitting room, he would dance to the Victrola for, and sometimes with, her while the crowd outside mobbed the front door and windows to watch their man Plootsy make moves with his long body that they didn't believe existed, even while standing there dumbstruck seeing him do them with nobody's eyes but their own God-givens.

When Plootsy came back to Plain View each year he always arrived during the days leading up to Christmas—bringing home hard-earned money, or "kale," a different car each time, and brand-new rags—and would leave out that next year on Easter Sunday night. But when he hit that rutted road out of Plain View that late Easter Sunday night in 1936, headed south for Florida and the awaiting 'mater crop, besides gas money, a zoot suit with shiny elbows and knees, and a shiny seat, frayed-collared shirt, and a pair of badly listing knob shoes, Plootsy Perryman had in his smoking, coughing, wheezing, and sneezing mufflerless car something else. Something else he surely ought not to have had. Doris Virginia.

They made it on out of Plain View while the Easter Sunday night program of choir and solo singing, children's recitations, and grownups' speeches was in progress at the church. This was the same Easter Sunday that the town of Appalachee's policeman, "Boots" White, shot to death the colored Big Man Thompson in Sam's Café there on the town's back street. Because of this, along with word about the Ku Klux Klan riding down from the policeman's home town —Yankee Town itself—to pay a visit to the town's colored section, the turnout for the Easter program had been poor. Yet the threat of grown white men who ought to have known better running around hiding under bedsheets and pillowcases wasn't enough to scare off Momma Rosiebellelee, who'd never missed a single one of these services, which she herself had inaugurated in her church that very first year. And when she got back home that night Doris Virginia was long gone, with just what she was wearing at the time and all her Tampa Red records.

Momma Rosiebellelee never even so much as mentioned the matter to anybody, and nobody ever dared mention the matter to her, even though most of the community was seemingly more concerned at the time with Doris Virginia's disappearance than Big Man Thompson's killing up in Appalachee. In those days in the South a colored man getting killed by a white man was as predictable as grits for breakfast. But the Mother of Plain View's baby daughter running off with Plootsy Perryman, road man and hepcat to boot, was something else—and then some more. Momma Rosiebellelee acted just like her daughter was still home rocking in the swing in the shade of the front porch, fanning herself in between long, cool sips of fresh spring water, while listening intently to the blues-moaning Tampa Red, nodding and flipping pages of her moviestar magazine, and silently watching the folks working over in the big cottonfield just across the road from the Hundred Acres. Either that, or Momma Rosiebellelee acted just like she had never even had a daughter named Doris Virginia.

It was on Christmas Eve of that same year that Doris Virginia came back home. Without Plootsy. But with another nigger. Blacker than her own sins. She also brought back a whole slew of new Tampa Red records, along with all the old ones she'd taken with her—not to mention a bellyful of baby. And that year for the first time since he'd gone away to do crop work as a young boy back long before the Big War, Plootsy Perryman didn't come home for Christmas. Yet when folks tried to find out why he didn't or where else he might possibly be, nobody got anything out of Doris Virginia . . . and even less out of her new nigger. She told everyone who asked that on that Easter Sunday night Plootsy had only taken her to the depot in Appalachee, where she'd boarded a train for the city she'd always wanted to see—Savannah, Georgia —and Plootsy, she reckoned, had driven on to Florida by himself. And, according to her, she hadn't heard a single word from him since. But when they asked where she'd got the money to go all the way to Savannah by herself—she shut everybody's mouth by saying it was none of their goddamn business. (When she took a mind to, Doris Virginia could cuss as easy as she'd light up a cigarette.) Meanwhile, her story went on, Savannah, Georgia, was where she met . . . *and* married . . . this here new nigger.

Though he was nearly a head shorter than Doris Virginia, Plain View's newest nigger had broad shoulders and a beautifully proportioned, muscular body—he looked plenty powerful but he still carried himself gracefully. But what made him different from any other Plain View man was his speech—a fast, clipped kind of talk, like nothing that anyone in Plain View had ever heard before, and even different from that of Northern-born niggers. So strange did his speech sound to Plain View's ears that *nobody* in the community could understand a single word the man said—though Doris Virginia kept telling everybody that she understood every word. His talk, she explained, was called "Geechie talk." Her nigger was, despite his boot-and-a-half blackness, not a *real* nigger, but a Geechie, which, according to her, the city of Savannah, Georgia, was full of. When they heard this and then took a look at this young man—who was so black that, as the local saying went, if you rubbed a piece of charcoal across his cheek it would leave a white streak—Plain View's blacks blanched.

Taken completely by surprise, Plain View didn't exactly know what to make of this here "unreal nigger" nigger. This included Momma Rosiebellelee, who most folks felt just wasn't too happy with all that blackness suddenly popping out of nowhere to take up under her roof. Unlike her children, Momma Rosiebellelee didn't think black was all that pretty.

Now the attitude of the new bride's still-numerous male admirers toward "Doris 'Ginia's Geechie" was a mixture of hatred and fear. They hated him for having "bigged" their princess, and they feared him because when Plootsy didn't show up that Christmas of '36, for the first time since long before the Big War, many people began to suspect that Doris 'Ginia's Geechie was the main reason *why* he didn't show. When he didn't come home that next Christmas, then the talk really got started about what must have happened between the two of them, and Doris Virginia, down there in Savannah, Georgia, since *nobody* in Plain View had ever known Plootsy to stay away from anywhere because of any man. That was when most folks began saying that Plootsy would never be seen in Plain View, or anywhere else, again. No, nobody felt up to messing with Doris 'Ginia's Geechie.

In spite of the sinister reputation he acquired early on, Doris 'Ginia's Geechie never bothered anybody and always was very polite to everybody, even though nobody ever understood anything he said. Also, he *loved* Doris Virginia, and was hardly ever away from her side. Sometimes, though, she could be real mean to him—like, especially, when it came to her cats, which she loved like those who knew said God must love His goodness. Ever since she was a child, her cats had eaten *and* slept with her; they ate right *on* the table, right off her plate. This never bothered Momma Rosiebellelee, an animal lover herself, nor did it bother Sugar Boy, just so long as no cat ate off his plate. It did bother the weak-stomached Speck, who made a point of eating either before or after his younger sister. And those times when he had to eat at the same table with her and her pride, he always shielded his plate with both elbows and a lowered head while eating fast with eyes closed.

Now, apparently, Doris 'Ginia's Geechie was not at all hep to cats, at least not to Doris Virginia's. The very first day he sat under Momma Rosiebellelee's roof with his feet planted beneath her kitchen table, a Doris Virginia cat jumped with all four feet, and tail, too, right into his plate, and just as quickly he backhanded her smack dab up against the kitchen wall. Well, some said later that if you got up close enough, the full imprint of Doris Virginia's right hand could still be seen pasted on her Geechie's left cheek. And as for the cat, Mae Sue—well, she bounced off the wall and onto the floor, delicately washed the affected spot, purred up to Doris Virginia for a pat of reassurance, and then leapt back up on the table, where for the rest of her long life she ate every one of her meals. And Doris 'Ginia's Geechie? He ate all of his meals sitting on the bench out on the back porch, alone except for the flies in summertime.

(Yet nobody ever learned what the husband's reaction was that first night in the bedroom, when he found the bed full of Doris Virginia's sleeping cats. No matter—the night sounds that started coming from behind their bedroom door didn't have anything to do with anybody getting slapped over some cat. In fact, these *human* grunts, groans, and moans soon had the cats meowing and scratching frantically on the bedroom door to get out of that cage. 'Ginia's Geechie's back porch revenge?)

And one last thing that people noticed about 'Ginia's Geechie was his willingness to work. He was nobody's lazy nigger, or Geechie—the only thing, many folks felt, that redeemed him in the eyes of Momma Rosiebellelee, and kept him under her roof. That very first week in Plain View he was out looking for work, though it took awhile for him to find a job because it seemed that even the white folks couldn't understand what it was he was trying to say. Yet he must have understood *them*, because it wasn't too long before he'd gotten himself a job up in Appalachee driving taxi for the newly organized Spence Taxi Cab Company.

The Spence Taxi Cab Company started out with one car, which was available for hire six days a week from six in the morning until midnight, and on Sunday from nine in the morning until nine that night. Those were 'Ginia's Geechie's working hours, seven days a week.

With her man driving taxi, Doris Virginia no longer sat all day in the shade of the porch during the hot summer months, fanning herself and watching the folks out in the field working. Now when her Geechie didn't have a paying customer in the car, the folks in the fields would look up and see him zooming by with Doris Virginia, looking straight ahead with her nose in the air, sitting up in the back seat. The very first time 'Ginia's Geechie drove down through the heart of Appalachee with her, and her red hair and pink skin, sitting all up close to his midnight black there on the front seat, the town's meanest policeman, Clyde "Boots" White, had stopped the taxi, dragged 'Ginia's Geechie out of the car, and whupped him over the head with his blackjack. Then the Man ordered the screaming, scared-shitless Doris Virginia out of the front seat—where, he announced, he never wanted to see any of her kind riding again—and into the back seat, where she stayed ever since.

The baby, a girl, born shortly after 'Ginia's Geechie started driving taxi, came out of her momma looking more like her daddy, and her black skin didn't exactly endear her to her grandmother, who was still impatiently waiting . . . waiting to deliver her Sugar Boy's firstborn. The baby was named by both parents—Savannah (by the mother) Carmen Maria (by the father). Doris Virginia, along with everyone else, called the child by her first name, Savannah, and only 'Ginia's Geechie called her by her two middle names, Carmen Maria. And when the child became old enough to talk, the father talked to her in that funny talk of his—which, to the surprise of everyone in Plain View, the little girl actually seemed to understand, *and* be able to talk right back at him. At the same time, though, she could still understand and talk regular Plain View talk, and the best explanation that Plain View people could come up with for this amazing gift was that the child must have been born with a double-jointed tongue.

Despite marriage and motherhood, Doris Virginia was still the foremost chick in the eyes, thoughts, and dreams of the vast majority of local males. And as the years shot past, there eventually or inevitably was scattered talk that—due to 'Ginia's Geechie's long and, especially, late working hours— on occasion one, or more, of these fantasizing males realized more of Doris Virginia than could be consummated in a dream. Much more. In fact, Doris Virginia, as most folks told one another, was the main reason her Geechie got the taxi-driving job from Mister Spence in the first place.

"You gonna bet me a nickel that Sugar Boy won't take Miz' Rockee Ryder today, Speck?"

"Naw, I don' think I will."

"You know something, Speck?"

"Wha'?"

"You wouldn't bet on a jackrabbit outrunning a cow. You ain't got no sport . . . no fun . . . nowhere in you. Ain't that right, Sugar Boy?"

But before Doris Virginia could get any affirmation from under the hood of the car, another, more urgent sound suddenly exploded from the back porch. Sugar Boy's fifteen-year-old "friend," Lucy Anna, was standing on the back porch. Lucy Anna's swollen belly had convinced Momma Rosie-bellelee to let her stay under her roof, where the expectant grandmother could supervise the birthing of her firstborn son's first child. Though everybody else assumed that Lucy Anna had been stung by Sugar Boy, his wife, Pecora, still sharing his bed and childless after ten years of marriage, was inclined to disagree—"the signs" had told her that that baby hadn't been put in Lucy Anna's belly by Sugar Boy at all.

Lucy Anna let loose again: "Doris Virginia! Doris Virginia! Momma Rosiebellelee calling for you!"

CHAPTER · FIVE

Built to its owner's specifications the year her Luvenia was born, Momma Rosiebellelee's house—beneath its pyramidal shingled roof and within what were now well-weathered, shingled sides—consisted of six spacious rooms, including the sitting room and kitchen, plus the front and back porches—all standing in the midst of a gigantic yard overrun year round with practically every kind of flower known to the region. The door leading into the front part of the house was cut dead-center in the front wall, and just a few feet to each side were two huge windows looking out from the sitting room onto the front porch, which except for the swing hanging in the left, east, corner, was bare of furniture. Clay pots, tin buckets, and wooden boxes full of flowers and plants scattered over the floor, hanging from the ceiling, and lining the railings took up most of the room out here. Also, on through the front door, the sitting room was a bit scarce on furniture, fixings, and hangings, except, of course, for a clutter of flowerpots and vases. The walls in here were still covered with the original wallpaper, a bleached out rose design. The largest piece of furniture in the room—an enormous davenport with fading, flower-patterned upholstery—hunched on the right side of the room facing out from the large stone fireplace cut into the rear wall and complete with firedogs, poker, and a long wooden mantelpiece that held a large kerosene lamp, flanked on each side by tall, flower-filled vases. Except for Momma Rosiebellelee's rocker, all of the furniture had at one time or another come from the Big House up on the old MacAndrew Plain View Plantation: the davenport, the nearly floor-length, tasteful but timeworn curtains on the four windows, a couple of straightbacks, several scattered stands holding vases of flowers and a high, mirrored dresser whose top was also covered with flower pots. And back over in the left corner of the room, nearest the window that looked out on the porch swing, stood the house's most fabled object. Doris Virginia's Victrola was a tall boxlike floor model, black with decorative gold trimming, standing on long narrow legs alongside several piles of uncovered phonograph records. Nobody was allowed to venture into this corner and touch any of the merchandise over here but Doris Virginia herself . . . and, of course, her numerous cats, who slept and played atop and behind both the Victrola and the piles of records. In fact, except for the Victrola, records, and cats, Doris Virginia kept this whole side of the room clear of all foreign objects, including vases and flower pots. This was the dancing side of the room.

In the middle of the rear wall was an open doorway into the hall which led to the house's four bedrooms, two on each side—the never-closed door of Momma Rosiebellelee's and the ever-closed door of Doris Virginia and her Geechie's on the right; on the left, facing the Momma's, was Sugar Boy and Pecora's, next to the one bedroom once occupied by Speck, later by Speck and Theophilia, and now by Lucy Anna. All four bedrooms had a window—Sugar Boy and Pecora's and Lucy Anna's facing east and the other two facing west. But Momma Rosiebellelee's room, since it was directly behind the sitting room, was the only one with a fireplace.

The open doorway at the far, south, end of the hallway led on into what was, as far as the Momma was concerned, the *main* part of the house—the kitchen. When she wasn't sleeping or watering and rearranging her flowers and plants, Momma Rosiebellelee spent little of her time in the rest of the house. The kitchen was her roost. Besides doing all her entertaining and holding her family conferences back here, she did *all* of the cooking. (Though she did relent somewhat by letting Pecora, and now Lucy Anna, do all the cleaning up afterwards.) The exact same size as the sitting room, Momma Rosiebellelee's kitchen had two windows looking out onto the back porch, plus one on each of the other outside walls. The curtains hanging in the windows back here were all hand sewn by Momma Rosiebellelee, regularly washed, starched, and ironed by Pecora, and altogether much brighter and cheerier than the faded Big House hand-me-downs in the sitting room. The northwest corner of the kitchen housed an imposing combination oil-and-wood cookstove, with cooking utensils hanging on both sides and rows of wall and floor cabinets chock full of even more cooking and eating utensils, but hardly ever holding much of anything to cook. Never the hoarder, the unantlike, and adventuresome, more grasshopper-type Momma Rosiebellelee was at her best when she had to scrounge food for her and hers on a day-to-day basis; she enjoyed her cooking, and eating, much more that way. The long kitchen table with its florid tablecloth and vase of fresh flowers stood across the room from the stove, right next to the east, or "sunup," window where Momma Rosiebellelee liked to sit and drink her first cup of coffee in the morning and wait for the sun to wake up Plain View's day. While there were several straightback, straw-bottomed chairs sitting around the table, the Momma had her own special "kitchen rocker" (as opposed to her "fireplace rocker" up front in the sitting room), where whenever she was holding audience with one of her subjects, or just sewing, she rocked, chewed her tobacco, and paused once in a while to spit into the shiny brass spittoon at her feet.

At one time the back porch had been a crowded storage place for farm equipment, but the only tools to be found out back here now (among the many flower pots and boxes) were those few the Momma needed to tend her flowers—an ancient hoe, a hand rake, and mattock being about the last of these remnants. Perhaps the most noticeable thing of all here was Momma Rosiebellelee's sizable collection of long dried-reed fishing poles that reached from floor to ceiling and filled one entire corner of the porch.

About fifty yards in back of the house stood the barn, with the necessary house just in back, both standing at the crest of the hill, thickly overgrown with shrubbery, that sloped down gently from the sides of the house about a hundred yards or so to the edge of a stand of young pines, Speck's former cotton and cropland on one side and on the other a forest of full-grown pines that stretched as far as you could see from the top of the Rosiebelle Lee Wildcat Tennessee Hill. Even with all those pines downhill from the house, there was not a single tree standing in or near Momma Rosiebellelee's yard, since when the house was built she had had every tree chopped down that she thought might someday throw some shade on her flowers.

Lucy Anna was still standing at the top of the six steps that led up to the back porch when Doris Virginia brushed by her without so much as a word or a glance. Lucy Anna's baby-faced beauty—along with that baby in her belly—had immediately won the heart of Momma Rosiebellelee. The girl's smooth apricot-toned skin (in contrast to Pecora's tar black), some said, would have been enough by itself to make her a *real* daughter-in-law for Momma Rosiebellelee, who, many folks suspected, wanted her children to choose light meat over dark every time. On the other hand, these same folk said, this was the very reason Doris Virginia didn't have much to do with young Lucy Anna, because the girl's beauty and, especially, color was a distinct rival to her own. Doris Virginia, like her momma, didn't like sharing the spotlight.

In the kitchen Pecora—who was doing all the cooking

now that *the* cook had taken to her bed—had stopped her cleaning to let her eyes follow Doris Virginia on down the hall until she turned the corner and zipped right through the open door of Momma Rosiebellelee's room. (Doris Virginia, Sugar Boy, and Theophilia were the only mortals who didn't stand on ceremony when they entered the Momma's room.) Lucy Anna had come back inside now and was standing quietly beside Pecora, also staring down the now empty hallway. Moments later Speck tiptoed through the kitchen door, stopped, and stood behind Pecora and Lucy Anna, looking over their heads down the hall. When Momma Rosiebellelee called *everybody* answered. That is, everybody but Sugar Boy, whose head was still planted under the hood of his '36 Ford out back by the barn.

Momma Rosiebellelee's room couldn't be called junky; there wasn't enough in there. The big, four-poster double bed —the only reason the Momma ever came in here—naturally dominated the room. It had been bought especially for her (and him) by Mister Mac, the very first piece of furniture brought into the house, and only minutes afterwards had been tested for durability right on the spot while Mister Mac's colored workers waited outside on the wagon in the hot sun until they were allowed to bring in the rest of the furniture. Standing in the middle of the room, the bed was flanked on both sides by several straightback, straw-bottomed chairs brought in by Pecora for the expected flow of well-wishers; Momma Rosiebellelee's Children would be coming all afternoon and into the night. The window by the head of the bed was always kept open and it had no curtains, screens, or shades—all obstacles, according to the Momma, to the free passage of sun and fresh air. Right underneath was a small stand holding only a water pitcher, drinking glass, and, naturally, a large vase of flowers freshly cut by Lucy Anna. Built into the room's north wall was the fireplace, now swept clean of all traces of ash, topped by a mantelpiece bearing a lone lamp with a smoke-blackened chimney and nearly dry of kerosene. The only other piece of furniture in the room stood against the south wall—a tall, dark-brown chifforobe with a glossy finish, which contained a stack of drawers on the left and on the right a gleaming full-length mirror on a door which swung open to receive the Momma's Sunday rags. The walls were papered in the same badly faded pattern of roses on a once-white background as the other bedrooms, and the narrow floorboards of finished pine were bare.

Despite the lazy heat of the day, the bed's top cover was a thin, brightly colored quilt whose four corners nearly touched the floor, practically hiding the big slop jar with its flower design that was sitting beneath the foot of the bed. Lying asleep at the foot of the bed was Doris Virginia's cat, Mae Sue. Momma Rosiebellelee was sitting up in bed with several pillows stacked between her back and the high wooden headboard. What all of her other years, eras, and epochs hadn't been able to do, Hard Times had. They had sprinkled her hair with gray, splotched her face with wrinkles while slowly leeching out the color from that acorn-brown skin, and even shrinking her down from her constant hundred twenty-five pounds. But even those lean, mean years of the Thirties hadn't carried enough ill wind with them to blow out the fire in the Momma's eyes.

"You want me, Momma?" Doris Virginia coming to a quick stop at the foot of her mother's bed.

"Come on up heah to me, child." Nor had the fire gone out of her voice. "You got yo'self all ready fuh t'day?"

"Yes, ma'am." Now moving around the foot of the bed.

"You took yo'self a bath?"

"Yes, ma'am." Slowly moving closer to the voice.

"You put yo'self on some clean drawers?"

"Yes, ma'am." This stopped her midway alongside the bed.

"Come on up heah 'n let me see you. Ain' see'n' too good t'day."

Doris Virginia edged up a few inches closer to the voice

while at the same time easing away from directly alongside the bed—but not quite far and fast enough. Momma Rosiebellelee suddenly leaned forward, and before Doris Virginia had a chance to holler out, that lightning left hand had streaked out and grabbed the hem of her blood-red, flared skirt and yanked it up around her waist.

"Whar's yo' drawers?" The Momma now pulling her daughter closer by the hem of her skirt.

"It's too *hot* for bloomers." Doris Virginia's face as red as the patch of hair peeking out just south of her navel.

"Hit's always too hot fuh you. Look in the bottom draw' of the chiffrobe ovah thar 'n git my silk ones. Luvenia's comin' t'day 'n you don' wan' her to think her baby sister ain' got no drawers to weah."

"She won't know."

"*I'll* know. Now go git them outa the draw' thar." Letting go of her daughter's dress, Momma Rosiebellelee sat back with a more amused than annoyed look in her eyes while watching a chastened Doris Virginia move around the bed and over to the chifforobe, open the bottom drawer, take out the Momma's special pair of pink step-ins, and do just that with them. "Now Luvenia won't come heah think'n we po'." A pleased Momma.

"Silk bloomers sho' ain't gonna make nobody rich." Doris Virginia walking back over to the bed, tugging at her unwanted underwear at each step.

"They sho' make you feel richer than the cotton ones do."

Doris Virginia, now back at the head of the bed, looking directly down into her mother's eyes. "Momma, do you love Luvenia better than me?"

"Hi could I, my child, when she been gone 'way so long 'n you been heah wit me all the time—'cept fuh the time you runned off wit that Plootsy niggah."

"Somebody must've loved Luvenia better than me 'cause she sho' got a heap more than me." Doris Virginia not wanting to get the talk off onto any nigger named Plootsy.

"Mist' Mac give her evahthin', I didn'."

"How come then he didn't give me what he give her? He didn't give me nothing. I was just as much his—"

"You ain' *his!* Mist' Mac a white man. You *mine!*" In a tone of voice Doris Virginia didn't recognize as the Momma's.

"Is Luvenia pretty like everybody say she is?" Doris Virginia quickly changing the subject, and softening her tone.

"She usta be real pretty. But, my child, I ain' seed her in ovah twenty yeahs." The old Momma's tone back.

"Prettier than me?"

"'Bout the same, I'd say."

"You just saying that."

"She might've been prettier than you then, but I bet you the prettiest now."

"I usta didn't be *this* pretty?"

"You *always* been pretty. But when Luvenia was little she always wore her drawers, even when hit was too hot. 'N I betcha she don' come down heah to see her Momma wit'out them on."

Bested at every turn so far, Doris Virginia plunged on. "I ain't gonna be calling her no Shirley Temple stuff when she gets here. She *ain't* no moviestar. I'm gonna call her all day Luvenia, Luvenia, Luvenia, *Luvenia, Luvenia, Luvenia!*"

"Is yo' Geechie gone to git her?"

"Yes, ma'am."

"Did he take hisself a bath too?"

"Yes, ma'am."

"Wha' he weah to pick her up in?"

"His Sunday suit."

"Is Savannah ready too?"

"Pecora gonna get her ready."

"When Luvenia is here I wan' her, you, Sugar Boy . . . 'n Speck too . . . all in heah t'gether, so I kin tell y'all all at the same time 'bout how I wan' the funeral did 'n who all to write letters to so they kin be heah."

"What funeral?"

"Mine."

"Oh . . ."

"Momma Rosiebellelee, the folks starting to come!" An excited Lucy Anna poking her head through the open door at Doris Virginia's back with this bit of news.

"Fo you let them in, Lu' Anna, go call my Sugar Boy—" The rest of Momma Rosiebellelee's request was drowned out by the roar of a car, belching smoke and backfiring, shooting past her window.

"He gone, Momma Rosiebellelee."

As the sound faded up the road the stillness was briefly interrupted by a loud whispering voice pleading from down the hall:

"Lu' Anna, tell the Momma I'se heah."

As if she hadn't heard Speck's offer of himself in place of her Sugar Boy, Momma Rosiebellelee turned her attention back to her daughter.

"Doris 'Ginia, go 'n see if Peco' got Savannah ready yet. 'N don' you go nowhar 'cause when all the other chilluns of mine been in to see me 'n I've seed the gran'chilluns, I wan' all my *real* chilluns heah by my bed. You heah? Awright, Lu' Anna, call Peco' to come empty the slop jar, then send in the folks."

Sugar Boy parked his car along the side of the road at the top of the rise on the town side of Haint Hills overlooking Sugar Creek Bridge to wait for Rockee Ryder. If his '36 V-8 was going to take her '42 Buick on the road between Appalachee and the Hundred Acres, Sugar Boy figured his best chance would be on the stretch through Haint Hills, where most drivers had a natural tendency to brake on the downhill slope because of the tricky ruts along there—but not Sugar Boy, who had the reputation of not slowing down for anything and who, despite his infamous Sugar Creek Bridge accident, felt he knew the Haint Hills ruts even better than the haints themselves. And especially than a *woman*. A *white* woman at that.

A good inch or so shorter than Speck, Sugar Boy was wider and more muscular than his baby brother. And while Speck's much lighter, softer, and smoother features gave him that almost-*too*-pretty look, more like Mister Mac, Sugar Boy's complexion was closer to Momma Rosiebellelee's. Even more than his rugged good looks, finished off by a pencil-thin mustache and a hint of a scowl, his most-talked-about physical feature (at least in polite company) especially among the area's females, was his ink-black, long and straight, or "blow," hair—so called by the local black folks because, and unlike "nigger natural," it blew wildly in the wind—a sight that got right down in the passion pores of most Plain View women and young girls old enough to bleed. And Sugar Boy, the complete opposite of Speck in most respects, *never* wore a cap and rarely ever got a haircut, so whenever he went speeding through Plain View with his car's top laid back, the wind would be swirling, twirling, flapping, and slapping those long strands of hair all over his head, just like it did the white folks'.

As Momma Rosiebellelee's favorite, Sugar Boy had wanted for little in his thirty-three years. He had replaced Luvenia atop Nigger Gal and his mother took him with her practically everywhere she rode the black mare. Then for his twelfth birthday, Momma Rosiebellelee bought him a brand-new Tin Lizzie, which he learned to drive on the very first day. And from that day onward he'd never been without a car, something he loved like Momma Rosiebellelee loved her Nigger Gal, Speck his mules, and later on, Doris Virginia her Victrola. Also for his twelfth birthday the Momma bought him a guitar which, to her great disappointment, he eventually traded for a harmonica, or "harp," whose sound he much preferred.

In a fatherless home, Sugar Boy quickly assumed the role of man of the house, and Momma Rosiebellelee treated him as an adult or equal. After he turned the farm over to Speck and his mules, and the boll weevils, Sugar Boy went looking for other work and for the next eighteen years he wouldn't accept any job that didn't have something to do with driving a car, truck, or tractor.

When he wasn't driving (or attending to his car in some fashion), Sugar Boy was usually found in the bottom of some female's drawers. He'd never had *any* trouble whatsoever in finding pussy. In fact, pussy came *looking* for Sugar Boy. From as far back as he could remember, females, both girls and women, single and married, even during his pre-puberty days, had thrown their pussies at him. But since he had always had all this pussy lying at his feet, or elsewhere, Sugar Boy had never had to fight for a single piece he'd ever gotten. It had always been there right in front of his nose, or wherever, and regardless if it was married, spoken for, spoken against, never spoken to, raw, overripe, cherry, or aged, he'd always gotten it. Sugar Boy took pussy as much for granted as grits. And as a result of all this easy-to-get tail, Rosiebelle Lee Wildcat Tennessee's older son respected very few women —these few being the Momma, Doris Virginia, Pecora, Theophilia . . . and the one he always tried not to think about, but always did. The one whose pussy he knew he would *never* get, but wanted something sinful.

As far as the local males went, Sugar Boy was admired, envied, and held in awe by most of them just as much as he was among the females—and this even though he was continually dicking their wives, sweethearts, sisters, nieces, aunts, daughters, granddaughters, mothers, and grandmothers. Still, none of them dared challenge or threaten Sugar Boy. Not that Sugar Boy had the reputation of whipping heads and asses but there was something in his makeup that made men not want to approach him about fucking their wives, sweethearts, and sisters—instead they would just beat the bitch. Also, Sugar Boy wasn't a talker. He was a doer. He had little to say to most; many of the women and girls who came to him to get serviced never got more out of him than a grunt or snort that signaled the culmination of their congress. And he especially didn't like people, particularly women, who talked too much. This near-total silence of his, along with his muscular, tank-type build and ever-present scowl, kept the jealous types in deadly doubt about what he might do if matters came to a showdown. But the scariest of these times came when Sugar Boy got drunk. Sugar Boy couldn't hold his liquor . . . some said this was because of the Rosiebelle Lee Wildcat Tennessee "Indian" in him. But, except for an occasional, masochistic female, he didn't do much damage to people physically, since everyone knew enough to stay out of his way. Everything else—furniture, doors, windowpanes, mirrors, and cars (other folks'), for example—that got in his way when he was drunk, he would demolish. Even on those occasions when Sugar Boy felt fit to enter Appalachee's notorious back-street hangout, Sam's Café, none of those who hung out there ever messed with him, and messing up folks was their business.

Unlike Speck, Sugar Boy didn't have a particularly strong need to be accepted by others; Sugar Boy did the accepting. Nor, like Doris Virginia, did he have to be surrounded by others most of the time. Sugar Boy was a loner. Despite this though he was the most popular person in Plain View and the most widely emulated, by *both* males and females. Still, Sugar Boy's only real friend was his car; few other things could hold his interest for very long. While Speck and Doris Virginia, like Mister Mac, loved reading books without pictures and such, Sugar Boy cared nothing for the habit. Sitting around reading was too dead for him. He liked movement, action—but he didn't mind the picture show too much, and he often drove Doris Virginia into Appalachee to it. But he only went if she promised him there would be a car in the show. Once she did fool him just to get him to take her; she always had trouble with the Man when she was seen on the street, or anywhere else in Appalachee, with a regular-looking colored man. That was the time he took her to see that old-style *Gone With the Wind* thing. She cried out loud for the women in the show and slobbered over the man moviestar while Sugar Boy just sat watching . . . and waiting . . . hoping to see a car, *any* car, even an old-style one . . . and he was glad as hell when the whole mess finally *went* with the wind more than three hours after it started blowing, because they didn't show even *one* damn car! He would never forget that picture as long as he lived. In fact, he didn't like any old-style picture because they never had any cars in them. Contrary to the tastes of most other local male picture-show-goers, he didn't even like cowboy pictures—no cars. Horses, or mules (Speck was still waiting for a picture show where everybody rode a mule), or even pistols, did nothing in the way of interesting Sugar Boy the way cars did.

When he was in his late teens and early twenties, with his seemingly endless supply of sharkskin slacks and his Rudolph Valentino slicked-down hair, parted in the middle, that had Plain View females moistening their Sunday silk step-ins, Sugar Boy had been Plain View's peacock. But when Hard Times hit he had trouble finding driving jobs, and he still refused to accept any other type of work—not that there was an overabundance of other types of work to reject. Then, when there were no driving jobs at all and he still had to keep his car and hair greased, he went into business for himself— moonshining. It was only about six months before he was on his way up the Oconee to the state prison farm at Yankee Town.

One word dispatched from the cabin in the woods over across the spring to the sheriff or the judge might possibly have kept Sugar Boy off the chain gang, but the blood between Sugar Boy and Mister Mac ran bad. While Luvenia had been Mister Mac's pet, Sugar Boy had been the Momma's— the Momma hadn't sent her pet up North. So, now she had both her pet *and* Mister Mac, and with Sugar Boy on the scene his jealous soul no longer had her all to itself, which was

BENNY ANDREWS
FEB 29 1974

one reason why Mister Mac didn't start bouncing little Sugar
Boy on his knee. Other than that they were both loners by
nature, the white man and his colored son had practically
nothing at all in common. Mister Mac loved hunting, the
woods, horses, hunting dogs, guns, and books. Sugar Boy's
chief interests were cars, clothes, and women. But the *real*
trouble between these two hot-tempered men came shortly
after Mister Mac's fabled move from the Big House into the
cabin in the woods back over across the spring. His pride was
stung to the quick, and the white man suddenly, and to everyone's surprise, started to take to the bottle. This was when his
demands on the time and energy of Momma Rosiebellelee
reached their height. Since at that time she was the only one
permitted by Mister Mac to put foot across the spring to care
for him and Missis Bea, this was taking up so much of the
Momma's time that she had hardly any left for anything else,
which was truly not Rosiebelle Lee Wildcat Tennessee's glass
of buttermilk. Then one night late she climbed the hill from
over across the spring; she was crying, and her face was
bloody. The Momma wasn't a crier. In a drunken fit, Mister
Mac had hit her for the first time ever in their many years
together. That was when Sugar Boy, who was crying by now,
ran downhill with the butcher knife on his way to "gut" his
white daddy . . . only to be stopped cold right at the spring.
Mister Mac was standing just over into the trees, cradling the
butt of a seven-shot pump shotgun whose barrel was aimed
dead at Sugar Boy's head. Sugar Boy started to back up, carefully picking his way on this moonlit night all the way to the
top of the hill and Momma Rosiebellelee's. The white man
and his colored son never spoke to each other again . . . nor
did Momma Rosiebellelee ever climb that hill from over
across the spring with her face streaked with tears and blood.
And Sugar Boy had never come down that hill to the spring
again.

· ——— ·

Sugar Boy didn't mind the chain gang nearly so much as the Momma had minded it for him. He'd been immediately assigned to the road gang, repairing, scraping, paving, and graveling roads throughout the area. Dump trucks were used on much of the road work, and it wasn't long before he had maneuvered his way behind the wheel of one of these. For a week during that summer Sugar Boy's gang even worked on the road that ran from Appalachee, through Plain View, and then on down through Muskhogean County. By the time the chain gang had worked their way down from Appalachee to Plain View, the banks and ditches along the road were filled with folks who had turned out to see what their favorite son looked like all dressed up in Georgia black and white. Many of the women and older girls were sporting face powder, lipstick, rouge, perfume, and even wearing their Sunday silk step-ins. Some had gone so far as to take a bath, and in the middle of the week to boot. Everybody who was there agreed that Sugar Boy's stripes fitted him just like they'd been painted on. When the chain gang reached the Hundred Acres, Momma Rosiebellelee herself led her flock of youngsters up to the road with buckets of cold lemonade, fresh and hot buttered, peppered, and salted roasting ears of corn, and cool, rich, and ripe watermelon for the convicts and the guards. Afterwards, the convicts sang the crowd a song. While all of this was going on, Sugar Boy, followed on each run by a whole passel of scrambling young Plain View boys, just sped back and forth down the long dusty road, hauling and dumping dirt as fast as the prison's noisy, battered dump truck—with no doors and a governor on the motor—would take him.

Sugar Boy had never once had the leather laid to his hide in his whole year at Yankee Town (they hadn't even made him learn to sing), and if the Momma hadn't insisted that he come straight home after his year was up—and if there'd been any pussy in Yankee Town—he probably would have asked to stay on just to drive the dump truck.

Still, Sugar Boy came home from Yankee Town a

changed man. The sharkskin slacks and slicked-down hair no longer seem to interest him. After her younger son had suddenly up and married before he'd turned seventeen, and right off started presenting her with a grandchild at two-year intervals (even though they were grandchildren that Theophilia wouldn't let her raise the grandma way), Momma Rosiebellelee was anxiously waiting for her Sugar Boy to marry and give her some grandchildren she would be able to love and treat *her* way. In fact, the Momma knew exactly whom she wanted, and didn't want, Sugar Boy to marry. And God in His heaven and Satan in his hell *both* knew that Momma Rosiebellelee hadn't wanted Sugar Boy to marry Pecora Moore. Not only couldn't the Momma figure out why Sugar Boy, who could have had his pick of all the women and courting girls in Plain View, hadn't asked *her* to help him make a selection, but nobody, man, woman, or haint, could figure out why he'd gotten messed up with Pecora Moore—a mismatch if there ever was one.

Born into perhaps the poorest and most superstitious family in or around Plain View, Pecora was what was locally referred to as "a FBI"—Fat, Black, and Ignorant. During those few hours she spent in school in her youth she was remarked on by her peers only for her superstitiousness and her big titties—the older she got, the bigger all three of these grew. But when she quit school to help out at home, everyone just sort of forgot all about her, except at those times when the subject of titties came up. And since the Moore family were not much for churchgoing, the whole clan—parents, eleven children, and a grandmother—was thought of by the community as being somewhat odd, keeping off to themselves the way they did in their three-room shack on Plain View's remotest, most desolate, and poorest patch of farmland. As if that weren't enough, there were also those who claimed that Grandma Sissie Moore worked spells, or "roots," on folks.

Then came the day that Sugar Boy came home. The first thing he did when he reached the Hundred Acres, after suffering several hugs and kisses from his womenfolks, was gas and crank up his old '28 Model-T and then go speeding like a young stud bull fresh out of the winter stall all up and down the dusty back roads of Plain View. He was a one-man show that brought folks out of their houses and out on their porches, stoops, and yards; the shut-ins peered out from their windows; those caught in the toilets hurried out without wiping or at least kicked open the door to watch; and the field workers came out from between the rows to the edge of the road to catch in their eyes, noses, and mouths some of that Georgia red dust, souvenir of the day Sugar Boy came home from the chain gang—the same day his long, straight locks started blowing in the wind. Bye-bye, slicked-down hair.

Sugar Boy sped around and around and through and through Plain View most of that afternoon until his car ran out of water and got so hot and steamed up that he had to stop. To stop at that far, desolate end of Plain View, right in front of the three-room shack of the poor family Moore. Now nobody in Plain View on that day was close enough to know what exactly went on when Sugar Boy's boiling and steaming motor pulled up in the front yard of the Moore house just tongue-hanging-out begging to be cooled off—not even the Moores themselves, who were all out working in the field. That is, all but for Grandma Sissie Moore . . . and young Pecora. Now many folks believed that old Grandma Sissie Moore worked her roots on Sugar Boy that day to make him do what he must have done. While others, menfolk, felt that Sugar Boy had been on the chain gang for so long that getting his first piece of tail in a year had just plain tetched him in the haid. Now whether he was under a spell, or just plain gone soft in the head, nobody could prove, but when Sugar Boy drove away from the poor family Moores' house *much* later that afternoon, sitting beside him on the front seat of his cooled-off Model-T, behind the two biggest titties Plain View had ever seen, was Pecora. And that very next Sunday she and Sugar Boy got married.

Not since the death of Nigger Gal had anybody seen
Momma Rosiebellelee in such a state. The Momma was
shocked—shocked first because her Sugar Boy had up and
gotten married without first consulting her before he took
such a serious step, and second because of the poor family
Moores' total lack of importance and total lack of everything,
in fact, and last because of Pecora's tar-black skin. Her two
sons, Speck and now Sugar Boy, the two lightest-skinned
nigger men in or around Plain View, had gone out and found
the two blackest women the Momma could imagine and
brought them both home to roost under her roof. Lord God,
she just hoped and prayed her baby Doris Virginia would
have more sense.

The very first thing Pecora did on moving under
Momma Rosiebellelee's roof on her wedding night was to
take a horseshoe from her pocketbook, which she proceeded
to nail up over the door to their bedroom to keep the haints
out. Haints taken care of, she went in to join Sugar Boy, who
was already waiting in bed, and for the rest of that night kept
him smothered in a ton of tittie.

Meanwhile, out in the kitchen, Momma Rosiebelle sat
smiling, forgetting for the rest of the night her great disappointment over the matchup, while rocking back and forth
. . . forth and back . . . back and forth . . . in perfect time to
the sensual sounds of creaking bedsprings stridulating down
the hallway from the newlyweds' bedroom, which created in
the Momma's head tiny images of little dancing, singing, and
laughing grandchildren. *Hers.* And the bedsprings just
creaked right on.

The night of the creaking bedsprings didn't bear
Momma Rosiebellelee any two-legged, grandchild fruit. And
as the years slid past the constant creaking of the springs, both
night *and* day, gradually began grating on the Momma's
brain, since the sound of all that grunting, groaning, moaning, crying, and screaming hard labor emanating from behind
her older son's bedroom door was, in Momma Rosiebellelee's

opinion, all wasted effort simply because not one drop of sweat of it produced *her* any grandchildren. The Momma—who had never before publicly expressed a belief or interest in signs, roots, or spells—blamed the situation entirely on Pecora, who she said was working roots on her Sugar Boy. Roots or not, the first ten years of their marriage brought no children for Sugar Boy and Pecora, yet rarely a night passed that they didn't give it at least one try with all they had.

However, Momma Rosiebellelee found plenty of other use for Pecora. Housework. Other than for cooking and sleeping, the Momma had never had any use for the indoors (she even preferred sewing out on the porch). And her daughter Doris Virginia—who didn't mind being inside at all just so long as she didn't have to work (except in bed) while she was in there—was no better. This just meant that the housework at Momma Rosiebellelee's had always suffered, to say the least. When Speck got married and brought Theophilia home to the Momma, the new bride had out and out refused to clean up anyone else's room. Then along came Pecora, who willingly cleaned house from front to back porch and from ceiling to floor, and cleaned well, thus giving the Momma—still the sole cook—more time with her flowers, sewing, fishing, and running folks. And Doris Virginia, who didn't seem to mind Pecora's inability to present her with nieces and nephews, now had more time to devote to her Victrola, moviestar magazines, courting, picture shows, and doing nothing. And Pecora went about her work everyday without so much as a grumble. Also, other than to step outside to do the porches and go out back of the barn, she stayed inside the house. She never went anywhere, at any time, including back home, nor did she receive *any* visitors from home or anywhere else. She seemed perfectly contented with her new lot: daily spouting her superstitions to all who would or couldn't help but listen (on haints and warnings and the importance of heeding signs, and so on) while cleaning Momma Rosiebellelee's house during the day and bouncing bedsprings with that same Momma's favorite son all night.

Meanwhile, Sugar Boy was spending more and more of his time with his car. No jobs at all were to be found now, much less a job driving. This was during those early, dark days of Hard Times, when the whole Hundred Acres lived out of Theophilia's Garden. Still, through all of these belly-growling years Sugar Boy kept his car going. There was nowhere to go and nothing to spend when he got there, but Sugar Boy was always the first there and the first back with his nothing. Finally, the WPA came along and Speck went to work with it the very first day it opened up its operations in the area. But not Sugar Boy. There was nary a driving job to be had, and what few were available were automatically given to the white folks. In fact, throughout Hard Times only two driving jobs were to present themselves to Sugar Boy. The first one was that of driving an ice truck—a good job, but one Sugar Boy didn't keep for long, simply because he was more interested in driving the truck than in selling the ice (which has been known to melt fast under a Georgia sun). On his return to the plant at the end of each day the owner of the plant felt the driver had too many more miles on his meter than ice money in his pocket. Then there came that second, taxi-driving job.

That started right after 'Ginia's Geechie landed himself a job driving Mister Spence's taxicab—and after he'd only been in Plain View for a couple of days at that. A driving job! Not Sugar Boy, but a black Geechie from way off in Savannah. Comes all the way to Appalachee and finds himself a driving job! Jealous of his brother-in-law's luck, Sugar Boy took off immediately to the taxicab company to find out whether another job was available. There was.

The taxicab owner, Mister Charm Spence, hired Sugar Boy on the spot and right away split the driving of the company's single car between the two of them. Sugar Boy reported in to work at six in the morning and was replaced behind the wheel at three in the afternoon by 'Ginia's Geechie, who worked until midnight; both worked seven days a week. The promise of a second taxi so that both drivers could have their own cars was made by the young white man who appeared *overly* pleased at having Momma Rosiebellelee's oldest son and *only* son-in-law working for him. Talk wasn't long in getting around Plain View, though, that the exceptionally handsome, bordering on beautiful white man hired 'Ginia's Geechie and then Sugar Boy to get next to Doris Virginia. But Sugar Boy soon found out that this wasn't true, a long way from it. From the very beginning Sugar Boy hadn't been really comfortable in Mister Charm Spence's presence—and not just colored man–white man uncomfortable. Something more than that. Like for a man Mister Charm Spence looked too soft and smooth-skinned to gain Sugar Boy's trust.

Then one day—after less than a year of driving taxi and to the complete astonishment of everyone who knew how much cars meant to him—Sugar Boy quit. This even after the promised second car had been delivered and broken in by him personally. And not only did Sugar Boy quit, but he never told one single soul—including Momma Rosiebellelee and Pecora—why right in the heart of Hard Times he just up and left a job he not only needed but loved so much. In fact, the reason why Sugar Boy quit driving taxi was something he not only didn't talk about but absolutely refused to think about. But everybody was quick to say that the reason for the quitting had to do with the good-looking young white man's designs on Sugar Boy's baby sister, who spent lots of time riding in the back seat of her Geechie's cab and hanging around the taxi garage itself. Still, 'Ginia's Geechie stayed on, though to the surprise of no one, since it was claimed that Mister Charm Spence, who'd gone to college over at Athens, was the only person in the whole county of Muskhogean who understood the funny talk 'Ginia's Geechie talked, at least until little Savannah Carmen Maria arrived, of course. But only Sugar Boy . . . and Mister Charm Spence . . . knew why he'd quit. And the colored man *couldn't* talk . . . and the white man *wouldn't* talk.

After this there were just no driving jobs to be found anywhere and all the driving Sugar Boy did now was on his own. And drive he did. All around and through Plain View his wheels sped daily, causing folks to get off the road and stand in the ditch whenever they looked up or back and saw a cloud of Georgia red rolling their way. *Nothing* on the road ever stayed in front of Sugar Boy for very long. All during Hard Times he owned a Model-T, A, and B, and finally the V-8, and only with the B did he ever have a wreck. Yes, Plain View's roads definitely *belonged* to Sugar Boy of the "blow" hair.

This was pretty much his life during the last years of the Thirties and into the Forties—until the Japs got around to bombing Pearl Harbor. First, Sugar Boy had wanted to join the army, especially since that day several weeks after the war got started when he just so happened to be in Appalachee in time and watched, for at least an hour, while a long convoy of military trucks and cars filled with soldiers passed through town on their way to California, which it was said the Japs were going to bomb next. Sugar Boy was moved—moved not by the fearless-looking, combat-ready soldiers on their way to protect the moviestars out West, but by the convoy of trucks and cars that was taking them there. He wanted desperately to get behind the wheel of one of those babies. Back home that night at the supper table he announced his intentions of joining the army. That was when Momma Rosiebellelee acted.

Before Pecora had even cleared off the table, the Momma had gone out the back door without a word to anyone, and on downhill across the spring and back into the woods to Mister Mac's cabin, where she stayed until right before daybreak. The next morning she climbed the hill to home and walked straight into Doris Virginia's room, woke up the heavily snoring 'Ginia's Geechie, and stayed right there until he had got-

ten dressed. Then she went out to the hill back of the barn
to watch as he drove his taxicab around by Speck's house, on
along the path running beside the hill down to the edge of the
spring. Mister Mac emerged from the woods, dressed in his
best, and got into the back seat while 'Ginia's Geechie held
the door. For the first time since the day he shot the redneck
twin Mike Nicholson back in '28 he was going into Appalachee, though this time not to kill but to keep his bastard son
from getting killed. He was off to see, for the first time in
many a year, his former partner in the bicycle business, now
longtime owner of the area's largest automobile garage, and
most important the head of the local draft board. Mister Mac
spent several hours talking and sipping Jack Daniel's before
he returned to the Hundred Acres, then back over across the
spring, where that night after supper Momma Rosiebellelee
once again crossed the footbridge, and didn't return until just
before sunup. She climbed the hill to her house and walked
straight into Sugar Boy and Pecora's room, shook her son
awake, and tearfully whispered that he wouldn't have to go
off out West to save the Hollywood moviestars from the Japs
or even to New York to save the Jews from the Germans,
because now he had himself a driving job, driving a sawmill
truck. Hallelujah!

　　Now sitting and waiting, watching his rearview mirror
for the first sign of that big, white, black-topped Buick, Sugar
Boy's thoughts were running back over those past several
months of driving the sawmill truck. After the logs had been
sawed into lumber, Sugar Boy and his cabmate loaded the
truck, then Sugar Boy drove it into Appalachee, where they
unloaded their cargo, stacking it there in the big lumberyard
over near the town's planer mill, before returning to the
woods for another load. Sugar Boy also drove the mill workers—excepting Speck, of course—back and forth from the
woods, and was even allowed to keep the truck parked out
back of the house right alongside the barn during non-work-

ing hours. And it was from this truck—and 'Ginia's Geechie's taxicab, parked out front of the house for those few hours he wasn't driving during the week—that Sugar Boy filled his own tank with hard-to-get war-rationing gas.

True, driving the sawmill truck had gone so well with Momma Rosiebellelee's older son that all thoughts of going off to war or driving an army truck to help save moviestars out West and New York Jews had left his mind altogether. But other things had entered. First, one rainy, windy Saturday night while he was speeding down through Haint Hills on his way home from Appalachee, alone (only the young, the foolish, and the drunk ever rode with Sugar Boy), he suddenly jammed on his brakes right at the bridge and nearly skidded off and over into Sugar Creek below. Standing in the middle of the bridge was a young girl, one he'd never seen before. Not knowing what else to do, he let her in the car and took her on out to the Hundred Acres. Nobody out here had seen or heard of her before either, and all anyone could get out of her was that her name was Lucy Anna and she was out on a "calling." Claiming to be fifteen, but looking a year or two younger, she was as pretty and as yellow as a ripe Elberta peach, with big soft-boiled eyes, quivering, blood-sausage lips, and a young body with baby fat still stored in all the right little-girl places. Doris Virginia *hated* all that pretty. Pecora said she was a haint and wouldn't go near her. But the Momma liked her style and put her up in Speck's old room.

No one came to claim the young Lucy Anna, and she just made her home there on the Hundred Acres, remaining a special pet of Momma Rosiebellelee. The morning she showed up at the breakfast table, obviously pregnant, everybody automatically assumed that the baby was Sugar Boy's, though he said nothing about it to anyone one way or the other. That is, everybody assumed but Pecora, who swore the baby was not her Sugar Boy's. Instead, she claimed it was the baby of the devil, sent by her dead brother Ezell, who had never approved of her marriage to Sugar Boy, to haint the Hundred Acres. Shortly after Lucy Anna arrived, Momma Rosiebellelee took to her sickbed.

Then something happened along Sugar Boy felt was much bigger than out-West moviestars, New York Jews, army trucks, the army, the war . . . haint babies. Much bigger. Somebody had come along and *stolen* his road from him. Rockee Ryder Nicholson.

Mister Nick might have gone all the way to town to get himself a wife, but the one he brought back was no stranger to Plain View. Born in Plain View and having lived there until entering her teens, she and her mother had moved into Appalachee, where a decade later she met Ike Nicholson, a tobacco-chewing, *nouveau riche* redneck, some thirty years her senior who everybody said was bent on buying up the whole county, names and all, including Miss Rockee Ryder . . . the older daughter of the former Amanda MacAndrew.

Life hadn't gone as well for Amanda's younger daughter. Valaria, cut from the same mold as her mother, was ultrasensitive and withdrawn, and she grew to have a minimum of self-confidence and a maximum of imagination. She had spent most of her young life wondering and daydreaming about a dead daddy she had never seen, and as she grew older, she began telling stories to the other children who had real live daddies about how he had loved her very much and talked to her when she was a little-bitty baby before going off and dying a hero's death in the Great War. The other children just started teasing her and calling her a "fibber." The meaner ones didn't stop there, saying to her and others that her ol' hermit uncle down in Plain View had a whole passel of nigger children, which meant that she had "Nigra" blood . . . which explained her curly hair. With no daddy to run home and cry to, and a mommy who couldn't cope with her tears, Valaria, at age fifteen, hanged herself.

Mister Nick's wedding was held in the old Plain View Plantation Big House and the groom's present to his young bride was a brand-new, black-topped, white-bodied 1942 Buick sedan. This was when Sugar Boy lost his crown as Plain View's king of the road, and lost it to a *woman* at that. A *white* woman to boot. Sugar Boy's first cousin.

When Rockee Ryder got married, Amanda, who was more afraid of loneliness than anything else, once again found herself alone, but this time not for long. Ike Nicholson drove his car in to pick her up personally and bring her back to her original home in the old Plain View Plantation Big House, to live with him and his new bride. Mike Nicholson's funeral was *almost* paid for.

Now Sugar Boy had only seen Rockee Ryder once when she wasn't sitting behind the wheel of her big Buick—but that one time was enough. He *couldn't* get her off his mind. She was the prettiest thing he'd ever seen—blonde, petite, and compact, with a fast, biting-at-the-bit gait, her head always held high, as if defiantly, all giving her an air of stuck-up daredeviltry. Sugar Boy had never before imagined, much less seen, a woman who was anything like that. To him she was just *asking* for it. And this woman, white or not, Sugar Boy knew *had to be taken* . . . on *his* road. Lord, have mercy!

Though it hadn't taken the heat along with it, the afternoon was steadily moving westward, and still no black-and-white Buick had flashed in Sugar Boy's right rearview mirror. Several cars, wagons, and folks on foot had passed his car there on the hill, most of whom he figured were heading out to the Hundred Acres to take their last look at the Momma. Sugar Boy's mind refused to hang on to this thought for too long, since he found it hard to envision a world without the Momma. Still, whenever he got around to imagining that world, he always imagined himself inheriting the Hundred Acres, and selling it all to ol' Ike Nicholson, since he'd often heard Mister Nick wanted that piece of land worse than God wanted His goodness and Satan his sin. Then he'd move into Appalachee and open up a garage and repair shop—the only thing in life Sugar Boy truly wanted.

One of the cars going past at that moment was a Spence taxicab, driven by 'Ginia's Geechie. The car went by too fast for Sugar Boy to get a good look at the lone figure sitting there in the back seat. Still no black-and-white Buick flashing in his right rearview mirror.

$\mathcal{T}$he folks were coming. First those who lived the closest came on foot. Then came the wagons, buggies, mules, and horses, tractors, and trucks. Then came the car crowd. Rosiebelle Lee Wildcat Tennessee's children were coming to see their big Momma before she crossed over, bringing with them their children, and *their* children, and a few of *their* children, all dressed in their Sunday best on this Saturday; they also brought along on that still, sunnyhot afternoon their food, *and* their drinks. Pecora and Lucy Anna were busily herding the long, never-ending line of folks—men, women, boys, girls, crying and sleeping babies, the old, the lame, the unborn—parading slowly and solemnly into the Momma's room to see, be seen by, speak to, be spoken to by, to touch, be touched, and blessed by Her. Now lying flat in bed while touching a bowed head here, an outstretched trembling hand there, having her own hand squeezed, kissed, and wetted with tears, the dying Momma Rosiebellelee was bearing up in typical Wildcat Tennessee style. Eating it up.

While Pecora and Lucy Anna were responsible for directing traffic in and out of the Momma's room, Doris Virginia was out in the living room single-handedly running the entertainment concession, regaling her own friends with her Victrola blasting out the blues of Tampa Red.

Baby I hate to go and leave you,
But how can I stay,
Your love is so cold baby,
I know it can't find its way.
Mercy, mercy, momma.

As the afternoon gradually ground down to dusk, the house and yard kept filling up with more and more people, many who were just getting off work and others who had finished up their Saturday business in town and were stopping by to pay their respects on the way home.

But long before dusk some of the folks sitting, standing, and squatting in the shade of the Momma's front porch swore they saw through the afternoon's thick heat maze something moving off the main road and onto the road running on down to Momma Rosiebellelee's. Several more minutes passed and these same self-proclaimed seers doubly swore they saw it move again. Then after another long wait the suspected movement was confirmed by a bunch of younger eyes there on the porch. Coming on down the road, walking so slowly that to those straining their eyes to see he seemed to be moving backwards—or, at best, standing still—was Cousin Tater, Plain View's most eligible bachelor, and Roosevelt, Plain View's oldest and most arrogant pig.

Said to be twice as slow as molasses rolling uphill on a cold winter morning, Cousin Tater was born back during the epidemic of 1918 and had been among Plain View's still breast-feeding newborns who'd nursed at Momma Rosiebellelee's community tits until their bedridden real mommas were once again well enough to handle the nursing themselves. But Cousin Tater's momma died from the sickness, leaving her firstborn there on the Hundred Acres where Momma Rosiebellelee took him to suckle alongside little Doris Virginia, until he was weaned and ready to be taken back home to his farmer daddy and brand-new momma, step style, where he

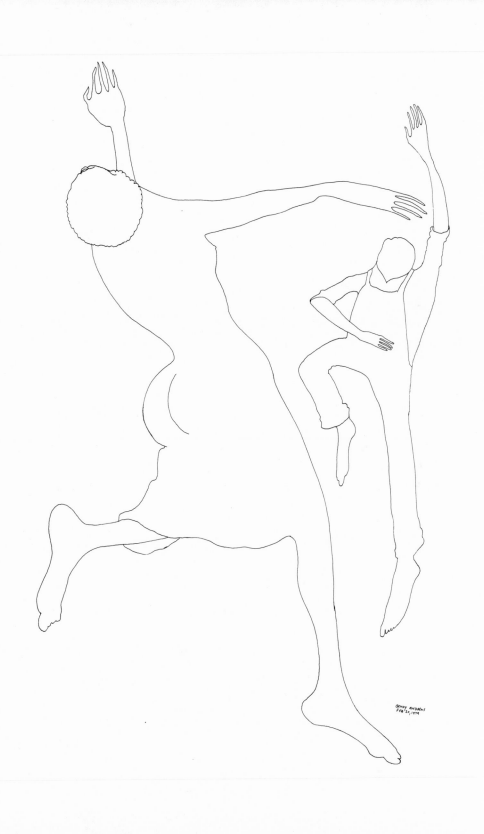

stayed until he got old enough to run away. And he ran right back to the bosom of Momma Rosiebellelee (How ya gonna keep them home milking the cow, once they've sucked the tits of Rosiebelle Lee Wildcat Tennessee, as the local saying went). The Momma rode him right back home atop Nigger Gal, after promising that even though he couldn't be her flesh-and-blood born, he would always be known to her and her children as "Cousin."

Hating farm life as he did, it wasn't long before the slower-than-syrup Cousin left home again. This time he ran, or walked, away to live in the old Lower Church, which since the death of the Reverend Willie Lee Williams had been left abandoned and unused, though its doors were still locked (the preacher, everybody figured, having taken the keys to open up those Pearly Gates—and then lock them right behind him). But he left the Lower Church windows unlocked. And from the time he was twelve it was back and forth through these windows of the Lower Church that the Cousin crawled to sleep by day and hunt by night. During Hard Times perhaps the most plentiful food around—along with grits and blackeyed peas—was sweet potatoes. And at a very impressionable age the runaway juvenile became addicted to the sweet potato (it, gritism, and "blackeye-mania" all being very common local addictions during Hard Times)—thus "Cousin Tater." First, he'd crawl out to feed his habit by hunting out a sweet potato patch for a fix and then on to the woods for the *real* hunting—possum hunting. Hating farming with slightly more than a passion, Cousin Tater decided early in life on a career in possum hunting.

Throughout the long history of man, possum hunting and farming have never jived. Whereas a farmer has to take bedcheck along with the chickens each night in order to rise with the rooster the next morning, the possum hunter doesn't begin work until long past sundown (that time of night when his prey comes out of hiding to seek its own food) and won't call quitting-time until the crack of dawn and then, while on his way home to sleep the whole day, meets the just rooster-awakened farmer on his way to the fields, where *he* feels that every God-fearing, decent, law-abiding *man* ought to been on his way to that time of the morning. Thus it was understandable that on these early morning encounters between the moonlight possum-hunting man and the sunshine farmer the two hardly spoke nicely to one another.

Sustained by his daily diet of sweet potatoes and possum, Cousin Tater kept living in the old Lower Church, which no one much minded, as they figured God Himself probably didn't want such a rundown building. And as far as the Cousin's *underground* food habit went, nobody much minded his digging in their sweet potato patch, or hill, because every time he stole a 'tater or two, the family would always find a possum in their mailbox the next morning.

Now Cousin Tater didn't have the Lower Church all to himself all this time. One early fall evening not long after he moved in, while he was out gathering his food, he found a pig digging in the same bed of 'tater that moonless night. The Cousin and the pig fought. Yet it was after digging 'taters together and then fighting that it happened that man and pig each suddenly dug t'other. That night the pig slept at Cousin Tater's holy house.

Nobody came to take the pig away nor would it leave on its own, something that caused the Cousin to believe the pig had been sent from God. Thus its name, Roosevelt, who the pig's new owner felt was about the closest thing the colored folks of Plain View had to God during those Hard Times. Now the Cousin had himself a fulltime 'tater-digging partner. And their first year together things went pretty well, at least until the local sweet potato patches had been harvested and hilled, since no one much minded the Cousin taking a 'tater or two from their hills every night, but *nobody* wanted a pig rooting around in there, and by now the man was refusing to go anywhere the pig wasn't accepted as well. Then came those long winter nights when Cousin Tater started wishing he could dissolve the partnership. The man and the pig spent many a cold, belly-grumbling night lying huddled together for warmth . . . Cousin Tater in his dreams smelling the pungent, undeniable aroma of hot barbecued spare ribs, fried pan sausage, boiling chitlings, ham hocks, knuckles, neck bones . . . while Roosevelt lay snoring . . . with one eye *always* open.

But with the coming of Roosevelt, Cousin Tater didn't need a dog for his possum hunting. Nobody's fat pig, Roosevelt, under the expert tutelage of Cousin Tater, had learned over the years how to tree a possum better than any dog in Plain View. The Cousin didn't go for hunting rabbit or squirrel . . . nor even birds . . . since that meant owning a gun, something he was deathly afraid of. But possum hunting only entailed having a dog (or a pig) to tree the possum, along with a pair of strong arms to shake it out of the tree, then a stick to hit it over the head with as soon as it dropped to the ground, and a sack to put it in afterwards.

About the only dog thing Roosevelt couldn't outdo the local possum hunting dogs at was baying at the moon, even though he gave it all he had and was rated by those who knew as the best of the non-barking animals at moon-baying (much better by far than the mule, cow, cat, or the other pigs). But once they had seen the pig treeing possums most of the community possum dogs began to develop a complex, especially the hounds, who constituted at least ninety-eight percent of the canine population of Plain View. In fact, matters reached a point where some of these hounds were overheard trying to snort and root up sweet potatoes in an effort to show up Roosevelt, who many of the dogs had come to believe was nothing more than a big showoff. This was an accusation that hurt the sensitive pig, since he had only started doing dog things out of deep admiration for these animals that folk seemed to favor so in an attempt to be accepted as an equal by them. But the only hounds he was able to get along with were the puppies and bitches. Also, the community's few non-hunting dogs just loved to death the coarse, vulgar pig who never failed to excite them. But Roosevelt took up no time with this minority group, which the hounds themselves looked down on and considered a bit queer on account of their non-hunting habits.

As for the pigs in Plain View, Roosevelt spent a little time around them when he first came onto the scene. These were the young ones who ran around in the open fields; he would occasionally pal around with some of them but he never wanted to get too friendly with their kind, for he was easily depressed by the strong smell of death they carried on them. Then came that time each year he always dreaded. This was the day when the young boars were cut by their owners and put away in the fattening pens. On these days Roosevelt would sneak away early in the morning (a morning with a cold, sharp steel smell in the air) and go deep into the woods to his favorite wading pond. Here for the whole day he would float around in the cool water, far away from the unnatural-like squeals of the young boars being cut by their owners' sharpened-for-the-occasion knives. Late that night Roosevelt would return from the woods back to the Lower Church and *never* would he go near the closed pens that housed these doomed half-animals, former buddies of his.

Man and pig were now close enough for the porch crowd to see Cousin Tater—a short, thin, black-as-sin, warm-eyed man with protruding, baked 'tater-brown buck teeth—all sheiked-up in his brand-new Sunday overalls, field straw hat, white guanosack shirt . . . and shoes, the reason why he was walking slower than his usual slower-than-cold-molasses slow. The black-and-white wingtips and the white spats had been brought to Cousin Tater that previous Christmas by his favorite male human being, Santa Claus, and were referred to by him as his "Santa shoes." (The Cousin's persistent belief in Santa stemmed from the fact that each Christmas morning

since he'd left home he'd awakened to find a present—a
bucket of fireplace-baked and still hot sweet potatoes, a union
suit, a colorful quilt, fruits and candies . . . shoes—on the
doorstep of his holy home. There were those skeptics who
believed the Cousin's Santa to be none other than Momma
Rosiebellelee, including an all-seeing Roosevelt, though he
wasn't talking.) Since Santa hadn't known Cousin Tater's
exact shoe size any more than the Cousin did himself, the
shoes turned out to be too tight for his feet, which was why
he'd cut open the outer seam of each shoe, thus freeing from
their cramped confinement both little toes . . . each of which
poked out of its respective shoe like guiding eyes for a pair of
feet still unaccustomed to shoes that kept shuffling unsurely
and slowly on down the road and on up to the packed front
porch of Momma Rosiebellelee's. Followed closely by a swag-
gering Roosevelt, whose graying coat was mud-free, due to
his having just waded out of his Saturday Sugar Creek bath
along with Cousin Tater. The pig came up almost to the
Cousin's waist and his lengthy body was accentuated by jet-
sweptback ears flattened close to his head, long, athletic,
skinny legs, and, set in deep sockets, a pair of beady, red-
rimmed eyes that stared menacingly down the sides of a long
snout from which dangled the pure-gold-looking nosering
that Roosevelt was already wearing when he came to live with
Cousin Tater. Protruding from the right corner of his mouth
was a long ivory tusk that curved upward in a sharp-pointed
arc. The left fang had been broken off at the root years earlier,
when Roosevelt had been challenged to prove himself no
possum-treeing fluke and had taken on and whipped deci-
sively a whole pack of Plain View's finest possum-hunting
hounds.

With the line to get in to see the Momma now extending
way out across the front yard, the man and his pig bumped
right into the end of it, which was moving slightly slower
than they were. Curled around Cousin Tater's neck on this

day was a young, live possum he was bringing to his *favorite* human being, the person he still believed to be his real mother, Momma Rosiebellelee.

While practically all of the doings were happening around at the front of Momma Rosiebellelee's on this day, the back-of-the-house *daily* drama was not to be interrupted, even by a dying Momma Rosiebellelee. From out of the woods, across the spring, and on uphill back of the barn Mister Mac was coming for his six o'clock supper.

Mister Mac had never been too gregarious, and once he'd moved into the woods of the Hundred Acres, he had practically become a hermit. When he and Missis Bea first took up housekeeping over across the spring, he had wanted Momma Rosiebellelee to come cook their three daily meals there in the log cabin. But at this the Momma said no, or "naw suh." She needed her *big* kitchen up at her house, the *new* Big House, to be able to move around in. Thus it was agreed that Momma Rosiebellelee would cook the MacAndrews' meals in her kitchen and bring them across the spring as soon as they were ready. And at this time *only* the Momma was granted permission to cross the spring for *any* reason. Now for the first year this worked out, with the Momma both doing the cooking and cleaning the cabin. But by that second year the Momma had put her "naw suh" to this plan and brought Sugar Boy's new bride, Pecora, with her downhill and across the spring to take care of all the cleaning work in and around the little log cabin. This became the arrangement that was agreed upon and carried out for those first few years between the black gal's house on the hill and the white man's log cabin across the spring and back into the woods.

But to Mister Mac, Momma Rosiebellelee, and even Pecora, it was very apparent that Missis Bea wasn't happy at all in her new surroundings. A born social butterfly, she never really adjusted to this secluded log-cabin living. And though she loved her son dearly, he'd *never* done anything that ever really interested her. His all-day hunting treks, hour after hour of reading, and most of all his not wanting people around (except, of course, for her . . . and . . . and that girl, who was still pretty enough, but not any the less a negress for all that) were things the former queen of the local social circle couldn't comprehend. To her it seemed her new home was always overrun with books, dead birds, and a *very much alive* negress. Then, to make worse even worse, shortly after moving into the log cabin her son started that o' nasty drinking habit. But what to her was even *nastier* and what she'd tried to close her mind—not to mention her ears—to was the things she'd heard him, her own flesh and blood son, and that negress doing—and *saying*—in there in his room those nights when they thought she'd already gone to sleep. And at their age, too! She thought people stopped doing *that* when they stopped having children. Oh, she just didn't want to think about it anymore.

On beautiful sunny days she took to dressing up in her still fine, but dated, clothes and strolling under her parasol down the narrow path leading to the edge of the woods, where she would look out through the trees over across the spring. One day while she was standing here she saw two very young boys, practically no more than babies, playing on the bank on the other side of the water while a woman, their mother apparently, was busily washing a tub full of clothes down closer to the spring. The taller boy's skin was coal black, like the woman's, while the younger one's skin was light . . . very light . . . white . . . like . . . hers. This sight upset her for the rest of that day, and for the next several days her mind continually fought against it, but the fact finally got through to her that those two little boys were *her* son's grandchildren. *Her* great-grandchildren. Her *own* flesh and blood! Just too much for a white lady. Honey, hush.

Missis Bea hadn't seen Rosiebellelee's offspring when they were children, because all such little unpleasantnesses were kept at a safe distance from the mistress of Plain View

Plantation. Even after seeing Sugar Boy, Speck, and Doris
Virginia (but never Luvenia) briefly as adults, Missis Bea
never thought of them as being her only son's children, much
less *her* grandchildren. But the two little boys she'd seen playing on the other side of the spring had caused some feelings
like she'd never felt before to grip her insides and not let go.
So affected had she been by the sight of the two children that
for the next three days she didn't even get up out of her
Napoleon bed.

But like a piece of lodestone, the spring drew her back,
and early that next Monday, washday, she was down at the
edge of the woods peeking out through the trees watching
"Little Darkie" and "Little Lightie" (her secret names for the
two little boys) playing together. From that day onward the
one thing she lived for was her Monday morning stroll down
to the spring. If the weather didn't permit washing, or the
children didn't come along with their mother, then Missis
Bea would go back to the log cabin, get under the covers of
her Napoleon bed, and pout for the rest of that day.

Then came that Monday morning when she was standing peeking through the trees, giggling softly to herself and
springing lightly up and down on her walking stick while
watching the two little boys running, jumping, and tum-
bling on the other side of the water. Suddenly, she heard
something behind her. Swiveling her neck, she saw her son
standing there, with a shotgun in one hand and a string of
still dripping blood birds in the other. He'd gotten home
from hunting much earlier than she had expected. Without
a word she hobbled right past him and on up to the log
cabin and jumped fully clothed under the covers of her Napoleon bed, from which she was never again to emerge.

When a week had gone by and she still stayed in bed,
with all her clothes and not a word to say to anybody, including her son, Mister Mac sent for the doctor. He found nothing
wrong with Missis Bea but old age, mixed with a strong dash
of stubbornness. Several days later Amanda paid her first visit

to the log cabin, bringing along two young daughters with her. Even the sight of her only official grandchildren didn't pull Missis Bea up out of her Napoleon bed. These grandchildren were teenagers, too big. Missis Bea wanted little-bitty . . . great-grandchildren . . . to play with.

Since she refused to leave her Napoleon, Missis Bea thus required the kind of attention accorded to the sick. After adamantly rejecting Pecora (offered by Momma Rosiebelle-lee) and the negress herself (offered by Mister Mac) as her attendants, the white lady called her son to her bedside and whispered in his ear the name of the one person she wanted to care for her. Mister Mac didn't know what to make of his mother's request, and when he told Rosiebelle Lee, she put in her "naw suh" all over again and stalked out of the log cabin that day—with Pecora trotting along right on her heels—madder than a pregnant bull. This left it up to Mister Mac, and that night for the first time since leaving the Big House, he walked through the woods and across the spring, and climbed the hill that night to Rosiebelle Lee Wildcat Tennessee's house, where he had to all but beg until he finally brought back to the log cabin the only person his mother wanted looking after her. The mother of Missis Bea's Little Darkie and Little Lightie. Theophilia.

If she hadn't been sick when she first took to bed, the white lady was now. Theophilia saw this right away, the reason why she hadn't presented too much opposition to Mister Mac's request. A no-nonsense sort from tonsil to toenail, Missis Bea's new nurse waited on her hand and foot, day and night, and made the white lady toe the mark strictly according to orders of the doctor, now a regular visitor to the cabin. Still and all, Missis Bea, as she knew she would, took an immediate liking to this unsmiling, black disciplinarian, and all she wanted to do was talk about children, little ones, with Theophilia, who at the time was carrying her fourth child. She eventually had to take time off from her nursing duties to have this baby, and then from across the spring uphill to

Rosiebelle Lee Wildcat Tennessee's came word from Mister Mac himself, by way of the Momma herself, that the baby was to be named Richmond. Theophilia, to the surprise of all (especially the midwife, Momma Rosiebellelee, and daddy, Speck), didn't let this ruffle her feathers one whit, because she *knew* exactly who over across the spring was doing the baby-naming. And late that very same night before she had even seen the newborn and three days after her eightieth birthday, Missis Bea died.

The undertaker was sent for, and from that point on every aspect of the funeral of the former mistress of Plain View was handled by her daughter, Amanda. The last rites were held in Appalachee's oldest Methodist church, which Missis Bea had joined as a young girl, before a sparse gathering made up mostly of family and those members of her select social set who were still living. The few others who were there had come mainly out of curiosity, to get a good look at Muskhogean County's most renowned recluse, Mister Mac. He didn't show. But later at the burial in the MacAndrew family cemetery—three acres of land way over in back of the Big House which had not been sold along with the rest of the plantation—just as the casket was being lowered into the hole that had been dug alongside the grave of George MacAndrew, some members of this even sparser crowd got a brief glimpse of the lone figure of a man, shotgun under one arm, a string of what looked like dead birds in the other hand, and a dog standing alongside him as he watched from far back at the edge of the forest before turning and disappearing back into the trees just as quickly as he had come.

After Missis Bea's death, Pecora's superstitious fear of the dead wouldn't let her ever again enter the log cabin. She claimed Missis Bea's haint came each night to the edge of the woods and looked across the spring, just standing there every night peeking and hainting out through the trees because, according to Plain View's high priestess of superstition, haints *couldn't* cross water. Now nobody ever remembered

Pecora offering a scientific explanation for this one particular haint hangup, mainly because nobody ever thought or bothered to ask her to. Still, no one went on record as having seen Missis Bea's haint on the Wildcat Tennessee Hill side of the water, either.

Thus it was left up to the Momma to go over and clean up the white lady's room, whereupon Mister Mac locked the door for the last time. Now Mister Mac was the last official MacAndrew left in Muskhogean County. Alone.

Prior to the Big War no self-respecting Southern white person would stoop to do service, or servant-type work, public or private. As a result in small towns throughout the Muskhogean region the overwhelming majority of these jobs in stores, restaurants, and other businesses, as well as in private homes, were held by colored folks, and this kind of work was referred to locally as "nigger work." Colored people also, along with a smattering of Jews, comprised the bulk of the area's small shopkeepers and tradesmen. The native-born whites were the landowners, and they practiced the key professions of commerce, law, medicine, and, of course, politics. The region's poor whites were practically invisible, restricted to small outlying farms and to the mountains and hills. Hillbillies. They had practically no contact with colored folks, who despite the end of slavery mostly continued living on and around the plantations and estates of the ruling landed gentry. Then came the boll weevil.

With the cotton economy destroyed, the exodus from the country to the towns and cities was on. Suddenly, "nigger work" was the *only* work, which meant the niggers were now *out* of work, and many of them headed North to the Promised Land. And the whites, who now owned and ran the stores, restaurants, and other small shops and businesses, made "nigger work" respectable by renaming it "serving the public."

But one person the little ol' boll weevil didn't put serving the public, or anybody else, was Mister Mac, who spent all his time now serving no one but himself, hunting, reading . . . and drinking. As master of Plain View Plantation, Mister Mac had been considered not only a gentleman farmer and huntsman, but a gentleman drinker as well. But in the old plantation days whenever he was hit by the urge to indulge privately in the spirits—which occurred anywhere from two to three times a year—he'd pack himself a bag and go off to Atlanta, away from the eyes, ears, and tongues of both friend and foe, where he'd stay for as long as a month, or as little as a week, however long it took him to wash the desire for drink out of his system. He always came home soberer than the Supreme Court itself, and nobody was ever the wiser. Then came the boll weevil who ate Mister Mac out of the Big House and home, and by the time he ended up in the little two-room log cabin downhill, across the spring, and back over into the woods *below* Rosiebelle Lee Wildcat Tennessee's house, he could no longer afford to ride off into the sunset on these mysterious little thirst-quenching trips. Being deprived of this outlet and at a time when he needed it desperately cut deeply into the white man's psyche, causing this most private of persons to reveal his heretofore secret drinking habit to his mother and black mistress, both staunch non-drinkers. That was when Mister Mac got mean. Real mean. Mean like nobody before had ever seen.

Six days a week, Monday through Saturday, year in and year out, rain or shine, hot or cold, sleet or slime, Mister Mac took to the woods with his shotgun and gun dog, Sport, in search of birds or, if they weren't in season, just tramping for hours and miles through the forest. After Missis Bea died, he started taking his meals up at Momma Rosiebellelee's. When he and Sport stepped into the Momma's kitchen for breakfast at six o'clock sharp, or for dinner at noon, or supper at six, nobody and nothing, not even one of Doris Virginia's cats, would be in the room but the man's hot food out on the table. Nobody had their breakfast, dinner, or supper before Mister Mac . . . and Sport, who ate his master's leftovers. Lying beside the white man's plate at each noonday meal was the still folded morning *Atlanta Constitution,* so he could read the front page while he ate.

He would read the rest of the paper that night in his cabin and return it to the breakfast table the following morning, to be picked up after he'd left by one of Speck's children so that each night their father could read yesterday's news. On Sunday, when the mailman didn't come, one of Speck's boys, Hamilton or Benjamin, would walk, come rain, shine, sleet, or slime, the four miles into Appalachee to buy the *Constitution*—or, if it was unavailable, *The Atlanta Journal*—at Mason's Drugstore and tote it all the way back to the Momma's kitchen, where she'd plop the fat Sunday edition filled with Hard Times and war news and funny papers on the table right alongside Mister Mac's steaming plate just as he was on his way up the hill. But it was not until Monday after work before Speck would be able to read what the fat paper had to say about Hard Times, the war, and cotton prices, which he never failed to follow, and the doings of his favorite funny paper folks. And his children had to wait until he had read everything in the paper he wanted to before they could touch the sacred scroll.

Come Saturday, right after his supper, Mister Mac, without his gun, and Sport would leave the log cabin for their one night out a week and not return home until early that next morning. Sunday was the man's day for reading, and Sunday night was when Momma Rosiebellelee, still dressed in her Sunday rags, would disappear out back of the barn on her way downhill and on over the footbridge, to vanish back into the woods and not emerge until the rooster crowed that next morning, sending her back across the spring and on uphill to start Monday morning breakfast for a still contentedly sleeping Mister Mac.

Now except for Mister Mac, Sport, and, of course, Momma Rosiebellelee, traffic across the spring was closed to all two- and four-legged creatures. So nobody knew what in the world Theophilia's cow, Peg, was thinking about the day she wandered away from her usual grazing grounds, on across the spring, back into the woods, and right up to the front door of Mister Mac's log cabin, where Theophilia finally found her at milking time—and not one second too soon. Mister Mac had just returned home from hunting, and when Theophilia walked on the scene he was standing right in front of the cow, loading his seven-shot pump shotgun, while Sport was running around in back, barking and dodging the well-aimed kicks of ol' Peg, who had completely eaten up the front lawn (always kept neat and tidy by a meticulous Mister Mac) and was now eagerly choosing dessert from among the luxuriant flowering borders (planted by the Momma). By the time the fuming, cursing Mister Mac got his gun loaded and aimed it to blow to Kingdom Come and a piece farther the sole supply of cream for his had-to-have-it early every morning coffee, Theophilia had run up and stood between the seven-shot pump shotgun and her family's sole supply of milk and butter, who had since finished up the flowers and already dropped several mammoth cowcakes on the barren ground in front of the log cabin, inadvertently splattering the fast-dodging and still-barking Sport. Theophilia stood motionless, staring open-eyed straight up the long barrel of that seven-shot pump shotgun, now aimed directly at her head by a cursing red faced Mister Mac. Well, neither Mister Mac, Theophilia . . . nor Peg . . . lost their heads that day, and cream for the coffee, milk for the children, and butter for the bread kept right on coming there on the Hundred Acres. But from that day onward ol' Peg wore around her neck a chain, one end of which was kept tied around the nearest tree or to a stake of some sort while she safely grazed in the pasture on the Wildcat Tennessee Hill side of the spring. Amen.

On this day of Momma Rosiebellelee's crossing over, Mister Mac climbed Wildcat Tennessee Hill, and came in and sat down in the Momma's kitchen, wearing a soft white straw

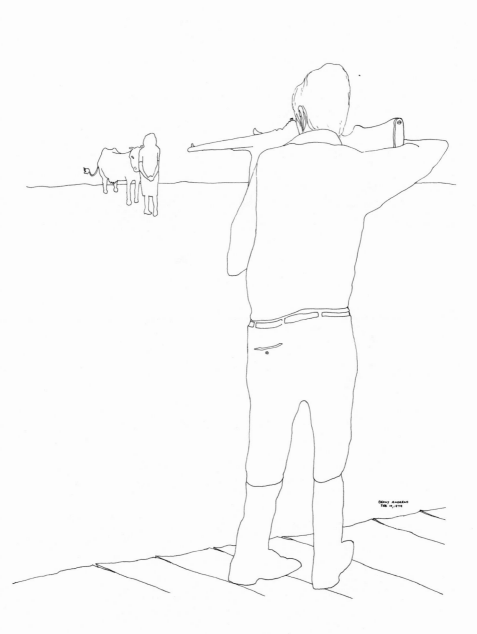

hat that shaded an all-khaki outfit—shirt, slacks, shoes, and socks. The kitchen was now empty of all but the seated white man and his white-and-black-spotted dog waiting under the table at his feet. Mister Mac took off his special dress hat and set it down next to his plate; the top of his head was almost completely bare—those few remaining strands clutching on to the edges of his bald dome by their fragile gray roots like dangling wisps of cornsilk. Years and miles of hunting and hiking had put a lot of weather in Mister Mac's face, transforming his soft, smooth, and boyish skin into a brown crust that was lined with deep wrinkles running up and down his freshly shaven face alongside that still prominent nose like furrows in a newly plowed field. The wire was still very noticeable in the rest of his lean body but was beginning to bend in some vital spots.

Taking from his right hip pocket a long white handkerchief, Mister Mac

HONK!

blew one nostril,

HONK!

blew the other one, glanced into the handkerchief, folded it loosely, and stuck it back into his right hip pocket. Saturday night supper on the Hundred Acres was thus officially underway.

As was the local custom whenever anyone visited the home of the dying or the bereaved, food was brought for the grieving family, who would've suffered an impossible task trying to feed a limitless number of guests under such circumstances. Thus, on this day Momma Rosiebellelee's kitchen was overflowing with baskets, buckets, boxes, jars, jugs, cans, and sacks full of all kinds and smells of eats and drinks that had been collected from the visitors and piled back here by Pecora and Lucy Anna. But Mister Mac sat in here, the air heavy with the aroma of foreign food, and ate only the food of the house, the only food his finicky stomach trusted.

Having eaten all he wanted, he set the plate, with its

mostly bread, vegetables, and pot liquor leftovers, under the table, where Sport immediately lit into it while his master leaned back in his chair, took out a Prince Albert tobacco can, and rolled himself a cigarette. He sat and smoked in between sips of coffee sweetened with thick, rich, cream from the tits of ol' Peg. Afterwards, the man took from his right hip pocket his long white handkerchief, and

HONK!

went one nostril,

HONK!

went the other nostril. Once again, he glanced into the handkerchief before folding it loosely and sticking it back into his right hip pocket. But on this particular day, rather than getting up and walking out the back door as he always did immediately after this final blow on his nose, Mister Mac remained seated another few minutes longer before calling, "Pecora!" In less than a flash she was standing in the hallway door, looking into the kitchen.

"I'm going in." And at these words she disappeared back down the hallway and began shooing folks out of the Momma's room, through the sitting room, and on back onto the front porch with the announcement, "Mist' Mac's comin'!"

After the all clear, the white man got up from the kitchen table (Sport remained behind as if realizing this was no time for a dog) and walked on down the hallway to his black gal's room. Hat in hand, he stepped inside and closed the door gently behind him . . . shutting out the voice of Tampa Red from the sitting room.

> *Though you break my heart every day,*
> *Just to pass the time away,*
> *But, baby, you're gonna miss me when I'm*
> *gone.*

More than half an hour later, Mister Mac emerged from the Momma's room and left the house by the back door, and with Sport trotting alongside, he crossed the backyard, and man and dog disappeared around the barn, the sounds of Tampa Red trailing behind them.

> *Baby, I'll never trust your love again,*
> *But if you ever need a friend,*
> *I'll be yours until the end.*
> *Baby, you're gonna miss me when I'm gone.*

Just minutes after Mister Mac crossed the spring and walked back into the woods, the folks gathered there atop Wildcat Tennessee Hill watched while a Spence taxicab turned off the main road onto the Wildcat Tennessee side-road. But instead of continuing on down into Momma Rosie-bellelee's front yard, the car suddenly turned left at Speck's house, drove on across his backyard, and then turned down the path running alongside Wildcat Tennessee Hill, finally braking right at the edge of the spring. 'Ginia's Geechie, dressed in his brown Sunday suit, popped out and ran around to the other side of the cab, and opened the back door for a woman whose face the watchers on the hill couldn't make out, because it was covered by a thick veil. They followed her every step with their eyes as she carefully, regally, made her way over the narrow footbridge; then the tall, shapely, straight-walking and well-dressed woman vanished back into the woods on the other side of the bridge. 'Ginia's Geechie got back into the taxi, to wait. Lordy, Lordy, Luvenia (aka Shirley Temple) had done come home.

CHAPTER · SEVEN

$\mathcal{E}$ight-year-old Richmond, Speck's and Theophilia's fourth child and third son, had long, skinny legs,
light-brown curly hair, fair skin, buck teeth, with a gap between the two front ones, and—on this particular day—he
had his back all up around his neck because his parents had
promised him that this Saturday he could go into town with
his older brothers, Hamilton and Benjamin, to the picture
show to see Johnny Mack Brown and Tex Ritter, playing
together for the first time ever in *Deep in the Heart of Texas.*
He'd been sitting on nails for more than a week in anticipation of seeing ol' Johnny Mack, his favorite cowboy, and Tex,
Benjamin's favorite (Hamilton liked ol' Buck Jones), draw
against each other and start shooting. All this time he and
Benjamin had been rehearsing daily with fists and cap pistols,
without caps, what they hoped and expected the two cowboys
would do to one another come Saturday. And when he'd been
told early that morning that because Grandmomma would be
crossing over that day, he couldn't go into town to the picture
show until the next Saturday, when o' Gene Autry was playing—and all *he* did was sing—he ran out of the house crying.

Now here he was down at Grandmomma's, all washed
up, wearing clean shirt, short pants—which he hated—and no
shoes, following right on the tail of his older brother. Benja-

min was almost twelve, short, leaning toward the stocky side, with a nest of uncontrollable blond curls, blue eyes, a pinkish face, and freckles. He was wearing *long* pants, at least, but was still barefoot, roving in, out of, and around their Grand-momma's house seeing what he could see, hear, or find to make up for his not having been able to go into town to the picture show to see o' Tex and Johnny Mack. And what had really put Benjamin's back all up around *his* neck was that he had bet Richmond that o' Hamilton, even though Momma had told him not to, had slipped off and gone to the show, since he still wasn't back from town. Man, he had wanted like the devil himself to take that grocery list into town, but since o' Hamilton was the oldest, he had been sent instead. Dog-gonit! Now he had to go and find something for himself and Richmond around Grandmomma's there that was worth missing the best picture show in a long, long time for. What-ever they found had better be good. Doggonit!

As for Richmond, he had no idea at all what they were looking for, and he couldn't possibly imagine finding *anything* down at Grandmomma's to make up for missing Johnny Mack and Tex. Not even peeping up dresses.

At age eight Richmond had earned hands down the title of Plain View's champion peeper. Anywhere in Plain View where women or older girls sat down with their hems raised high, it always seemed that little Richmond would pop up from out of nowhere to peep under their dresses. Now Rich-mond didn't understand himself why he'd gotten so partial to peeping, but he most certainly remembered when. He'd taken his very first peep just that previous Christmas Day, when he'd been down on the kitchen floor on all fours playing with the little toy car Santa Claus had brought him when something suddenly made him look up (the devil?) . . . and right smack dab under the dress of his Aunt Doris Virginia, who'd stopped by to wish them all a merry Christmas and was now out in the kitchen talking to his momma while she cooked breakfast. Aunt Doris Virginia was sitting with the hem of her dress raised up to its usual height—raised so high on this merry Christmas morning that young Richmond saw all the way up to something he'd *never* seen before. Aunt Doris Virginia had a whole nest of hair growing up under her dress! And just lying there staring with his mouth hanging open at that patch of hellfire-red hair nesting under his Aunt Doris Virginia's dress had given young Richmond the funniest-all-over feeling that he in his few years here on earth had ever felt. Richmond was hooked.

And from that day onward, Richmond had tried to peep under *every* dress he saw, maniacally curious about the nest of hair growing wild up there, though seeing it again hadn't turned out to be easy. True, he roamed the far corners of Plain View peeping under the dresses of young and old, but not once since that first peep had he sighted hair up there again . . . simply because bloomers blocked his view. (That is, all except for those little girls, most of whom, especially during the summer, didn't wear bloomers, but he never felt the same funny feeling as he did with older girls and women. He knew this was because for some strange reason hair didn't grow under little girls' dresses.) He didn't mind seeing bloomers either, especially the pink ones, but they didn't exactly leave him with that same indescribable feeling that first time had. He had even gone so far as to share his discovery with Benjamin and Hamilton, who—rather than expressing shock and disbelief as he'd expected them to when they heard such —had just laughed at him in a strange, knowing way and told him that menfolk *got* that. Not only had he not understood how grown men *got* hair while it was well hidden under grown women's dresses, he also couldn't understand just what in the world they would *want* with it in the first place. The more he thought on the subject, the funnier he felt.

Richmond also liked titties, but they were usually harder to see than bloomers, though easier than underdress hair— except, of course, for those women who nursed their babies out where everybody could see, and somehow Richmond could never keep his eyes off their titties. Once he had even reached out and touched one when one of those women was nursing her baby, and she smiled at him just for a second before slapping him hard across the hand. He hadn't touched a tittie since.

Now today he was determined to peep, peep, and peep under *every* dress he saw to try and make up for missing Johnny Mack and Tex. And there was a whole heap of dresses there at his Grandmomma's that day just slobbering at the hem to be peeped under. But he *knew* the one he really wanted, the one he *knew* the hair grew wild under. Aunt Doris Virginia. Honey, hush!

Trailing on Benjamin's heels through and around the house all afternoon, Richmond missed nary a peep; old under the dress, young under the dress, and even *too* young under the dress. And whenever he heard a baby cry he'd stop peeping and immediately rush to the spot, since he knew from experience that wherever there was a crying baby, there was sure to be a tittie. And on that Saturday afternoon of his Grandmomma's crossing over, Richmond followed the cry of the baby until he started thinking he was in peeper heaven, as titties kept plopping out all around him at record pace— fat titties, skinny titties, tiny titties, puny titties, long titties, short titties, wide titties, flat titties, pretty titties, wrinkled titties, dark titties, light titties, bragging titties, bashful titties . . . *titties!*

And it was on that crossing over Saturday that he got caught peeping under a beautiful, young dress (he hadn't taken the time to see whose head the underdress belonged with) by his daddy. Backing off from that deadly parental glare, Richmond had quickly moved from his ringside seat on the porch on around to the side of the house—but not before looking back for one peep for the road, only to have his view blocked by the back of his daddy's head. Speck had taken his son's ringside raised-hem seat there on the porch and was sitting and peeping like nobody's business. Daddy, Richmond thought, must've known about the hair up there, too. He wondered, his father being a grown man, whether he was going to *get* it.

But still no Aunt Doris Virginia under-the-dress peep for young Richmond, as the Tampa Red blues were keeping her busily on her feet dancing. Richmond was slowly beginning to hate that o' Tampa Red something close to sinful.

Just then around at the side of the house he saw a too-short Benjamin jumping up, trying to look into their Grandmomma's window. Then spotting Richmond, the older brother whispered loudly, "C'mere and let me hold you up so you can look in and see what they doing in there."

"Who's that in there with Grandmomma?" Returning the whisper.

"Mist' Mac's in there with her. Can you see them?" Holding his younger brother up to the window by the legs. "What they doing?"

With his chin just above the sill of the open window, Richmond didn't answer for fear of disturbing the scene that met his bulging, disbelieving eyes. He couldn't see his Grandmomma's face because it was covered by her hand, and her shoulders were shaking. But what his young eyes were bulging about was the sight of Mister Mac down on his knees on the floor alongside the bed . . . holding the Grandmomma's other hand in both of his and kissing it with his mouth. And Mister Mac was crying!

"What they doing in there . . . gump?"

Doris Virginia hated bloomers, and she kept tugging at the unfamiliar and uncomfortable elastic of the Momma's Sunday step-ins that was tightly smothering her ass. Doris Virginia was also getting bored despite Tampa Red wailing there in the living room. Yet even she knew her place was right there beside the Momma on this day, and it would be a sin for her to be anywhere else at such a time. Still, sin or no sin, she would've given a tit to be right that moment in the car beside Sugar Boy when he took that high-stepping white heifer. Doris Virginia wanted something to get up and go, some carrying-on. That was about when she stopped dancing long enough to walk over and look back down the long line of folks who were still pouring in through the front door to see the Momma. And standing at the very end of the line, with a pig by his side and a possum around his neck, was Cousin Tater. Doris Virginia wondered. Standing there in the doorway tugging at her too-tight drawers, she suddenly found herself remembering when she'd been going to school and all the other boys jived Cousin Tater about his having a thing the size of a mule's. Damn, she thought, those step-ins were some tight . . . and Lord, Lord, hot!

Along the ditches on both sides of the road running the two miles through Haint Hills, and even atop the hills themselves, the drink, talk, and laughter flowed—along with a smattering of betting—where those, mostly males, gathered to see their king take *his* road back from the unwelcome, white-woman intruder.

Then she was coming. Sugar Boy, gunning his motor, sat watching that all-too-familiar cloud of Georgia red forming slowly and silently in his right rearview mirror, growing larger and larger in the glass and moving closer and closer to him like a huge dust storm. Then he heard it. Like a howling tornado, that big black-and-white Buick came screaming down the road from Appalachee pulling on its tail that mountainous cloud of Georgia red. Rockee Ryder was here! Here, just like she was down on her bended knees *begging* to be taken by the true king of the Plain View Road himself, Sugar Boy.

Shooting out onto the narrow two-lane road right alongside her, Sugar Boy could see from the corner of his eye the surprise in the white woman's face as his car suddenly pulled up right next to hers. The surprise and her instinctive reflex to slow down for the mile downgrade to Sugar Creek Bridge was just enough for Sugar Boy, mashing the footfeeder all the

way to the floor, to shoot right past her. Looking in the windshield mirror, Sugar Boy saw nothing but Georgia red. God-
damnit, he had taken the bitch on *his* road! He could feel for
the first time in many a month his hair blowing in the wind.
Honey, hush!

Then just as if it had suddenly caught on to what was
happening, the brand-new white '42 Buick sedan abruptly
emerged from the dust and was now running right alongside
the little black '36 V-8 Ford convertible, and the Sugar Creek
Bridge stood down there at the bottom of Haint Hills . . .
waiting. Neck and neck, nose and nose, the colored man
turned his head and looked right over at the white woman,
and she, without blinking a pretty blue eye in the storm of
dust and gravel swirling between the two speeding cars and
around her rolled-down window, looked straight back at him.
Eyeball to eyeball. Sugar Boy and Rockee Ryder. First cousins. Lord, have mercy!

Then it happened. Staring dead on into the prettiest face
he'd ever laid eyeball on, Sugar Boy saw through the flying
dust and gravel the white woman's tight, blood-red lips suddenly soften into a warm, tooth-glistening smile. Now all this
time, even while he was looking straight across at the white
woman, Sugar Boy *knew* he had complete control of his car.
He knew his car along with every rut in the road running
through Haint Hills better than the haints themselves. In
fact, he was just waiting for Rockee Ryder to hit a rut the
wrong way . . . his *only* chance, he also knew, of retaking his
road from the white woman and her big black-and-white
Buick. Without realizing it, Sugar Boy suddenly felt his dead-
pan face relaxing, to return the white woman's smile. But
before the smile could quite get to his lips, Sugar Boy looked
over out of the corner of his eye and saw the nose of the Buick
veering slightly to the left. Instinctively, Sugar Boy swerved
his V-8 farther to the left on the narrow road, then waited for
a chance to turn back to the right, but he couldn't . . . the big
Buick now had the middle of the road and was fast taking up

all of it. That's when the two speeding cars hit Sugar Creek Bridge. Nose and nose.

After Sugar Boy shot over the left side of the bridge, taking that last railing down with him into the creek below, the big black-and-white brand-new '42 Buick didn't slow down for one instant . . . speeding right on ahead of that cloud of Georgia red, hauling back to the Big House the new, just *officially* crowned queen of the Plain View Road. Miz Rockee Ryder. Amen.

Richmond hadn't known *what* to think of Benjamin's daring. The mere thought of it had scared him. He had often wondered what was it like over there but had always been too scared to even think of going over to find out for himself. And all the children had been told time and again *never to go 'cross the spring.* Now, having followed Benjamin across to "see what Aunt Luvenia Shirley Temple looked like," as his older brother put it—here he was. Scared. They hadn't been able to see their way too clearly over here because it was dark now, and there was no moon out yet. He'd just followed in Benjamin's tracks across the plank over the water and then along the narrow footpath running through the woods up to the front door of the log cabin. Feeling their way around back of the unfamiliar building, he and Benjamin now stood side by side, looking in through a big open window, covered by a screen, that was cut low enough to the ground so that he wouldn't have to be held up to see into the cabin. Standing on tiptoes, he could see that what little light there was in the room was coming from a kerosene lamp sitting on the middle of a large, unfinished, wooden kitchen table. On one side of the table, with his back to the window, sat Mister Mac, while on the other side, but unable to see them because of the light shining in her face, was a woman. Aunt Luvenia Shirley Temple! The prettiest woman Richmond had ever seen in his whole life! Even prettier than his Aunt Doris Virginia! But before Richmond could enjoy more of this pretty face, much less hear what the two were talking so softly to each other about, he and Benjamin heard a dog bark. A bird-dog bark! By the time Richmond split the spring waters running for all he was worth, he didn't know where Benjamin was, in front or behind him; all he had on his mind by the time the cool water was splashing around his fast-pumping legs was whether his oh-so-pretty Aunt Luvenia Shirley Temple, like his pretty Aunt Doris Virginia, grew hair under her dress, too.

Folks called him Tree. Nobody ever saw him until Saturday night. Wherever there was a party, or a sizable gathering for sin, Tree was sure to show up. Drunk. Tree *came* to parties drunk. And uninvited. So drunk would he be that no one dared strike a match too close to him for fear that Tree would go up in flames. Yet just his drunkenness in itself wasn't the main reason why he was never invited, and always unwelcome, in Plain View's homes on Saturday night, especially by the womenfolks. "Treetop-tall and guaranteed to fall from wall to wall," went the saying, because Tree was a *faller.*

The instant his long shadow would fall across the front porch of some unsuspecting hostess, she would quickly dispatch her husband to the front door to keep the faller out— or at least upright, since when Tree came into a room he *leaned.* Meanwhile, the lady of the house would be starting to panic, scurrying around helter-skelter, dragging furniture to the farthest corner of the room away from the spot where Tree stood drunkenly leaning—north, south, east, then west —before being quickly shoved into a chair by a fast-acting host, or falling. And when Tree fell, he took *everything* down with him, especially glassware and those fragile household objects so precious to hostesses' hearts. And *wherever* Tree fell, he slept, until late Sunday morning when the family whose floor he'd chosen to fall on the night before would oftentimes have to step around and over the long, loudly snoring Tree on their way out the door to church.

And on this Saturday night of the crossing over of

Momma Rosiebellelee, Tree was sighted leaning his way on down the road in the direction of Wildcat Tennessee Hill.

Benjamin was doggone heavy! Since Benjamin had held Richmond up before so he could see into their Grandmomma's room, he had talked his younger brother into squatting down so he could stand with both feet on his shoulders and look over into the window of their Aunt Doris Virginia's room. Despite straining with all of his eight-year-old might to hold up his much heavier brother, Richmond still had enough strength, and curiosity, left to ask, "See anything?"

But with eyes and thoughts absorbed by the goings-on inside, Benjamin wasn't answering. Now Richmond could hear through the open window the sound of the Victrola from the sitting room.

> *Now if you want yo' baby,*
> *To treat you right,*
> *Woo her early in the morning,*
> *And late at night.*
> *You gotta woo yo' baby.*

Then someone was talking. It was their Aunt Doris Virginia.

"If you want some, then you better git that o' pig outa here right now."

"Whar I is, Roosey heah is too." After a long pause.

"Is that Cousin Tater in there, too?" Richmond whispering louder, but still no reply from Benjamin up top. Aunt Doris Virginia was still talking:

"All right, the pig can stay. Just don't let it come near me. But if you wanna stay in here, then you better take that damn o' possum from 'round yo' neck."

"What they doing in there, Benjamin?" No reply from up top. But after a short silence Richmond heard his Aunt Doris Virginia's voice again:

"Lord, *it's* l-o-n-g!"

"What they doing?" Still no word from up top.

Then after another long silence, the now seriously curious and slowly weakening Richmond heard the voice that sounded like Cousin Tater's:

"Wha'cha doin' gwine so fast?"

"I'm *shooting* it up to!" A strange, husky, Aunt Doris Virginia voice Richmond had never before heard.

"Jes leave hit theah, I'll git hit."

"What they doing, huh? What they doing, Benjamin? *Is he looking under Aunt Doris Virginia's dress . . . gump?*" Just a second before Richmond shoulders crumbled.

> *When you woo yo' baby,*
> *Woo her with a thrill,*
> *'Cause if you don't,*
> *Some other man will.*
> *You gotta woo yo' baby.*

Nobody liked him, and he didn't like *any* of them. But everybody knew he would be there, making fun of everybody and everything all the time. Yet everybody wanted him there —in fact, was waiting for him. Crazy Coot.

He had once been tall, but now his broad shoulders were a little hunched over, his hair and beard were gray and scraggly, and he had piercing cynical eyes and a mocking, tobacco-stained, bucktoothed grin; Crazy Coot was, some said, closing in on his one hundredth birthday. His last. The story told by Pecora, who'd heard it from her Grandma Sissie, was that as a young boy Coot had made an agreement with the devil. He'd boiled a black cat alive, and then, while standing in front of a looking glass, picked the cat's bones from the pot and held them all in his teeth for a second, one by one, until he found the one that would make him invisible—and then he couldn't see himself in the glass anymore. Then he swallowed that bone whole, and his image suddenly reappeared in the glass.

Thus, besides not having to go to church ever again, he was guaranteed one hundred years of life and good health here on earth by the devil, whose *only* demand in return was that at the end of this time Crazy Coot's soul would belong to him. Whenever anybody asked him about this, Crazy Coot would just wink and flash that broad, tobacco-stained, bucktoothed grin of his. Yes, like they said, ol' Crazy Coot sure as hell had the devil in him.

Born a slave, Cootney Leguin couldn't recall his parents, who had either been sold off by their master or died before he was old enough to remember. After slavery the young Coot went North . . . to Atlanta, but unlike most Freedmen he eventually returned home, to Plain View. He came back knowing how to read, though the most important thing that he brought back from Atlanta was a picture taker. Thus began Coot's reign of craziness—always saying a lot of book words nobody else in Plain View knew the meaning of, drinking his own homemade muscadine wine (even during the week when everybody else was out working), and going around saying—without even being struck down right in his tracks by lightning—that there was *no* God at all up there in heaven (though he never did say who it was that was up there). Still, he spent more time reading and talking about the Bible than all of the long line of Plain View preachers put together. *Nobody* liked him, but *everybody* wanted him around, because he took their pictures with his picture taker for a dime if they kept the snapshot . . . and for a nickel if he kept it.

Crazy Coot owned thirty acres of some of the richest land in Plain View, but instead of planting cotton, or even corn, like the Good Lord intended all decent-minded farmers to do, he raised chickens. Yes, chickens! His one-room rusty tin-roofed house, built with his own hands, sat about in the middle of this acreage, the yard completely overgrown with practically every kind of grass and weed known to the area. And clucking, crowing, pecking, scratching, laying, and hatching amongst this dense undergrowth were Crazy Coot's countless free-ranging chickens. He didn't own a single chicken coop or henhouse for them. Came Friday he would roam his thirty acres collecting eggs from the nests scattered all over his land, and even beyond. Early Saturday morning he would hitch his blind mule up to his one-horse wagon and haul the eggs into Appalachee, where he'd sell them from door to door. He also had a gigantic pecan tree on his land, whose produce he peddled to the townfolks during the fall and winter months. As far as raising food went, Crazy Coot never bothered, since he was never known to eat anything other than chicken, hard-boiled eggs, and pecans.

Plain View's children loved Crazy Coot though most of their parents tried to keep them as far away as possible from a man who went around talking about there being *no* God in heaven. But he often took pictures of them, which he hung on the wall of his house, and they could come and look at themselves, along with everything else he took pictures of, any time they wanted to. And it was Crazy Coot who put a stop to these same children picking on Cousin Tater. Whenever they saw the little man and his pig out walking, they would taunt him by calling him bad names and chunking rocks at both him and Roosevelt; some even went so far as to break out the windowpanes of Cousin Tater's holy home, the Lower Church. But these children weren't about to start anything up with Crazy Coot—big, wide, and well over six foot tall as he was, with a headful of unkempt hair and beard, a thunderous voice, a gut-rattling laugh, and barefeet—the whole year round. On those few occasions when he decided to visit Plain View Baptist Church, and only for the midsummer night revival meetings, rather than coming in and sitting on the mourner's bench where the rest of the sinners sat, Crazy Coot preferred to stand outside looking in through an open window while guffawing and bellowing encouragement at the preacher up in the pulpit to whup the Bible on the souls of every single hypocrite sitting there in that church. He would

pause every so often, throw back his head, and partake of his personal communion straight from the pint bottle of home-made muscadine wine he kept in his hind pocket at all times, carefully wrapped in pages torn from the Bible to keep it chilled. Hallelujah!

Due to his unpredictability and, mainly, his size, no one tried teaching this devil's disciple churchgrounds decorum. In fact, besides the neighborhood children, few folks dared go anywhere near Crazy Coot, other than to have their picture taken. But one who did was Cousin Tater, who thought that Crazy Coot—next to Momma Rosiebelle-lee, of course—was the most fascinating person alive. The Cousin just loved going over to Crazy Coot's house, where for hours on end he would walk around looking at the pictures that covered all four walls. Hanging here on nails were, unframed, pictures of practically everything: folks, chickens, cows, pigs (several of Roosevelt in various poses), possums, horses, mules, cotton, corn, trees (some with colored men hanging from them), convicts, guards, flowers, grown women in their underwear, and everything. Crazy Coot went everywhere to take these pictures —all over the county, and sometimes even outside it, taking pictures of everybody and everything. Someday, he always claimed, he was going to buy himself one of those picture-show picture takers. (Another thing that added to Coot's craziness in the eyes of Plain Viewers was his shameless love for the picture show and he went *every* Saturday afternoon as soon as he was done selling his eggs and pecans there in Appalachee.) He was always telling the Cousin, and anyone else who got within earshot, that he was an *artist*. But whenever this claim of Crazy Coot's was mentioned around Speck, Plain View's expert on all such arty stuff, he would explain that an artist was a man who *drew* pictures of naked women, not *took* pictures of them. Crazy Coot had tried to strike up a friendship with Speck, who was also Plain View's closet reader, but Speck

naturally shied away from such a highly controversial
figure and laughed at the Coot's craziness along with everyone else.

Crazy Coot never married, but over the years more than
two dozen women had come to live with him in sin at one
time or another, ranging in duration of stay from fifteen
minutes to fifteen months. But they *all* left. The reason for
this, as talk had it, was all those pictures hanging and lying
around everywhere, and Crazy Coot's homeless wild chickens
roosting all over, around, under, and even inside his little
one-room shack. But, according to other talk, the main reason
why these women came in the first place and stayed as long,
or left as soon, as they did was that ol' Crazy Coot *lapped pussy.*
Honey, hush yo' mouth!

The hulking, thunder-voiced Crazy Coot—with his picture taker dangling on a long string of twine around his neck,
barefoot even in the wintertime and followed by a chicken or
rooster or two, towering over the much shorter and slenderer
figure of Cousin Tater, capped off by a field straw hat and
with the faithful Roosevelt at his side—got to be a very common sight around Plain View.

But even more so than these long strolls of theirs, Cousin
Tater—who just loved listening to the many strange words he
never understood booming off the tongue and out through the
thick lips of his friend—looked forward to Saturday night.

Crazy Coot's house had only one door, at least one opening where a door was supposed to be, since he'd never gotten
around to putting one in, and hanging curtain-fashion over
the opening instead were two croker sacks sewn together end
to end. (The very proud Coot didn't believe in entering other
folks' houses by the back way, much less his own.) His house
also had no windows, as he claimed they took up too much
precious wall space needed for picture hanging. Other than
the pictures on the wall and the stacks of books, with and
without pictures in them, in the corner farthest from the
door, about the only things of any importance in Crazy Coot's

shack were the pallet on the floor and the gigantic fireplace, which he did all of his cooking in and entertaining in front of. And it was in front of this huge fireplace that Cousin Tater enjoyed many of his most memorable moments. Before a roaring Saturday-night fire he would sit there with a mouth greasy from hot-off-the-flames possum meat and baked-under-the-coals sweet potatoes, while over at the other side of the fireplace, roasting his weekly chicken while munching hard-boiled eggs and cracking pecans in his teeth, would be Crazy Coot. And sitting in the middle of these two good friends, wearing his soft white straw hat, which he *never* removed, and roasting a pheasant, would be the little one-room shack's honored Saturday-night guest—Mister Mac. Farther back in one corner of the room lying flat out, snoring heavily, slept Roosevelt, covered with a roosting chicken or rooster or two. Sport, eyeing the snoring pig dubiously, occupied the opposite corner, sleeping with one eye open. This was the scene every Saturday night at Crazy Coot's.

Not much at the talking game, Cousin Tater still very much enjoyed listening to Crazy Coot and the white Mister Mac talk and argue about, seemingly, everything under the sun . . . moon . . . *and* stars. A jug of muscadine wine always sat on the floor between the Coot and Mister Mac (Cousin Tater didn't drink); Mister Mac always took the first pull of the night and afterwards always wiped off the mouth of the jug with the palm of his hand after the colored man took a drink. The Cousin never understood exactly what the two men were talking and arguing so vehemently about all the time, but over the years he did catch passing between them a few words about God, war, baseball, Joe Louis and Jack Dempsey, President Roosevelt, white and colored folks, money, Jews, Hitler . . . and something they called "sex," which they both always seemed to laugh a lot about. Sometimes the Cousin even got a little scared for ol' Crazy Coot as the night went on and the muscadine wine went down, and the arguments between them got hotter than the logs in the fireplace. The Cousin figured that they must be arguing about all that stuff they read in all those books they spent so much of their time reading. But before the white man and the colored man could get up to hit one another, one or both of them would pass out right there on the floor from too much muscadine wine. An hour or so later the house rooster would wake up from Crazy Coot's pallet on the floor and go out to the stoop and do his Sunday morning crowing, which would awaken Mister Mac and send him reeling home, Sport leading the way. Later that day he'd do some reading in his books without pictures for ammo for that next Saturday night, when sitting before the big fireplace, wearing his soft white straw hat, roasting pheasant, and guzzling muscadine wine, he'd talk to ol' black Crazy Coot about God, war, baseball, Joe Louis and Jack Dempsey, white and colored folks, money, President Roosevelt, Jews, Hitler . . . and something called "sex" . . . until the rooster woke up and crowed the next morning.

They were still waiting on Wildcat Tennessee Hill, the womenfolk and girls in particular, looking every so often up to the main road, waiting . . . waiting for the devil's man, Crazy Coot, to come and take their picture.

Then there he was. Women's powder puffs and lipsticks popped out of purses; hands reached up and down to straighten hats, dresses, and drawers. The men coolly rolled cigarettes, lit up, and then let them dangle from the corner of their mouths. Everybody was ready for their pictures to be taken by ol' Crazy Coot. Suddenly from inside the house word came down the long line that was still slowly marching in that the Momma wanted her picture taken too! When told of this, Crazy Coot said there wasn't enough light inside the house to make a good picture, so the Momma sent word back down the line for some menfolk to come pick her up on her mattress and bring it out into the front yard so she could have one last picture taken before crossing over. Delighted, Crazy

Coot went in himself and swooped the Momma, along with her sheet and quilt, right off the bed into his massive arms while others, led by Speck, followed with the mattress. Now the Momma felt just a bit evil being this close to a man of the devil only hours before her scheduled arrival outside the Pearly Gates. Other than for having pictures taken, she'd never had much to do with Crazy Coot, though he often gave her chickens, eggs, and pecans, as she never quite trusted this big man with his bucktoothed grin and those dark, devil eyes that looked right through a body . . . not realizing that all ol' Crazy Coot had ever wanted from the Mother of all Plain View and queen of Wildcat Tennessee Hill was just one time to get down to the bottom of her drawers . . . with his tongue. That leering, tobacco-stained, bucktoothed grin stayed on his face all the way out to the front yard.

Several folks had passed Cousin Tater in the line, but he'd finally made it in to see for the last time the woman who he still thought of as his real momma. Approaching her bed, he took the possum from around his neck and wordlessly handed it over to the Momma; she gratefully accepted it and put it down with the many other presents given her that day by her countless children, which by now took up most of the bed. Tears flooding his eyes and with hat in hand, the Cousin knelt beside the Momma's bed, and with her free hand she first blessed him by touching him on top of his balding head before doing the same to Roosevelt, who acknowledged the benediction with a soft, reverent grunt. Still not having uttered one word, Cousin Tater slowly rose, and as he turned to leave the room, the Momma blinked away the thick tears that now blurred her vision, and saw dangling from one of the Cousin's hind overall pockets a pair of the prettiest pink-silk Sunday step-ins she'd ever laid eyeball to.

Long about sundown someone down at the house noticed for the first time that somebody was sitting on the grassy bank

on the Hundred Acres side of the main road right past the
mailbox going toward Haint Hills. It was a dark-skinned,
gray-headed old man whom nobody at Momma Rosiebellelee's seemed to know, wearing a pair of brand-new overalls
and a clean but well-worn brown sports jacket and playing on
an old, but still tuneful guitar and softly singing,

> *Boll weevil's here, baby,*
> *Boll weevil's everywhere. . . .*

CHAPTER · EIGHT

$\mathcal{F}$irst, a stunned, shit-shocking hush smacked the
crowd there atop Wildcat Tennessee Hill right dab in the
middle of its big loud mouth. *Nobody* wagged a tongue . . . or
beed a bop. The word had just reached the Hundred Acres by
the fastest of feet. Sugar Boy had gone over the Sugar Creek
Bridge! His V-8 had been pushed off by Miz' Rockee Ryder's
Buick, taking the last railing down with him. Then . . .
women cried, grown men took mansize swallows from their
bottles before starting to cuss, then hauling off and kicking
the sides of the porch, and young girls wet their Sunday
bloomers. Having delivered the news, Fast Foot, who hadn't
hung around long enough to find out whether Sugar Boy had
survived the crash or not, struck out at full gallop for Haint
Hills, followed by a whole passel of folks led by curious young
boys and wailing women, Doris Virginia in the lead here.
Left behind atop Wildcat Tennessee Hill were only the old,
the lame, sleeping babies, Cousin Tater and Roosevelt, still in
with Momma Rosiebellelee, and Pecora, who from the instant
she first heard *knew* the why of this new Haint Hills tragedy.
When Speck heard the news of this second Accident on Sugar
Creek Bridge, he started to run in the other direction, around
back of the barn to find a hiding place. Nobody told Momma
Rosiebellelee anything.

But just at that moment nobody was needed to tell the Momma about her oldest boy going off Sugar Creek Bridge, V-8 first, since she was going to be too occupied with *special* company who were right then moseying on down the road toward her house. White folks company.

As lean as a stalk of Georgia sugarcane, but still as hard as the times, spear-featured, and with a head of still thick though slowly graying brown hair capping off an overall-clad body, and showing off the international farmer's suntan— burnt brown from the neck up, elbows out, and knees down (except for the back of his neck, which was an immutable red) —coming to pay his respects that Saturday night to Aint Rosie before she crossed over was ol' Cotton Eyed Joe.

With him on this crossing-over night was his smoke-haired, milk-skinned, puffy-lipped, electric-blue-eyed teenage daughter, Betty Jean, dressed in a white floursack blouse and a guanosack skirt—tight packaging for a body that was already busting out in all directions lawfully allowed; her legs were bare, and her feet were stuffed into her mother's only pair of high heels. Slung over her shoulder was the Prickards' most precious possession, the family guitar. San Antone!

By the time these two unexpected guests had crossed the yard and started up the front steps, an awkward silence had settled over those few who were left behind here at Momma Rosiebellelee's. The old menfolk who could stand, stood, while the rest who were too old or lame to scrape or shuffle anymore just removed their hats out of respect—even the babies who'd been deserted for Sugar Creek Bridge abruptly stopped their crying as the white man and his pretty young daughter silently and gingerly made their way up the steps, across the porch, and on into the house as the eyes, rather than the words, of the old blacks directed them.

Speck didn't know how long he'd been hiding out back of the barn, but his soft crying was brought to a sudden halt by a voice, a voice *singing*. He didn't know where this singing voice was coming from, but he knew doggone well *who* it was coming from! Lord, have mercy!

> *I'm nothing in the world,*
> *But just an ol' country girl.*
> *An ol' country girl who knows,*
> *She ain't as pretty as the girls in the picture*
> *   shows.*
> *But an ol' country girl who can tell*
> *The difference 'tween a croker sack and a cow-*
> *   bell.*

Speck's eyes were dry now, but he felt sure his ears were starting to give him trouble. He couldn't believe what he was hearing, but he still started walking slowly around from behind the barn and on around, toward the house, following that voice that sounded so sweet to his soul.

> *Just an ol' country girl,*
> *Who goes to town in the wagon on Saturday,*
> *To church in that same ol' wagon on Sunday,*
> *Then back home pea-picking, 'tater-cooking,*
> *   and corn-canning on Monday.*

Entering the house through the kitchen, Speck naturally didn't see or even hear the crowd that was already returning from Sugar Creek Bridge. When they heard this strange voice twanging out from their Momma Rosiebellelee's house, they cautiously slowed both their mouths and feet while moving down the main road heading back to the Hundred Acres. But by now this twangy, affecting voice was the only sound to be heard atop Wildcat Tennessee Hill this crossing-over Saturday night of the full moon as it rang out through Momma Rosiebellelee's bedroom window on past the barn, and on downhill to vibrate in the ears of 'Ginia's Geechie who was still sitting down there in his taxicab and on across the spring, where the crickets along the banks had stopped chirping, and back into the woods, where the white man and his colored daughter sat across the table from one another, and out over to Speck's place, where the penned-up hog stopped grunting and snoring long enough to listen, and ol' Peg paused momentarily while chewing her cud so as not to drown out the foreign sound, and on up to the main road where the Sugar Creek Bridge crowd were now completely silent, then back to reverberate in Speck's outstretched ears as he stood in the doorway of the Momma's bedroom, watching and listening to his favorite singing sound coming from the mouth of the prettiest girl he'd ever seen in his life.

> *I'm nothing in the world,*
> *But just an ol' country girl.*

Frozen for he knew not how long there in the doorway, Speck watched while Betty Jean finished up her song, bent down, and gave the misty-eyed Momma a hug, and while a self-conscious Cotton was getting his hand squeezed by the Momma. Then they turned toward the door, where for the first time the colored man and the white girl met face to face. Staring head on at all of this forbidden pretty was suddenly proving to be too much for Speck. His knees started to knock, teeth chatter, hands shake, heart pound, and eyes blink. And she was looking at *him!* Lord, have mercy! But . . . *was* she looking at him? No! She was staring at something over his right shoulder. But staring at *who?* Knocking knees, chattering teeth, shaking hands, pounding heart, blinking eyes, and *all* weren't enough to keep Speck from wheeling around to see just who in the world *his* Betty Jean could be staring at so intently over his right shoulder. He saw. Lord, he saw. Standing just in back of Speck, wet, muddy, scratched and cut up here and there, and with his blow hair a mess . . . stood Sugar Boy . . . staring hard right back at Betty Jean to beat the band. Lord, Lord.

·———·

Before the crowd had reached Haint Hills, it had met a group heading the other way, led by Sugar Boy himself. Crying and wailing, all the womenfolk and young damp-bloomered girls had rushed up to him and in kissing, hugging, touching, grabbing, squeezing, and clutching him had nearly torn his clothes off—this, not the car wreck itself, had left him all ragged, scratched, and bruised. White lady or no white lady, Sugar Boy was still these folks' king of the Plain View Road.

Standing on the porch now watching ol' Cotton Eyed Joe and Betty Jean pick their way carefully through the crowd in the front yard, Sugar Boy reached slowly into his water-soaked right front pocket and brought out his harp. Shaking it free of water before sliding it softly across his lips a few times, he then cupped it in both hands, and began blowing gently. Now Sugar Boy didn't know many pieces to play, as he never took up much of his time learning any, but whenever he took out his harp to play, folks always listened. And on this particular Saturday night, when for the second time in his life he'd lost his best friend to Sugar Creek, he reached into his pocket for his next best friend, his harp. He started to blow as he walked down off the porch, through a once-again-silent crowd, on across the front yard, and on up the narrow road right behind ol' Cotton Eyed Joe and Betty Jean, harping it all the way. By now Sugar Boy's harp was beginning to affect the rest of the crowd, which suddenly began moving across the yard and on up the Wildcat Tennessee Road on the heels of their harp-blowing king. Once they reached the main road, Cotton Eyed Joe and Betty Jean crossed over to the other side; the father kept on walking toward their house, but the daughter stopped . . . turned, and by the light of the Saturday night full-moon stood watching and listening to this strange-looking Nigra man, who came to a halt right at the edge of the Hundred Acres side of the road and with his followers at his back stood blowing his harp like a man suddenly gone mad-dog mad while standing right face to face with this white, young, and pretty hillbilly gal.

Meanwhile, suddenly hit by the catching spirit of Sugar Boy's harp, with a trace of smell on his breath and a thin trickle of tobacco juice burning a crooked path from the wrong corner of his mouth, Speck jumped out from the crowd and ran right out into the middle of the main road, where he broke into a wild "buckdance."

The instant his daddy broke away from the crowd up front, young Richmond, who'd been walking at the tail end of the group, ran over and snatched something hanging from the hind pocket of Cousin Tater and ran back down to and on around the back of his Grandmomma's house where he handed the thing he'd snatched—something soft—to a waiting Benjamin, who'd sent him to snatch it in the first place.

By now Sugar Boy's harping and Speck's buckdancing had the crowd popping fingers, clapping hands, and stomping feet. Meanwhile, Speck was feeling nobody's pains (just Crazy Coot's muscadine wine and Cousin Tater's chewing tobacco) and doing the buckdance of his life, which, to the delight of the crowd, he'd interrupt from time to time to break out into a mad hambone-beating fit—left hand, right hand, both hands, off the right leg, off the left leg, off both legs, and off the chest. *Nobody* could beat a better hambone than Speck. And with the crowd popping, clapping, stomping, and hollering him on, Speck—on this crossing-over Saturday night of the full moon there in the middle of Plain View's main road, buckdancing and hamboning to the harp music of his big brother for a crowd of folks that he more than anything else in the whole wide world wanted to be one of, wanted on this night to *approve* of him—felt like he was on top of the world. Move, buckdancing feet, move . . . jump up and click your heels two times before you come down, something *no* other two feet in Plain View could do . . . blow, sweet Sugar Boy, blow . . . beat hambone off the leg, beat hambone off the chest, beat, hambone, beat . . . move, buckdancing feet, move . . .

when I say move . . . move, buckdancing feet, move . . . Lordy, Lord, doggone!

Not feeling like she was anywhere near the top of the world at that particular moment, Doris Virginia stood in the crowd listening to Sugar Boy's harp, which she loved to death, but not flexing one finger to pop, hand to clap, toe to stomp, or lip to holler for Speck's buckdancing, which she *didn't* love to death. It was something that just made her embarrassed . . . or jealous. She didn't know which, and before taking any of her time to think about it, she dashed out of the crowd and into the middle of the main road where ol' Speck was having the time of his life, buckdancing and hamboning it, and with one quick motion grabbed his Sunday cap from his head, turned, and disappeared with it back through the crowd, running like hell. *Nobody,* especially a silly ol' Speck, buckdance and all, went around stealing Doris Virginia's Hundred Acre stage! Honey, hush!

Abruptly, the crowd stopped popping, clapping, stomping, and hollering to stare openmouthed at a sight most had never seen and the rest had all but forgotten. By the bright light of the full moon they *all* saw Speck standing out there all alone in the middle of the main road. Bareheaded! Those long strands of ashblond blow hair hanging down in his face. Both stunned and humiliated as never before in his life, Speck tried desperately to cover his naked head with both hands, then took off right through the heart of the crowd on the tail of his baby sister, running like hell.

Meantime, Sugar Boy was totally unaware of everything going on around him, and with the crowd whooping him on at his back, paying no attention to anyone now but him and the hillbilly gal. He just kept blowing his harp across at Betty Jean, and by now she was picking her guitar right back at him, while to her comely rear her folks were standing, sitting, and squatting on the porch and stoop and in the front yard of their darkened house. At first they listened impassively and self-consciously to the playing out at the main road, but now were fervidly hooting and hollering her on in the Saturday-night battle that was building up between the Hundred Acres mean and low-down blues-blowing harp and their toetapping, knee-slapping, authentic fork-of-the-chick-style guitar. And now with sore lips and a tired tongue, Sugar Boy, both hands cupped tightly, just kept right on blowing and slobbering all over that overheated, moaning, groaning, hot-sounding harp, and kept staring feverishly over across the road at that pretty-as-peach-pie hillbilly gal, who was playing just as hard and as hot right straight back across at him, with her fiery fingers gripping the long neck of that ol' guitar like if she was to loosen her hold upon it just one mite that strange-looking Nigra man looming over across the road would slip away from her forever. Blow on, Sugar Boy, blow on! Pick it, Betty Jean, pick it! Lord, have mercy! San Antone!

Just on past the mailbox up the road a piece, the old black blues-playing man just kept right on singing and playing on his old guitar,

Well, I would go to Arkansas City,
Lord, boll weevil's over there. . . .

Breaking out of the other end of the crowd, Speck didn't see any sign of his baby sister. Doggonit, Doris 'Ginia! And, man, he was madder than anyone had ever seen him. Yes, honey, Speck was some mad. By the time he hit Momma Rosiebellelee's front yard he was going full speed and three flying steps took him up to the stoop, across the porch, and on into the house where Lucy Anna was helping the last of the old, the sick, and the afflicted in to see the Momma. He threw open the door of Doris Virginia's room where the only sign of life he could see in there by the dim light of the kerosene lamp was a pile of purring, snoring cats and kittens sleeping in the middle of the big double bed. Speck also thought he sniffed a faint odor of pig and possum. Both hands

back covering his head, he ran on down to the kitchen, but the
only people back here were Pecora and little Savannah Carmen Maria. A moonfaced, inkspot beauty, the only grandchild of the house sat in her best Sunday dress, a red-and-
white polkadot sewn by the Momma, eating her supper at one
end of the big dining table while at the other end sat Pecora,
talking quietly about haints and pigs seeing the wind to an
inattentive Roosevelt, who was busily slurping from a big
bowl of Saturday-night-special slop on the floor.

"Doris 'Ginia been heah?" But before waiting for an
answer, Speck, hearing something out back, hit the back
porch with one foot and the ground with the other one. Dropping directly in front of his two sons, scared out of their skins,
Benjamin and Richmond.

"Wha' y'all doin' back heah?"

"No ... no ... nothing, sir!" Benjamin answering while
Richmond turned tail and ran as fast as he could for the front
of the house and home.

"Did yo' Aunt Doris 'Ginia come back heah?"

"No ... nosir!"

"Wha' you hidin' 'hind yo' back?"

"No ... no ... nothing, sir!" Benjamin, with both hands
behind his back, began taking slow steps away from his
daddy.

"Did yo' Aunt Doris 'Ginia give y'all somethin' to hide
from me?"

"No, sir! She didn't give us nothing!"

"Then let me see wha' you hidin' 'hind yo' back, boy."

"I ain't *hiding* nothing back there, sir!"

"I said, let me see!" One giant Speck step had him right
on Benjamin, and he reached a long arm around and snatched
from his son's hands whatever it was he'd been keeping from
his father. But instead of a Big Apple Sunday cap, he now
held in his hand something much slicker than his cap ...
something soft that felt ... and looked ... more like ... like
a woman's bloomers ... *step-ins!*

"Whar . . . whar . . . whar the devil you git these, boy?"

"Uh . . . uh . . . Richmond found them in Cousin Tater's pocket."

"Cousin Tater?"

"Yessir!"

"Don' you lie to me, boy. I'll give ya the whuppin' of yo' life if you do."

"That's the truth, sir. You ask Richmond here." Only to look around and find no Richmond.

"Y'all go back round to the front 'n stay thar. Whar's Ham'ton? Did he git back from town yet?"

"I don't know . . . I ain't seen him, sir!"

"Doggonit! Tha' boy betta not gone to tha' pictur' show! Now you leave from round heah 'n I don' wanna heah nud'n else outa you or Richmond, 'cause if I do I'm gonna git my belt to both of ya. You heah? 'N I'll . . . er . . . ah . . . give these heah back to Cousin Tater. Now git!" Gone.

Caressing the soft step-ins gently, Speck suddenly held them up to his nose and he gave them a deep, lingering sniff before stuffing them into his right hind pocket and heading out to the barn, still in pursuit of Doris Virginia and his Big Apple Sunday cap.

No trace of Doris Virginia was to be found anywhere in, around, under, or atop the barn. Nor was she downhill at the spring, or in the taxicab where her Geechie was still sitting and waiting. Speck didn't ask him about his wife's whereabouts, though, because he knew he would've gotten from the funny-talking man an answer that he wouldn't have known the answer to. So Speck just looked in the rolled-down window himself, greeted 'Ginia's Geechie, and then looked under the car. No Doris Virginia.

Looking across the spring, he wondered if she'd run back into the woods with his cap. But he wasn't so angry at his sister that he'd dare to cross over the forbidden waters to see if she was hiding somewhere over there. His fear of Mister Mac was total. Absolute. Doggonit, Doris Virginia! He stood down here listening to the noise of the crickets that all but drowned the sound of the water trickling downstream, and thinking, for the first time ever, something hard about his baby sister. She was *always* picking on folks. Joking. Especially on him. Now she had all the folks up at the main road laughing and joking about his light, straight hair. She didn't have to go and do that. Doggonit, he *needed* his cap back! Without it he felt buck-naked. He didn't know what in the world to do. He couldn't go back up on Wildcat Tennessee Hill and start looking for her up there, because right then he could hear the crowd returning from up at the main road back to the Momma's, and he couldn't chance being seen bareheaded by them again. He could go home and get his old leather work cap, he knew, but he'd never wear it in to see the Momma, since Doris Virginia had told him the Momma wanted to see her *real* children all together one more time before she crossed over sometime later that night. Maybe then she'd split up the Hundred Acres between Sugar Boy and him. The *men* of the family. Doggonit! He starting to panic, because the Momma could be calling right that minute for them to come in to see her for the last time, and here he was down at the spring. Bareheaded! Then came the time when he *knew* there was only one thing left for him to do. Turning toward home, running, passing the ghostly silhouette of the taxicab, and wondering how much longer it would be before Luvenia . . . er . . . Shirley Temple left the cabin and climbed the Hill to see the Momma. Lord, time was running out!

When he came running into the back door of his house, Theophilia and all the children were sitting down at the kitchen table eating a supper of fried fish, fried Irish potato slices, buttered cornbread, and buttermilk. And all were talking and laughing. Led by Hamilton, who'd just arrived from Appalachee on the grocery delivery truck. A black beanpole from the Crawford side of the family with an alert, expressive face, Hamilton was busily regaling his envious and interested younger brothers and sisters with tales of his big Saturday in town. Although absolutely nothing was mentioned by the narrator about the forbidden picture show, he still hadn't gotten around to filling in the two hour gap in his account of his experiences in Appalachee. And Benjamin and Richmond weren't about to bring up the matter in front of their momma, who still hadn't asked her oldest son herself if he'd gone to the picture show against orders not to. They just kept dogging down their fish and 'taters while encouraging the abnormally slow-eating Hamilton to do the same just in order to get him outside so he could tell them all about the Johnny Mack Brown and Tex Ritter show which they both just *knew* he'd gone to see. But the moment Speck popped through the screendoor all talk, laughter, and even chewing and swallowing came to an abrupt halt . . . while six sets of astonished eyeballs took dead aim on his bare head.

"Where's yo' cap?" Theophilia wanting to know.

"Doris 'Ginia stole hit. She been heah wit hit?"

"She ain't been here. What in the world she want with your cap? All y'all folks been doing down there the whole day and night is cutting the fool."

"The grocery truck come?"

"It been here and gone."

"Hit brought the rutabagas?"

"It brought *everything* on the list Hamilton took in. You ready to eat?"

"Ain' got time. Why ain' y'all down at the house? Git yo'self 'n the chilluns ready 'n git on down thar fo hits too late! Ham'ton, hi come hit took you so long to git back home? You betta not went to that pictur' show!" Running straight through the kitchen on into the other room while flinging these words back over his shoulder.

"Before it's too late for what?" Theophilia pushing her chair back from the table and following her husband on into the next room. The children went back to their food, Hamilton suddenly having become the quietest of the lot. "When Mrs. Rosiebelle Lee *calls* out mine and the children name to come and see her, then we'll all go. But I'm *not* going before that, you hear? That place down there right now is like a Sam's Café on a Saturday night."

"'Oman, don' always be so doggone proper *all* the time. The Momma liable to . . . er . . . cross over any minute now, but fo she do she gonna split up the Hundred Acres 'tween Sugar Boy 'n me, the *men* of the family. So hur' up 'n git yo'self 'n the chilluns fixed up 'n go on down to the house to be ready when she do call. You wan' to farm agin, don'cha? Evahbody else is already down thar 'cept you 'n the chilluns . . . 'n . . . 'n Lu . . . er, Shirl . . . er, Luvenia who still over wit Mist' Mac yet."

"You mean to stand there and tell me that Luvenia ain't been to see her sick momma yet? *What* in the world are you doing?" Theophilia coming to a stunned standstill in the doorway of the bedroom.

"None of yo' doggone bizness! Jes git cho butt outa heah 'n start gitt'n ready. . . ." But before he could complete his command, Theophilia had raced up to where he was standing in front of the fireplace and snatched the scissors from his hands . . . though not before he'd cut from the top of his head a handful of that long and straight ashblond blow hair.

"You *losing* yo' mind, man?"

"Gimme back them scissors, 'oman! Wha' I do wit my hair is my own bizness 'n nobody else!" But with the long, sharp scissors now pointed menacingly at him by a never-more-deadly-serious Theophilia, Speck suddenly developed second thoughts about trying to wrestle them away from her (with her being pregnant and all) and instead flung the clipped hair into her face before dashing around her and on out through the front door. Speck's only thought now was to find Doris Virginia and his Big Apple Sunday cap before the Momma called him and Sugar Boy in to split up the Hundred Acres. Maybe, he thought, all of a sudden, his sister threw his cap away somewhere . . . like . . . like somewhere up at the main road right after she snatched it off his head. With this maybe in mind he just kept right on running straight on up to the main road.

Back in the bedroom, Theophilia was on her hands and knees sniffling softly as she went about collecting every single, silken strand of ashblond hair she could find there by the light of the lone kerosene lamp. And out in the kitchen Hamilton had suddenly found his voice underneath the fish, 'taters, and buttermilk and was once more talking "town."

CHAPTER · NINE

$\mathcal{E}$xcept for the old blues-singing and playing man
still sitting down beyond the mailbox toward town, picking
and mumbling softly, the main road up here was now empty
of folks. The Hundred Acres crowd had returned to the
Momma's and the white folks were back over at Cotton Eyed
Joe's raising their own hillbilly hell. Standing in the middle
of the road, Speck was trying to map out in his mind the spot
where Doris Virginia snatched his cap and to figure out in
which direction she might have taken once she broke through
the crowd. Considering that she could have flung the cap in
the air while she was running, he began by searching for it
along the bank and ditch on the Hundred Acres side of the
road at the approximate spot where she turned off the main
road and ran through the crowd. He even walked down the
side road leading to the Momma's, checking both sides of the
lane in search of his security baldachin but stopping about
midway down lest his ashblond dome be spotted by a member
of the mob yet milling around down in the front yard of the
house. Frustrated, he searched his way back up to his original
starting point and now, at a loss as to what else to do, he
wandered over to the opposite side of the main road where he
started hunting all over again. He was working on the chance
that, after shooting through the crowd, Doris Virginia had

circled around them and ended up on the other side of the road (rather than running for the house, as he had automatically assumed she had). And as he now remembered it, he *never* once saw her again after she shot into the crowd with his cap waving in her hand. With this fresh hope, he got down on his hands and knees and began making a serious search for his cap all up and down the bank and ditch on the hillbilly, or Ike Nicholson, side of the road. And it was while he was moving on down the road away from town groping on his hands and knees through the tall grass and weeds in the ditch that he thought he heard something. He stopped for just a moment and sat up at the side of the ditch. By now he'd moved a ways down from the sounds that were coming from the front yards of the houses of both the Momma and Cotton Eyed Joe. What he was listening to was the sound of his own breathing; he'd inhaled a lot of the road dust that covered the thick foliage of the ditch and bank. Speck's breathing there in the still night didn't seem to him to be subsiding any, even though he had caught his breath by now—and what little air that was out at that time of night had already cleared the dust out of his nose. And the farther away from the Hundred Acres crowd he got, it seemed, the less his heart pounded. Yet the sound of his breathing seemed to be getting louder and louder now. . . . Then all of a sudden he realized that that loud breathing wasn't even *his*. What in the devil! Following his ears but against his better judgment, a now-apprehensive Speck began crawling, or was drawn, slowly on hands and knees along the ditch toward where the heavy-breathing sounds were coming from. Yes, they were coming from the ditch itself! Now he had started breathing loudly himself . . . though this time not from exhaustion, but from anticipation . . . and fear. Now he was almost on top of the source of the thick sounds . . . like someone who was having trouble catching his breath. Stopping again, Speck began to focus both his eyes and mind upon a moonlit sight in about the deepest part of the ditch and directly below the spot where he was lying, breathing heavier and heavier, atop the bank. There was somebody down there in the ditch! *Two* somebodies! A man . . . and a woman! And they were doing something . . . something peculiar! It was a white man and a white woman! Wait! The man was . . . was Sugar Boy! Yes, Sugar Boy! And the woman? Who was the white woman? Please. Lord, don't let it be . . . please don't let it be! But it was! It *was* HER! *Sugar Boy was down there in the ditch fucking . . . no . . . no . . . not fucking . . . but . . . but . . . lapping his Betty Jean! Lapping her up like a hound dog lapping honey!* Honey, hush yo' mouth . . . doggonit!

When Speck came racing up the road like a crazed jackrabbit, his hair flying in his face and almost covering his eyes, he nearly ran smack into the car pulling out of the Wildcat Tennessee Road. Speck felt so far away, confused, scared . . . and mad at that precise moment that he nearly collided head on with 'Ginia's Geechie's taxicab, and when it swerved past him, he didn't even look over into the back seat as the cab pulled up onto the main road and turned off toward town.

The veiled figure in the back seat took one last look out of the rolled-down window at the silhouette of a man sitting all alone there on the bank of the road right below the mailbox and then drifting up into her ears came the soft singing sounds from a time long . . . long ago.

> *Boll weevil, boll weevil,*
> *Cut down all my cotton and corn . . .*

The silhouette, the song, the Hundred Acres . . . and Plain View, all behind her now, the veiled figure turned to look straight ahead through the windshield of the taxicab, now nearing Haint Hills on its way to Appalachee to make that last train to Atlanta. There, she would change for Cincinnati, Ohio, her home. Her *only* home. Lord, Lord, Luvenia (aka Shirley Temple) had done gone home.

I'm gonna pack my suitcase,
And down the road I'm going.
Boll weevil, boll weevil. . . .

"Momma! Momma! Luvenia done gone! Geechie just now left with her in the taxicab heading back to town! She *don't* wanna see me! And o' Speck's gone crazy. He got that o' shotgun of his and done ran Theophilia and the children right outa the house! I always said he was crazy, hiding all that real pretty hair under that ol' cap of his all the time—"

But before Doris Virginia had a chance to get Momma Rosiebellelee's reaction to the sudden, startling doings of her older daughter and younger son, from down the hall came a loud, long reverberating crash that spun her around on her heels and sent her shooting back out through the Momma's bedroom door, headed pell-mell for the living room, and short seconds later her piercing, shrieking, screaming voice resounded all across, up, and down Wildcat Tennessee Hill.

"You goddamn som'bitch, motherfucker black bastard shit!"

The Tree had fallen, taking down with him Doris Virginia's Victrola and three stacks of records. Tampa Red hushed. Doris Virginia cussed. And Tree snored.

But just moments later from up Wildcat Tennessee Road a piece, by Speck's house, came still another sound . . . a loud, booming sound. The unmistakable sound of a shotgun.

"Lu' Anna! C'mere 'n tell me jes wha' in the devil's gwine on out thar!" The Momma sitting straight up in bed, as if she herself had been shot from the shotgun. Lucy Anna dashed in through the doorway, but before she even had a chance to give her version of what was happening out there, the Momma was swinging her legs down off the side of the bed.

"Git me my dress, my child."

"Momma Rosiebellelee! You can't git outa bed!"

"Hush up 'n git me my dress. My *new* one."

"Yo' *new* dress? You mean yo' . . . yo' bury'n dress?"

"Git it!"

"But you can't weah that one befo' . . . befo'. . . . It's bad luck!"

Wearing her colorful new frilly and flower-patterned burial dress, designed and sewn by herself, Momma Rosiebellelee fought off many dissuaders, tightly gripping her rarely used walking stick with one hand while shooing away all offers of assistance with the other hand, stepped out of her front door on this beautiful-for-a-crossing-over, moonlit Saturday night, and began her long, slow walk up Wildcat Tennessee Road. Each side of the road was lined with folks —the old, the young, the lame, all still, silently and sorrowfully watching their Momma make what they dared not say but knew deep down in their bellies would be her last walk. She was on her way up to see for herself just what in the devil her speckled baby was doing, shooting his shotgun on the very night that his own momma was busily preparing herself and her loved ones for her crossing over. Lord, Lord, ol' Speck ought've been ashamed of himself!

With the ends of her long hair—now with scattered streaks of gray—beating softly down across her butt, Momma Rosiebellelee made it to the front yard of Speck's house. She brushed off those many hands up here who were trying both to help her and hold her back from her dangerous mission, hobbled up on the porch by herself, and with her walking stick banged heavily on the wall right next to the screendoor.

"Speck! Open up in thar!"

"Momma, tha' *you?*" Following an unbelieving pause.

"Open this heah do'."

"Hit's open, Momma."

Pulling open the screen door with one hand and pushing open the door to the bedroom with her stick, Momma Rosiebellelee walked head on into a loaded shotgun. As the door closed behind her, the crowd out in the yard held its breath in anticipation of the explosion. But the Momma's mind was elsewhere.

"Speck, whar's yo' cap?" She was standing near the door,

and Speck was standing in front of the fireplace, with a double-barreled shotgun pointing straight her way on one arm
and his other arm thrown up to try to cover his bare head.
The hearth was covered with broken glass, and looking up
over the mantelpiece the Momma saw a big hole occupying
the spot where ol' Hamilton Crawford's head had once stared
out into the room. The picture frame was still hanging there.
In the other corner the Joe Louis boxing pictures still hung
. . . unscathed.

"Doris 'Ginia stole it."

"Wha' the devil she do that fuh?"

"'Cause I was buckdancin' to Sugar Boy's harp 'n she
don' know hi to buckdance."

"Buckdancin'! Hi in the name of God kin I cross over like
I oughta be doin' if y'all gonna go 'round cuttin' the monkey
lak this? Y'all my *real* chilluns. Wha' other folks gonna think?
'N wha' in the world you doin' wid that ol' shotgun? Stop
pointin' that thin' at yo' momma. You gittin' bad as Mist'
Mac."

"Mist' Mac got a seven-shot pump. This heah is jes—"

"Whar's Theophilia 'n the chilluns?"

"They . . . they . . . got scared 'n run outa heah up to the
main road. They be back."

"Hi come yo' bran' new ov'alls all dirty down the front
thar? You fall?"

"No, ma'am. I was lookin' fuh my Sunday cap."

"On yo' belly?"

"Jes to look ovah in the ditch up off the main road whar
I thought Doris 'Ginia might've throwed hit."

"Wha'cha doin' wid that ol' shotgun? You gonna shoot
my baby?"

"No, ma'am. I jes got all mad 'cause of what I saw . . . up
thar in the ditch."

"Wha' you see?"

"I can' tell you that."

"You mean to tell me you can' tell yo' own momma

standin' right heah fo she cross over wha' that you saw up thar in the ditch that made you git yo' shotgun 'n run yo' family outa the house?"

"No, ma'am." Speck's eyes now, like the twin barrels of his gun, pointing down at the dusty toes of his Sunday slippers.

"Then I'll jes go up thar to tha' ditch 'n see fuh myself." The Momma's voice sharp and determined as she turned toward the door at her back.

"No, ma'am! Don' go up thar to the ditch, please, Momma, don' go!"

"Then tell yo' momma wha' you saw up thar in the ditch then." Turning back to face Speck.

"I . . . I . . . I saw somethin' bad."

"Bad? Wha' bad?"

"*Real* bad!"

"Now, son, you tell yo' momma fo she cross over wha' the o' bad thing you saw up thar in the ditch t'night."

"Momma, please don' make me tell you, 'cause hit's too bad fuh you to heah."

"*Tell me!*"

"Momma . . . oh, Momma . . . I . . . I . . . I saw Sugar Boy up thar in the ditch."

"*Sugar Boy! MY* Sugar Boy? Lawd, God! Is he hurt? Is he . . . dead?"

"No, ma'am, he ain' hurtin' or nud'n."

"Wha's he doin' up thar in the ditch then? Is he drunk? *Tell me, boy!*"

"He's . . . he's . . . he's in thar wid . . . wid somebody else."

"*Who else?*"

"Er . . . er . . . ah . . . Betty Jean."

"*Betty Jean?* Cotton Eyed's young gal?"

"Yes, ma'am."

"She a sweet child. Sung me a song 'n then gimme a big ol' hug t'night. Lawdy, Lawd, that Sugar Boy of *mine.*" Here the Momma, an expression of great relief showing on her

face, stood for a while, staring at nothing in particular and
shaking her head from side to side at the same time, with her
tongue letting go with several clucks of pure amazement.

"But Momma . . . he's . . . he's liable to git hisself kilt."

"You gonna kill him wid yo' shotgun thar?" A now
deadly concerned Momma.

"No, Momma! I . . . I . . . I mean the white folks up thar
will kill'm if they catch'm."

"Nobody gonna kill *my* Sugar Boy! Now you jes put that
o' shotgun down 'n stop actin' lak a crazy fool while I go up
to the road heah 'n git *my* Sugar Boy."

"Momma, you can' go up thar! They liable to kill you too!
On yo' cross-over night!"

Too late. The Momma had opened the door and was now
out on the front porch, which still was neck deep in folks, but
as soon as they saw Speck standing in the doorway, still holding his double-barreled, they began scampering and scattering in all possible directions. The Momma hobbled down by
herself off the porch and began making her way, slow but
sho', on across the front yard, heading up to the main road to
get *her* Sugar Boy.

Left standing alone in the doorway, and even forgetting
all about his exposed head for the moment, Speck began hollering after the retreating figure of the Momma.

"You always did love Sugar Boy mo' than you love
me!" This surprising accusation startled the crowd outside
the house so much that they stopped running for cover
long enough to listen to what else the suddenly bold Speck
might just be hollering out next on this crossing-over Saturday night of the full moon. And as he had sensed that
the crowd, his kind of folks, was listening to what *he* had
to say, ol' Speck just kept right on hollering out into the
moonlit night.

"You love Doris 'Ginia mo' than me, too, 'n she jes a girl!
I'm a *man!* You nevah did love me! When Sugar Boy was a lil'
bitty boy, you rode him wid you on Niggah Gal lak you usta

ride Luvenia all the time fo she went Nawth to Cincinnati, Ohio! But you *nevah* did ride me wid you on Niggah Gal! You even rode Doris 'Ginia wid you, 'n she was jes a girl! I was a *boy!* You usta put me on Niggah Gal by myself 'n I'd be so scared I'd cry, 'n you 'n Sugar Boy would jes laugh at me! Then when I was up on her back, she would head right fuh that low-limb tree down the hill back of the barn 'n run right under hit jes as fas' as she could, 'n evah time that ol' limb would knock me right off on the ground 'n evah time I came home cryin' y'all would jes laugh some mo' at me! I *hated* Niggah Gal! I was glad when she went blind! 'N I was even gladder when she died! I *hated* her! I *still* hate her! I hate *all* horses! They's mean! Not good lak mules! I *love* mules! I usta love ol' Red 'n Clyde to death! But you went 'n sold 'm jes 'cause Sugar Boy din' wanna farm no mo'! If Sugar Boy hadda wanted to farm, you wouldn've let Mist' Mac plant them o' pine trees all over the Hundred Acres! *I* wanted to farm! But you didn' love me! You love Sugar Boy! 'N Doris 'Ginia, 'n she jes a girl! I'm a *man!* I bet jes lak Theophilia said, when you cross over, you gonna give the whole Hundred Acres back to Mist' Mac . . . or to Sugar Boy, 'n he don' even wanna farm! *All* Sugar Boy wanna do is drive them o' cars 'n trucks 'n . . . 'n . . . 'n mess 'round wid other menfolks' women! He don' wanna farm! All I wan' is a lil' piece of land to farm on 'n a mule to plow wid. *Please,* Momma, don' give *all* the Hundred Acres back to Mist' Mac . . . or to Sugar Boy. *Please* gimme enough land to farm on! I don' wanna go over to Mist' Nick's side! I *love* the Hundred Acres! 'N I *hate* the sawmill! *Momma, please, I want me a mule!*"

When the Momma reached the main road, Speck's screaming diatribe bouncing off her back every slow step of the way, she could just make out there in the moonlight a small group gathered right near the mailbox.

"Theophilia, tha' y'all?" The Momma coming to a stop while her old eyes peered into the darkness.

"It's me and the children. Mrs. Rosiebelle Lee, you oughta be home in bed . . ."

"I'se lookin' fuh my Sugar Boy. Y'all seed him up heah?"

"He ain't been up here since we come."

"All y'all all right?"

"Yes, ma'am, we all right. I just had to sit down here. Can't run like I usta."

"Hi you feelin'? You 'bout ready?"

"It won't be long, I think."

"Then I betta stay heah wid you." The Momma hobbling over to where Theophilia sat on the dewy grass of the bank, her back resting up against the mailbox post. With the help of Hamilton and Benjamin, the Momma lowered herself down and sat beside her. "O' Speck didn' hurt nobody, did he?"

"No, ma'am, he didn't. I got all the children out just as soon as he came running into the house hollering something about he was gonna get his gun and go blow *both* of them to Kingdom Come. I don't know what he was talking about."

"Nud'n. O' Speck was talk'n 'bout nud'n. Jes lissen to him now, down thar holler'n up a storm all 'bout nud'n."

"Ain't everything he's down there hollering is about nothing. You *did* treat Sugar Boy and Doris Virginia better than you did him. And *still* do. He oughta done some of this hollering a long, long time ago. Now it's too late."

"I love Speck jes as much as I love Sugar Boy 'n Doris 'Ginia. Hit's jes that when he was little, Speck was all the time hangin' on to my dress tail when the other chilluns was out playin'. I had to keep makin' im go play wid the other chilluns, 'cause all he wanted was to stay in the house wid me. Lak a girl. 'N Lawd knows I jes didn' have no time fuh that all the time. I had a whole churchful of folks, and some mo' on top, to see for. Make sho' they all had 'nough to eat, clothes on they back, a bed to sleep in . . . 'n the white folks didn' mess wid them all the time. Wid you, yo' chilluns come fus'. Wid me Plain View come fus'. All mommas ain' the same way. Now when they was little, Sugar Boy 'n Doris 'Ginia both was always out playin' wid the other chilluns 'n not hangin' on to my dress tail lak Speck. Luvenia . . . now she was somethin' else herself. *Always* wid Mist' Mac. She love Mist' Mac. 'N Mist' Mac love her. He never tole me, but I knowed. But Luvenia, she'll be back in the maw'n . . . you jes wait 'n see . . . she comin' back. . . ." The last words trailing off, as if the Momma was sitting there talking to herself. Then—"Is tha hi come you married my son, 'cause you didn' think I love him? Did *you* love him or jes took pity on him?" There was a sudden lull up on the main road, where the distant sound of Speck's yet ranging voice competed with strands of Betty Jean's guitar suddenly starting up over across the road at their backs. Then, like a haint, Sugar Boy appeared from out of nowhere and with nary a word walked right past the little group by the mailbox on down Wildcat Tennessee Road toward the house.

"He had the nicest manners of all the boys." Theophilia breaking the silence. "And was the prettiest. Oh, that hair! Long, straight, and ashblond! I usta sit for hours on end out there in the hot sun on the terrace in the field, just watching Speck plow. Everybody always said that Mrs. Rosiebelle Lee had the prettiest children in the world, and I wanted mine to be pretty just like yours. I was young then and didn't know . . . but Poppa and Momma *knew.* Yet nobody could plow or handle mules like Speck could. He treated and loved o' Red and Clyde better than he did me . . . his children . . . or hisself. Lord, if I hadda only known. But like I said, I was young then and so foolish that even if I hadda known what was ahead of us, I guess I still would've married him. But I still love *all* my children . . . even if he still ain't the same to me no more. You been blessed. I guess you ain't *never* had anything like that happen to you, Mrs. Rosiebelle Lee."

"Yes, Theophilia, I'se blessed. But I ain' *always* been blessed. Let me tell you somethin' I ain' *nevah* tole nobody else 'n I'se only gonna tell you 'cause I know you don' go 'round talkin'.

"I don' 'member my momma, 'cause she died when I was born up thar in Monroe. But they all said she was 'bout the prettiest thing you ever did see. She was lak my chilluns, had a white daddy 'n a cullud momma. Lawd, I always felt so bad 'cause I nevah knowed her. The white folks raised her, but when she married Poppa, a tramp Injun man from up at Chattanooga, Tennessee, they throwed her out. 'Cause he was a Injun, Poppa couldn't talk good, 'cept Injun talk, so he never did say much to nobody 'bout nud'n. Folks thought he was stuckup 'cause he didn't always talk to them. But he jes didn' know hi to talk our talk too good. But he was a worker. The bes' wood chopper for miles 'round. He chopped wood for evahbody. All over Walton County 'n outside of it. He was never wi'out his axe. He had a horse too, Injun Man, that he rode from choppin' job to choppin' job. 'N as fah back as I kin 'member he took me on Injun Man wid him on all his choppin' jobs. He would chop the wood for the fireplace, stove, or heater, 'n I would stack hit or take hit inside the house or shed of the family he was choppin' fuh. Some o' them logs was heavy, but I was strong. But this way, we had no good home. We never stayed one place long. Many times Poppa would chop wood jes fuh us 'n Injun Man to git somethin' to eat 'n a place to sleep. I musta slept in every barn in 'n 'round Walton County. I never did go to no schoolhouse. 'N Poppa didn' know hi to learn me to read 'n write, 'cause he didn' know hi to hisself. But he did learn me to count, ride a horse, chop 'n then measure wood, put a good edge on a axe, 'n to fish. Yessuh, we had some *real* good times together. But he never learn me his Injun talk. I think 'cause he didn' wan' folks thinkin' I was stuckup if I talked hit, lak they thought he was. Po' Poppa. He was such a good man. My Sugar Boy looks jes lak he did.

"Then one early mawn'n Poppa got his axe and rode ol' Injun Man, 'lone out on a choppin' job somewhar 'n nevah come back. To this very day every time I heah somebody choppin' wood, I think hit's Poppa.

"When Poppa didn' come back, I went to the house whar Momma had been raised 'n worked 'n got myself a house job, my fus' one. By now I was gittin' nigh on to becomin' a woman—I was always big for my age, you know, in the buzum 'n the hips—'n I was in need of company. Man company. But I didn' wan' all them white men all the time lookin' me over lak I was a mule or somethin', 'cause I was scared o' them. They took wha' they wanted, 'n if they didn' git hit, they kilt somebody. But at this house the cook, Miz' Luvenia, who was lak a momma to me 'n who learn me hi to cook 'n sew, had a son, Willie Henry, who played the guitar 'n who all the time talked 'bout gwine off to Atlanta to play 'n sang for the folks up thar whar, he said, he heard they knowed wha' good singin' was all 'bout. I usta sit night aft night aft night lissenin' to his guitar pickin' 'n sangin'. But his guitar was wha' I love. Lawd, he sho' could pick pretty. I lak'd him. He lak me too 'n was all the time axin' me to run off to Atlanta wid him. Many a time I had a good mind to go wid him but, bein' the daughter of a wood-choppin' man, I won' so sho' 'bout some guitar-pickin' man. Now if that guitar hadda been a axe . . . Anyway, we got 'long real good thar, 'n pretty soon we was talkin 'bout gittin' married. He was the fus' man since Poppa who I thought I could trus'. 'N he trus' me. 'N we finally 'cided to git married 'n go off to Atlanta, so he could sang 'n pick. But us gittin' married jes won' God will. Lawd, Lawd, it sho' 'nough won'.

"'Spite gwine wid 'n bein' set on marryin' Willie Henry, I was bein' messed wid by the oldes' white son o' the house whar I worked. He wouldn' keep his hands offa me. I didn' wan' nud'n to do wid him no way 'n even tole him so. But that jes made him try mo' harder. At fus' I could git 'round him all right, 'cause I could tell he was still young 'n didn' know the ways of womenfolks lak I knowed the ways of menfolks, 'specially white menfolks. So I thought, wid him I won' have no trouble 'mount to much. But then when he heared I was gonna go off to Atlanta wid the cook's son, he got real mad wid me. He tole me that I *couldn't* leave his family to go to Atlanta, or anywhar else, wid a shiftless niggah. Tha's when I tole him that I could go to Atlanta or anywhar my foots would take me wid anybody I wanted to. Lawd, why did I wanna say that? He tried right then 'n thar in the kitchen whar I was busy cookin' his family's supper to git me, but I got loose from him after pointin' a butcher knife in his face. I was scared. And, Lawd, did he git mad. He lef' the kitchen redder than a coal of fire bakin' in hell 'n sayin' that no niggah was gonna take me 'way from him up to Atlanta, or anywhar else. Tha's when I thought hit was 'bout time this heah o' gal got her guitar-pickin' man 'n headed for Atlanta, or somewhar fo thar be trouble. White folks trouble. After supper I went lookin' fuh Willie Henry to tell him. But I couldn' find him nowhar. The nex' mawn'n they found him.

"They didn' kill him lak they did to mos' cullud men. Him, they *cut* . . . lak you would a hog for fattenin'. He was no mo' good as a man. Lawd knows, I was sorry for wha' happen, 'cause I love that man lak nobody bizness, but Miz' Luvenia 'n everybody else blamed me for wha' happen' to Willie Henry. 'N he wouldn' see 'n talk to me, 'cause he was so 'shamed. Lawd, hit hurt me too. I said to myself that no mo' was I gonna be the cause of a cullud man gittin' cut, or kilt, by the white folks 'cause no mo' would I ever let myself love a cullud man lak I love Willie Henry. I was jes gonna mess 'round wid white men, 'n if they cut or kilt they own 'cause o' me, then that was white folks' bizness. All the cullud folks 'round blamed me for them cuttin' Willie Henry, 'n they even stopped talkin' to me. That made me feel real bad, 'specially when Miz' Luvenia didn' talk to me no mo'.

"I lef' that house one night after dark 'n never went back. 'N evahwhar I went afta that house, I went lookin' for the riches' white family I could find, 'cause I knowed no matter whar I went the white menfolk was gonna be afta me 'n thar won' nud'n under God's sun any cullud man could do to help me, lest they kilt him, 'n I won' gonna have that happen agin to me. I knowed by workin' for rich white men, if I evah did have one of they babies, they could 'ford to feed, clothe, 'n house me 'n my chilluns wid no trouble. Make them pay for wha' they git, 'cause they sho' won' gonna let me have another cullud man.

"I was young, sassy . . . 'n pretty, Lawd, Lawd . . . then 'n I soon learn to be the bigges' hellraiser 'round. But a hell-raiser only wid white men, rich white men. No cullud or po' white trash 'lowed. I was rich white stuff. But no matter what else I done, I paid the white folks back for wha' they done to Willie Henry. I ain' tellin' you heah t'night but God in heaven knows I paid them *all* back fuh what they done to my Willie Henry 'n had some change lef' over.

"But when I lef' thar 'n come heah, I won' mad at nobody no mo'. White folks, cullud folks, Injun folks, no folks. I come heah to live. But I still knowed I couldn' marry or fool 'round wid no cullud man. When I fus' got heah fo the white menfolk could git me 'n do wha' they wannit wid me, I went right to the top myself 'n got the big white man hisself, Mist' Mac. When you got the big white man, ain' no other white man gonna mess wid you, lest he git hisself kilt. Lak Mist' Mike Nicholson did. But he was the change left ovah from Monroe. But tha's white folks bizness. No cullud man got kilt, or even whupped, heah in Plain View 'cause o' me. I'se right proud of that.

"Mist' Mac been good to me. Better than any other white man. But I don' know if a cullud woman is 'lowed to love a white man. I jes don' know . . . but *they* kin love all they want. . . . Long afta I come heah, thar was almos' some trouble when one night Willie Henry showed up wid his same ol' guitar outside my front do'. Lawd only knows hi he found me, but he did. All the way from Atlanta whar he'd gone all 'lone right after he got well. Thank the Lawd, Mister Mac was off on one of his trips 'n Willie Henry spent the night. But he still won' a man . . . if you know what I mean. But he won' mad at me and didn' hold me 'sponsible for wha' they done to him. This was back when all the tramp singers and dancers usta come through. He was one of them. But he knowed only to come 'round when Mist' Mac was away. I even bought him a guitar that he took wid him all the way back to Atlanta right after the boll weevil come. He never did come back to see me afta that. God bless him. He was one man I sho' 'nough love . . . even after they cut him."

The Momma's talk had tired her out. She sat holding a sleeping Joe Louis in her lap, while Theophilia held Marian Anderson, also fast asleep, in hers. Olivia lay sleeping between them, but there was no sign of Hamilton and Benjamin, both having sneaked off during their Grandmomma's talk to go mix with the crowd that was now slowly drifting back down Wildcat Tennessee Road from in front of Speck's. By now he had finished his tirade and sneaked unnoticed out the back door. Sometime around midnight, wearing something pink to cover his ashblond blow, Speck was seen toting a bucket of red paint, a heavy-size paint brush, and a ladder, all the time carrying on to himself about "putting the world's biggest airplane on the big barn up at the Plain View Plantation Big House."

Meanwhile, young Richmond had sat up through his Grandmomma's whole talk and, stubbornly fighting sleep, sat right beside her waiting for more. From over on that side of the road came the slow, soft twang of Betty Jean's guitar, while down at the house Sugar Boy's harp was answering back with a low moan.

"I feel it." Theophilia's time had come.

"You sho'?"

"I've had enough of them to know by now."

"Le's go home, *my* child."

"Now, Mrs. Rosiebelle Lee, you ain't in no shape for this." The old stern, firm, no-nonsense Theophilia was back.

"Richmond, go down and tell your Uncle Sugar Boy to come and get his Momma and put her back to bed where she belongs. This is no time for a sick woman. There's some women down at your house, Mrs. Rosiebelle Lee, who ain't cutting up who can help me. Richmond, go on!"

"Theophilia! I know me 'n you ain' never seed eye to eye on mucha nud'n, but would you let me bring my *las'* grandchild into the world t'night fo I leave hit? I sho' would 'preciate that." There in the moonlight on the bank of Plain View's main road while the guitar twanged and the harp moaned the old, dying woman sat staring into the eyes of the young mother, whose face and voice suddenly softened as she spoke again.

"Richmond, come back here and help me pull yo' Grandmomma up. This baby, if it's a boy, you gonna name it . . . after yo' poppa. But if it's a girl, I'm gonna name it . . . after you. Let's go home . . . Momma Rosiebellelee . . . it's kicking to see you."

> *I ain' gonna pick no mo' cotton,*
> *I declare, I ain' gonna pull no mo' corn . . .*

EPILOGUE

*A*fter the baby was born, the Momma, rather than be carried back home, insisted on walking herself. But instead of going down Wildcat Tennessee Road to her house, she turned the other way, heading back up to the main road. Nobody dared mess with her now, they just stood around watching her hobble her way on up. Nobody had the slightest inkling as to where she was going, nor what she was going to do once she got there. But one thing they *all* knew. And that was that their Momma Rosiebellelee knew exactly where she was going and what she was going to do once she got there. Amen.

"Tha' you, Willie Henry?"

"Hit ain't the bear."

"You come back."

"'Bout time, I'd say."

"You fine?"

"Fine as wine. You look great as cake."

"No mo'. I'll jes set down right heah if you don' mind none. G'won sangin'."

> *I ain' gonna dig no mo' 'taters,*
> *Oh boy, I ain' gonna pick no mo' peas. . . .*

Suddenly above the soft sounds of the guitar and the singing, the Momma heard different sounds, sounds from long . . . long ago. Growing louder and louder. Looking up, she could see something coming down the main road. It was growing larger and larger. She could see the cloud of dust, smell the Georgia red up her nose. Then she saw them. Two horses! One was . . . was Nigger Gal! And atop her sat a young, beautiful Rosiebelle Lee Wildcat Tennessee, her long black shiny hair stretched straight out like a rope in the wind back of her head. The other horse was white. A white stallion! She knew who this one belonged to. But no! That wasn't Mister Mac in the saddle. It . . . was a black man. *Willie Henry!* And he had a guitar slung over his shoulder, and above the louder and louder-sounding hooves of the two horses, she could hear them both laughing and by looking into their happy, young faces, she could tell that they were on their way to Atlanta! Rosiebelle Lee Wildcat Tennessee crossed over smiling. Lord, have mercy!

I've been walking, I've been walking. . . .